Y0-CBB-361

Stephen Crane was born in Newark, New Jersey, on November 1, 1871, the fourteenth child of an itinerant Methodist minister. He was schooled at Hudson River Institute at Claverack, at Lafayette College, and for one semester at Syracuse University. While in the Delta Upsilon fraternity house at Syracuse he wrote the first draft of *Maggie: A Girl of the Streets*. In 1895, the young author, who had never seen a battle, published *The Red Badge of Courage*, the extraordinary revelation of the mind and heart of a raw recruit that made Crane famous. In that same year, Crane traveled through the West and Mexico as a correspondent for Irving Bacheller's newspaper syndicate, and in 1896 he was assigned to cover the Cuban Revolution. While waiting in Jacksonville, Florida, for the boat trip, he met Cora Howorth Stewart, the hostess and proprietress of the Hotel de Dream. She and Stephen fell in love, and as his wife she lived with him in England during his final three years. On New Year's Day, 1897, Crane was shipwrecked en route to Cuba, a disaster which he recreated in *The Open Boat*. Later assignments took him to Greece to cover the Greco-Turkish War and to Cuba to report on the Spanish-American War in April 1898. Returning to England and Cora in mid-January of 1899, he found himself threatened by bankruptcy. He tried desperately to write himself out of debt, but he never succeeded. Plagued by tuberculosis, he collapsed in early April 1900 and died at Badenweiler, Germany on June 5, 1900.

ABOUT THE EDITOR:

FRANK BERGON teaches English at Vassar College and lives in Highland, New York. He is the author of *Stephen Crane's Artistry* (1975).

THE
WESTERN WRITINGS
OF
Stephen Crane

EDITED AND
WITH AN INTRODUCTION
BY

Frank Bergon

A SIGNET CLASSIC
NEW AMERICAN LIBRARY

TIMES MIRROR
NEW YORK AND SCARBOROUGH, ONTARIO
THE NEW ENGLISH LIBRARY LIMITED, LONDON

SIGNET CLASSIC TRADEMARK REG. U.S. PAT. OFF. AND FOREIGN COUNTRIES
REGISTERED TRADEMARK—MARCA REGISTRADA
HECHO EN CHICAGO, U.S.A.

SIGNET, SIGNET CLASSICS, MENTOR, PLUME AND MERIDIAN BOOKS
are published *in the United States* by
The New American Library, Inc.,
1301 Avenue of the Americas, New York, New York 10019,
in Canada by The New American Library of Canada Limited,
81 Mack Avenue, Scarborough, Ontario M1L 1M8,
in the United Kingdom by The New English Library Limited,
Barnard's Inn, Holborn, London, EC 1N 2JR, England

First Signet Classic Printing February, 1979

1 2 3 4 5 6 7 8 9

PRINTED IN THE UNITED STATES OF AMERICA

Contents

Introduction

What is remarkable about Stephen Crane's Western stories is that they were written before the modern Western was born. Equally remarkable is that these shoot-'em-up tales of lynchers and bushwhackers are perhaps the only Westerns ever written to be praised primarily for their literary value. Admired by such proponents of high art as Henry James and Joseph Conrad, Crane's stories make us aware of the tensions and terrors normally obscured by the formulas of popular fiction. They are Westerns that shine with intelligence, and they remind us of how much subsequent writers and film makers have ignored in their portrayals of the Wild West.

Stephen Crane went in search of the actual West in 1895. He was then on the verge of becoming known as the boy who had written a great book about war without ever having seen a battle. He was only twenty-three, and the serial publication of *The Red Badge of Courage* by America's first newspaper syndicate cleared the way for him to go West as a correspondent for that same syndicate. His trip took him into the heart of the Great Plains and across the Rio Grande, but after less than four months of travel through Nebraska, Texas, and Mexico, he found himself returning to New York to add his name to the long list of Easterners responsible for inventing the Western.

Such meetings of East and West rarely produced works of art, but they did breed durable fantasies and mythical archetypes. From the first moments there was a shadowy place out yonder called the West, Americans seemed to demand that it be quickened with large, thrilling figures and deeds. It was as if there were a hole in the American psyche, a need shared by a people without history or mythology or tradition. Easterners ranging from the New York country gentleman James Fenimore Cooper to the metropolitan New York dentist Zane Grey seemed to respond to this national need for culture heroes by inventing mythical frontiersmen and cowboys. An adventuresome promoter named Edward Zane Carroll Judson, better remembered as dime novelist "Ned Buntline," brought the mythical West eastward when he persuaded Buffalo Bill Cody to appear on a stage in Chicago in 1872. In 1903 Edwin S. Porter brought the Wild West farther east when he filmed *The Great Train Robbery* on the tracks of the Delaware and Lackawanna Railroad in New Jersey. This early motion picture made in the East, along with an Easterner's novel, Owen Wister's *The Virginian* (1902), normally marks the birth of the Western as we have come to know it in fiction and film. Because many discussions of the development of the popular Western have overlooked Crane's stories as too original, and because many assessments of Crane's literary achievement have failed to see his stories as bona fide Westerns, it is important to identify the popular Western characteristics of his work. But it is equally important to see that as one of the creators of the modern Western, Crane was also one of its finest critics. He wrote anti-Westerns before the Western became a formula.

The showdown between a gunfighting hero and an outlaw on a long, empty street in a Western town identifies the horse opera so completely that it is now difficult to imagine that Stephen Crane's comic rendition of this moment occurred long before the two-man gunfight at high noon or sundown had become a staple of Western melodrama. According to Bernard DeVoto, this obligatory scene of the horse opera which Hollywood calls the walkdown was invented by Owen Wister, and the first walkdown took place in the early twentieth century when Wister's cowboy hero shot down badman Trampas in the closing pages of *The Virginian*. In anticipating this classic walkdown, Crane's face-off between the marshal and desperado in "The Bride Comes to Yellow Sky" also makes clear that the walkdown evolves out of a three-sided drama. The third essential role in such a Western, besides those representing outlaws and heroes, is that of the townspeople who advocate a new civil existence for their community. As shown by studies of the modern Western, such as John Cawelti's *Six-Gun Mystique*, the Western town itself lingers somewhere between anarchy and social order. Without the town and its community in the background, the gunshooting adventures of many recent Westerns, including several Italian-made Western films, have no resonance, for the actual conflict of the traditional Western is between the outlaw and the community. In "The Bride Comes to Yellow

Sky," disruption comes to a sleepy Texas town in the form of drunken Scratchy Wilson, a wizard with six-guns, who, like those earlier representatives of Western savagery, the Indians, seems to emerge from the landscape itself. Scratchy is an outsider who is "the last one of the old gang that used to hang out along the river," and he moves "in the direction of his desire, chanting Apache scalp-music." In conflict with Scratchy's old way of life along the Rio Grande is the social order being brought to Yellow Sky in the form of a train bearing a new bride, the civilized trappings and fittings of railroad parlor cars, the customs of porters, and the values of husbands. Crane anticipates the methods of the cinema by presenting this thematic conflict through a kinesthetic image: "To the left, miles down a long purple slope, was a little ribbon of mist where moved the keening Rio Grande. The train was approaching it at an angle, and the apex was Yellow Sky." The man caught in the middle of this conflict is the Western hero, and like the Indian or outlaw, he, too, stands outside the normal community. Despite his recent marriage and his residence in the town, Marshal Jack Potter enters the story as an outsider who is coming into town like a Leatherstocking or a Gary Cooper to settle (with a comic twist) the conflict between the gunslinger and Yellow Sky. As the marshal and desperado confront each other, the marshal announces that he is unarmed:

His enemy's face went livid. He stepped forward and lashed his weapon to and fro before Potter's chest. "Don't you tell me you ain't got no gun on you, you whelp. Don't tell me no lie like that. There ain't a man in Texas ever seen you without no gun. Don't take me for no kid." His eyes blazed with light, and his throat worked like a pump.

"I ain't takin' you for no kid," answered Potter. His heels had not moved an inch backward. "I'm takin' you for a———fool. I tell you I ain't got a gun, and I ain't. If you're goin' to shoot me up, you better begin now. You'll never get a chance like this again."

So much enforced reasoning had told on Wilson's rage. He was calmer. "If you ain't got a gun, why ain't you got a gun?" he sneered. "Been to Sunday-school?"

"I ain't got a gun because I've just come from San Anton' with my wife. I'm married," said Potter. "And if I'd thought there was going to be any galoots like you prowling around when I brought my wife home, I'd had a gun, and don't you forget it."

"Married!" said Scratchy, not at all comprehending.

"Yes, married. I'm married," said Potter distinctly.

"Married?" said Scratchy. Seemingly for the first time he saw the drooping drowning woman at the other man's side. "No!" he said. He was like a creature allowed a glimpse of another world. He moved a pace backward, and his arm with the revolver dropped to his side. "Is this—is this the lady?" he asked.

"Yes, this is the lady," answered Potter.

There was another period of silence.

"Well," said Wilson at last, slowly, "I s'pose it's all off now."

"It's all off if you say so, Scratchy. You know I didn't make the trouble." Potter lifted in his valise.

"Well, I 'low it's off, Jack," said Wilson. He was looking at the ground. "Married!" He was not a student of chivalry; it was merely that in the presence of this foreign condition he was a simple child of the earlier plains. He picked up his starboard revolver, and placing both weapons in their holsters, he went away. His feet made funnel-shaped tracks in the heavy sand.

Without the ritualistic spatter of gunfire at the end of the drama, the story as a Western may seem as incomplete to some readers as would a mystery story that ends with the detective still scratching his head over an unsolved crime. "I thirst for his blood," Henry James wrote to Owen Wister in objection to the Virginian's marrying—in James's words— "the little Vermont person" instead of dying with his boots on. The Western buff may object even more vehemently to the ending of "The Bride Comes to Yellow Sky," but what Crane's story lays bare is the unstated premise of both *The Virginian* and the legendary West. The real destroyers in this West are not gunslinging desperadoes or corrupt Eastern capitalists or encroaching railroads. The world of the Western has accommodated any number of villains, but it cannot succumb to the domesticating woman and still survive as the legendary West. As soon as the Virginian puts on a straw hat and Scotch homespun suit, he is no longer a cowboy. Supporting a common American literary dream of the free, undomesticated, independent male are the images of Leatherstocking leaving Mabel Dunham and fading into the wilderness and the Lone Ranger riding toward the invariably setting sun. It is certainly the violation of Jack Potter's idea of himself as the lone, peacekeeping marshal of Yellow Sky that weighs him with the guilt of a "heinous crime" as he heads home with a new bride. Crane's story makes brightly clear that the world the bride destroys is one belonging to "a simple child of the earlier plains" like Scratchy Wilson, who protests that he isn't a kid even as he acts out a boy's dream, making the town his toy and stomping around in red-topped boots beloved by little boys in New England.

As attractive as the legendary West is in its simplicity, it cannot satisfy our sense of the historical West, and one of the pleasures of Crane's Westerns is that they give us glimpses of historical complexities that the fantasies of most horse operas cannot support. Even before Crane went West he wrote in "Billie Atkins Went to Omaha" about offshoots of industrialization such as the railroad hoboes and bindle stiffs who were crisscrossing the same country as cowboys on horseback. The simple view of the railroad as the intruding machine that spoiled the pristine West and robbed the cowboy of his freedom and independence is complicated by the fact that the extension of railheads into Kansas made the era of the cowboy and the long drives from Texas a possibility in the first place. Crane, sensitive to such ironies, presented the interpenetration of the industrial West and the Wild West through the career of the ex-cowboy in "A Man and Some Others." As a mine owner, Bill was originally part of the corporate, industrial West that quickly replaced a fleeting initial period of individual prospecting in the 1850s. As a cowboy, Bill became not a free spirit but a hired hand, and as an ex-cowboy he became a hired goon for the railroads during the hobo wars that had begun with the Omaha and San Francisco walkouts in the 1877 national railroad strike. Crane knew that the pastoral Wild West whose passing is so often mourned in fiction and criticism is simply a West that never existed. Even as a sheepherder on the barren plains of southwestern Texas, Bill cannot escape the effects of industrialization and the modern world; there he is in equal "danger of meeting horse-thieves and tourists." Besides tourists, the railroads brought homesteaders to a land advertised as a garden of the world, but in Nebraska, Crane found men battling nature. He flattened the myth of an Edenic West where self-sufficient men live in harmony with nature. Despite faith in nature's renewal that helped some Nebraskans endure brutalizing droughts and blizzards, Crane saw that without government aid there was "looming eventual catastrophe that would surely depopulate the country." He probably knew that only a few years earlier, between 1888 and 1892, over half the people in western Kansas straggled eastward in wagons bearing signs, "In God we trusted, in Kansas we busted."

What appears in many Westerns as the lamentable encroachment of civilization into a resistant Old West is revealed in Crane's Westerns to be the result of Westerners wooing Eastern investors and settlers. "Every small American town is trying to get population and ideals," Sinclair Lewis wrote in *Babbitt,* and Western small towns, as Crane shows, were trying to get ideals in order to get population. In both "Twelve O'Clock" and "Moonlight on the Snow," Westerners complain that the community's reputation for bloodshed is scaring away Eastern capitalists: " 'When these here speculators come 'long flashin' rolls as big as water-buckets, it's up to us to whirl in an' git some of it.' This became the view of the town, and, since the main stipulation was virtue, War Post resolved to be virtuous." What such virtuous demeanor might attract is shown in "A Christmas Dinner Won in Battle," another Western that Crane wrote before he went West. The prairie town of Levelville in this story welcomed first the surveyors, then the railroad, and in "an incredibly short time, the town had a hotel, a mayor, a board of aldermen and more than a hundred real estate agents, beside the blueprint of the plans for a street railway three miles long." Along with "civilization" and the "five grades of society," the railroads also brought to Levelville what many Westerners did not welcome, civilization's underbelly, the "Slavs, Polacks, Italians, and Hungarians . . . men with dark sinister faces who had emerged from the earth, so to speak." As the author of *Maggie,* the first American novel to treat slum life seriously from an insider's point of view, Crane might have done the same for the lives of these new Western workers. In this story it has been suggested that he instead chose to parody John Hay's *The Breadwinners,* a social novel that begs the question of industrial strikes through sentimental resolutions, producing an evasion of the labor issue which Crane's story—even as parody—must also share. It is instructive to see, though, that by setting alien scenes of industrial mob violence in the innocent spaces of a prairie town like Levelville, Crane showed himself prepared to understand the complexities of the West even before he visited it in 1895.

The actual West of Crane's visit had seen sixty thousand Western members of the American Railway Union walk out during a series of strikes in 1893 and 1894. Like the young, romantic hero of "A Christmas Dinner Won in Battle," many Americans had never seen the "sinister faces" of these strikers before; they seemed to emerge from the earth as "the men usually so sober, industrious, and imperturbable were running in a wild mob, raving and destroying." The extent of these strikes and sympathy strikes shocked many Americans in 1894, the same year that the newly formed Western Federation of Miners waged a two-front strike in the Colorado mines of Leadville and Cripple Creek. During these same years thousands of unemployed Westerners followed the lead of Coxey's Army and began marches to Washington, D.C., from Texas and California. When Crane arrived in the West, almost a half-dozen years had passed since the United States Superintendent of the Census announced that population had increased to the point where it was no longer possible to consider any part of the West a frontier. Certainly Crane also knew Richard Harding Davis's claim in *The West from a Car-Window* that by 1890 the West differed only to the stay-at-home Easterner who read reports by travelers tending to "show the differences that exist between the places they have visited and their own home. Of the similarities they say nothing. Or he has read of the bandits and outlaws of the Garza revolution, and he has seen the Wild West Show of the Hon. William F. Cody." Before his trip Crane wrote a spoof of such a legendary West in the form of a tall tale called "In a Park Row Restaurant." Two years earlier, in 1892, Francis Parkman had written a new preface for the fourth edition of *The Oregon Trail* and mournfully announced that the world of his book could now exist only in memory: "The buffalo is gone, and of all his millions nothing is left but bones . . . The wild Indian is turned into an ugly caricature of his conqueror . . . In his stead we have the cowboy, and even his star begins to wane. . . . The Wild West is tamed."

Crane was well-prepared for his trip, and yet his immediate response to the West as found in his journalism may surprise many readers. Missing from his newspaper sketches about Texas is the equanimity or laughter or controlled irony with which he treats the "wave of progress" in the Western fiction he wrote both before and after his trip. In the sketch he wrote about Galveston he seems at first calmly to echo Richard Harding Davis in a complaint that "travellers tumbling over each other in their haste to trumpet the radical differences between Eastern and Western life have created a generally wrong opinion. . . . It is this fact which has kept the sweeping march of the West from being chronicled in any particularly true manner." But in that same sketch Crane seems angry that Texas is not the truly different place of legend. He rails against the "almost universal condition of yellow trolly-cars with clanging gongs" as the most reprehensible product of the metropolitan, corporate, industrial society sweeping across the country. His references to purple pigs and children born with china mugs instead of ears are the uncontrolled metaphors of a man who seems spitting mad at finding so little in Galveston except square brick business blocks, mazes of telegraph wires, and reposeful men on the streets. Like the disappointed traveler of his sketch, Crane imaginatively "goes out in the sand somewhere and digs in order to learn if all Galveston clams are not schooner-rigged." It is significant that in a later sketch Crane refers to himself as "the archaeologist," for as he moves toward San Antonio, the symbol of "the poetry of life in Texas," he finds himself digging deeper and deeper for what remains from the past. He notes that in San Antonio the business edifices of stone and brick and iron are reared on ashes, and among them he finds a few remains, little old buildings, that have escaped the whirl of modern life and yet "despite the tenderness which San Antonio feels for these monuments, the unprotected mass of them must get trampled into shapeless dust which lies always behind the march of this terrible century." Crane's swing from sarcasm and anger to tenderness for monuments lapses into sentimentality at the discovery that "the Alamo remains the greatest memorial to courage which civilization has allowed to stand." Finding little color in the drabness of modern life, Crane finally fled the "Americanisms of San Antonio" and turned toward Mexico.

Going to Mexico in the late nineteenth century seemed to many Americans a way of going farther West. Texas, California, and most of the American Southwest were part of Mexico until almost mid-century, and after that time projections of the Wild West gradually shifted south of the border where, as Crane said, "southern Texas was being repeated." Either as the Wild West or as what Crane called "the land of flowers and visions and all that," Mexico seemed to offer flight from the industrial middle class. Crossing the border into Ciudad Juarez on a Sunday in 1882 was to Helen Hunt Jackson, writing in the *Atlantic*, "to escape from America and the nineteenth century as from place and time"; and thirty years later Ambrose Bierce still found that "in America you can't go east or west anymore, or north, the only avenue of escape is south." Crane could find the Wild West by riding into the badlands south of Mexico City, or he could escape to the Mexico of romance by taking a boat ride down the Viga Canal to the Xochimilco gardens, but a return to the city would quickly remind him that everything he had fled in the States was now coming to Mexico. Tourists and investors were both made welcome under Porfirio Díaz's dictatorial reign from 1876 to 1911. While bringing progress to Mexico and prosperity to a few, Díaz sold three-fourths of the country's mineral resources to foreign speculators, built roads, railroads, and telegraph lines, seized communal lands, granted them to favored *hacendados*, and laid the conditions for the revolution of 1911. At the time of Crane's visit in 1895, everything seemed peaceful. Englishmen and Americans owned industries, mines, *ranchos*, haciendas, oil fields, and as Crane said, if an American tourist who wanted a drink would go out into the street and yell: "Gimme a Manhattan!" about forty American bartenders would "appear of a sudden and say: 'Yes, sir.' "

The disappointment and nostalgia apparent in Crane's journalistic response to the wave of progress in Mexico and the West must be seen as understandable parts of a divided sensibility that gives all of his work its personal stamp. Often seen only in his role as an innovator and iconoclast, it is important to see Crane also as the defender of what he called the solemnity of tradition and history. Until he died of tuberculosis when he was only twenty-eight, he remained both an ironist and an idealist. A character description in a later war story, "This Majestic Lie," might serve as a portrait of Crane himself:

> Somewhere in him there was a sentimental tenderness, but it was like a light seen afar at night; it came, went, appeared again in a new place, flickered, flared, went out, left you in a void and angry. And if his sentimental tenderness was a light, the darkness in which it puzzled you was his irony of soul. This irony was directed first at himself; then at you; then at the nation and the flag; then at God. It was a midnight in which you searched for the little elusive, ashamed spark of tender sentiment.

Sometimes you thought this was all pretext, the manner and the way of fear of the wit of others; sometimes you thought he was a hardened savage; usually you did not think but waited in the cheerful certainty that in time the little flare of light would appear in the gloom.

It was as a storyteller rather than a journalist that Crane eventually achieved a balance between sentimental tenderness and irony of soul to give us without nostalgia or anger the best stories we have of the fading Wild West. "I understand," he wrote to a friend, "that a man is born into the world with his own pair of eyes, and he is not at all responsible for his vision—he is merely responsible for his quality of personal honesty." It was this personal honesty that would not let Crane surrender to the myth of the West as did Wister, Remington, and Roosevelt. But it was this same honesty that would not allow him to swing to the opposite extreme often identified with the Western "realism" of his friend and early mentor, Hamlin Garland. The harsh world of Garland's *Main-Travelled Roads* (1891), with its blighted lands and broken farmers, became a model for fiction that purported to represent the West with historical accuracy. Gunslingers and showdowns would be left to the mythmakers as serious writers identified themselves by the degree to which they either ignored the legendary Wild West as subject matter or treated it as bunk. In our own time the discrepancy between horse operas and serious fiction has so extended that Bernard DeVoto could justly claim, "The novelist can have the Old West myth or the historical West but I judge he can't have both of them at the same time."

But that is exactly what Crane wanted in his fiction: both at the same time. Neither Garland's view of the "realistic" West nor Roosevelt's view of the romantic West could fully satisfy Crane's own experience of both Wests. Nor could a simple division between "myth" and "reality" accommodate Crane's more profound understanding of the actual West, for he was one of the few writers in the late nineteenth century to recognize how the myth of the West had become part of its historical reality. In the 1890s, an Easterner prepared to visit a West that was the opposite of his mythic expectations would be surprised to find people out West who knew the myth and lived by it, creating a situation worthy of a Jorge Luis Borges. Before Crane went West he showed an early awareness of how the historical West might be shaped by its myth. In a newspaper article he wrote about Indian slayer Tom Quick, Crane ironically shows how Quick's exploits in dime novels colored the attitudes, if not the exact actions, of future Indian slayers, moving westward. Frontiersmen apparently began imitating their mythic counterparts as early as the eighteenth century when, according to the biography of John Bakeless, the real Daniel Boone began to model his public pronouncements on those of the fictional Daniel Boone as portrayed in 1784 by John Filson in *The Discovery, Settlement, and Present State of Kentucke.* In the twentieth century, a novel as late as Willa Cather's *My Ántonia* confirms Crane's observation that even realistic Westerners were always playing (or playing down) roles of legendary Westerners. When Scratchy Wilson puts on his fancy, decorated, maroon-colored flannel shirt made by some Jewish women on New York's East Side, he steps into a stereotypical role, but despite his ludicrous appearance, he becomes no less a whizz with his pistols. Jack Potter is no less the marshal of legend when, unarmed, he faces Wilson's drawn pistol and his heels do not move an inch backward. The triumph of "The Bride Comes to Yellow Sky" is that while it banishes the purely legendary West to the realm of fantasy, it quietly affirms the role of that fantasy in creating the historical West. It would be a denial of historical fact to write realistically of the West without including the Potters or Wilsons or those others who become Westerners by playing the roles of Westerners.

Crane's struggle to write fiction that tested the Western myth without totally rejecting it or accepting it began with "One Dash—Horses," the first Western he published after his trip. In following his own experience and telling the story of an Eastern dude who is initiated into the ways of Western life, Crane was adopting what had become a typical situation of much Western writing. Washington Irving, Francis Parkman, and other writers before Crane had all found themselves in this position of the dude coming into the West where things were supposed to be truly different, a situation that has since generated plots of countless horse operas. Crane's own initiation into the adventures of the Wild West, according to his first biographer, Thomas Beer, occurred in the badlands south of the Valley of Mexico when Crane and his guide, Miguel Itorbide, were chased on horseback by Ramón Colorado and his bandits. This actual event imitates what has become another cliché of Western writing, the chase and rescue. Forms of frontier pursuit extend as a commonplace from those indigenously American narratives of Indian captivity in the seventeenth century to the equally indigenous Western films of John Ford, Howard Hawks, and Sam Peckinpah in the twentieth century. Many people find the chase scene as obligatory to Westerns as others find the walkdown, and Sam Peckinpah goes furthest in saying that all stories are Westerns to the extent that they "put the hare in front of the hound and let the hound chase the hare." Crane's own gallop from bandits came to an end with the fortuitous appearance of *rurales*, "that crack cavalry corps of the Mexican army which polices the plain so zealously," as Crane says, "a fierce and swift-moving body that knows little of prevention but much of vengeance." The passage offers a true enough account of the thugs who made up the *rurales* during the Díaz regime, but the sudden rescue of Crane's story also produces a reversal typical of Western fiction and film as Crane's pursuers become the pursued.

Crane suggests in "One Dash—Horses" that he was thinking of other tales similar to his own as he wrote his story of this race for life. One such tale might have been "Kaweah's Run" in Clarence King's *Mountaineering in the Sierra Nevada*, published in 1872. Often overlooked as a maker of American literature, Clarence King, who is presented in *The Education of Henry Adams* as "the best and brightest of our generation," culminated a career of scientific exploration of the West as the first director of the United States Geological Survey, which he was largely responsible for forming in 1879. His literary career placed him in a triumvirate with Mark Twain and Bret Harte, a group that by the 1870s had brought a new literary professionalism to the treatment of Western materials. The miners, mountaineers, and desperadoes, as well as the landscapes and adventures found in Mark Twain's *Roughing It*, Bret Harte's *Luck of Roaring Camp and Other Stories*, and Clarence King's *Mountaineering in the Sierra Nevada*, shaped the initial outlines of what has remained our most tenacious vision of the legendary Far West.

Just as Clarence King named "Kaweah's Run" after his horse, Crane gave the honor of his story's title, "One Dash—Horses," to his guide's battered black horse and his own "little insignificant rat-colored beast," who, like Kaweah, emerge as the true heroes of their run. Other similarities between the two stories are remarkable. Both King and Crane work with what has become the assumption of twentieth-century cowboy fiction—that the Westerner and his horse go together as naturally as a man and a woman. Crane's explicit use of this simile stresses the intimacy expected of Western heroes with the natural world, for it is through its animals and natives that the Westerner comes to know the mysteries of the wilds. When King finds himself, like Crane's protagonist, chased by Mexican bandits, King finds the moment thrilling: "Kaweah and pistol were my only defense, yet at that moment I felt a thrill of pleasure, a wild moment of inspiration, almost worth the danger to experience." To evoke the sensation of such a run, both Crane and King put the reader on horseback, as it were, looking over the horse's ears. Crane's protagonist Richardson swings into the saddle next to his guide José. Richardson feels a thrill of confidence in his mount as side by side the two horses race down the village street and into the desert:

> Richardson, looking down, saw the long, fine reach of forelimb, as steady as steel machinery. As the ground reeled past, the long, dried grasses hissed, and cactus plants were dull blurs. A wind whirled the horse's mane over his rider's bridle hand. . . .
> Richardson, again looking backward, could see a slanting flare of dust on the whitening plain. He thought that he could detect small moving figures in it. . . .
> . . . As a matter of truth, the ground seemed merely something to be touched from time to time with hoofs that were as light as blown leaves. Occasionally Richardson lay back and pulled stoutly at his bridle to keep from abandoning his servant. José harried at his horse's mouth, flopped around in the saddle and made his two heels beat like flails. The black ran like a horse in despair.
> Crimson serapes in the distance resembled drops of blood on the great cloth of plain.

What distinguishes Crane's writing are these details—the hiss of dry grass, the dull blur of cactus plants, and the pursuing riders in the distance perceived as small, moving figures in a slanting flare of dust on the whitening plain. The use of such details marked Crane as the American writer who had brought fictional prose as close as possible to reproducing immediate sensation and perception. Unlike King, Crane uses his skills to evoke the thrill of Richardson's run only as a brief moment in what is actually a welter of rage, terror, and hatred. "The long horror" that underlies most of the adventure shapes the ominous vision of distant serapes as drops of blood on the plains. Unlike King, Crane also stresses the role of chance in the outcome of this drama, as suggested by the title—"one dash"—which appears in other Crane stories as slang for one roll of the dice. Crane's concern with the importance of luck in the outcome of individual showdowns differs from that of most Westerns, where victories are traditionally due to merit. Most distinctive of "One Dash—Horses," however, is that at moments of the story's greatest intensity, the author breaks into the narrative in his own voice with a direct address to the reader or a comic aside or an unexpected wisecrack that destroys the immediacy of the drama. There are few readers who have not been troubled by the interruption that occurs as Richardson lies in a dark room and listens to voices on the other side of a doorway discussing plans to murder him. Richardson feels his skin draw tight around his mouth and his knee joints turn to bread. As he slowly comes to a sitting position he looks like a corpse rising in wan moonlight that gives everything the hue of the grave. At that moment Crane breaks into the story and addresses the reader: "My friend, take my advice, and never be executed by a hangman who doesn't talk the English language. It, or anything that resembles it, is the most difficult of deaths." The self-consciousness of such mannered prose pervades "One Dash—Horses," as if Crane does not know whether to treat his story seriously or comically. He cannot adapt quite as comfortably as Clarence King to the role of the Western hero riding with grace and confidence through his Wild West adventure. Crane keeps testing the validity of that legendary West at the same time that he measures himself against it. Like his protagonist, Richardson, "he remembered all the tales of such runs for life and thought them badly written." He refuses to let his story and central character fall into the simple heroics of those badly written stories, but as his comic or sarcastic voice successfully punctures the story when it is about to balloon into the falsely heroic, it also unsuccessfully deflates the dramatic intensity of the immediate moment.

In three stories written between the time of "One Dash—Horses" and "The Bride Comes to Yellow Sky," Crane's intertwining of the mythical West with his own experience took a new turn. All three stories, written in 1896, combine the education of the dude with the showdown (or some other contest based on a bet or dare) to produce Westerns that are as much stories of comprehension as of action. Through his initiation the dude acquires new skills, but he also acquires new ways of seeing. In "The Wise Men," a story that H. G. Wells described as "a perfect thing," two dudes called the New York Kid and the San Francisco Kid (and a third named Benson) engage in a series of bluffs and bets with true Western bravado until they are potentially deep in debt unless an older man can beat a younger man in a race down the Paseo de la Reforma. The Kids win, but what matters is their attitude. The third kid, Benson, loses both money and a handkerchief tied in a string marking the race's finish line, but after a momentary disgruntlement, he composes himself to affect a Western stance. Asked how much he lost, he laconically replies, "Oh, not so much," while the Kids offer exactly the same response to Benson when asked how much they won. "Well, I'm damned!" says an observer. Like Larpent, the Western gambler in "Moonlight on the Snow," who is about to be hanged for murder, the Kids become themselves most when least concerned about themselves. Larpent's apparent indifference to his fate makes him "handsome and distinguished—and a devil." The Kids' disinterest in the result of the bet lets them share a minor part of that dignity that goes beyond victory or defeat.

The situation becomes more serious during a showdown on a dark Mexican street in "The Five White Mice" when these same Kids, entangled again by bets, dares, cold bluff, and chance, expose something new about themselves and their darker-skinned enemies. In the West in 1895 there were no Indians left to chase Crane across the desert, but there were Mexicans, and in the dime novels and folklore of the time, the Mexican often replaced the Indian as the stereotypical dark, mysterious savage, the supposed opposite of the white man. The Western hero, though, remained the man in the middle. Just as mountainmen like Kit Carson and Jim Bridger once defined themselves by adopting the dress and ways of Indians, so the new Western hero, the cowboy, was one who adopted the skills and outfit of the Mexican *vaquero*. A significant example of this change occurred when Buffalo Bill Cody prepared to avenge Custer's Last Stand during the closing phase of the Indian Wars. According to biographer Richard Walsh, when Buffalo Bill rode out to duel Yellow Hand and take "the first scalp for Custer," instead of wearing his customary suit of buckskin, he appeared before reporters wearing a Mexican stage outfit of black velvet slashed with scarlet and trimmed with silver buttons and lace. With less extravagance, Crane's dudes also wear sombreros and large, flashing spurs, and during their adventures, Mexicans fill the role of natural antagonists as Indians once did in the Wild West fiction of the past. The most extreme stereotypes of the Mexican appear in Crane's journalism, especially as objects of easy satire, but such stereotypes are jarred in both "The Five White Mice" and "A Man and Some Others," two of the finest stories Crane ever wrote. In "A Man and Some Others," the story that Joseph Conrad admired most, Crane violated the dime-novel formula in a way that offended the mythic expectations of a future president of the United States. "Next time I want you to write a story," Theodore Roosevelt said in a letter to Crane, "in which the frontiersman shall come out on top. It's more normal that way." Roosevelt's mythic (and racist) assumptions are exposed in "The Five White Mice," called "one of the great short stories of the world" by Ford Madox Ford. During his showdown the New York Kid learns something about the combination of honorable manhood and fear and the five white mice of chance that allows his gun to rise from its holster and cause his Mexican antagonist to back down from a fight. The New York Kid then becomes angry as he recognizes the "equality of emotion" he shares with someone he took to be a fearless, knife-wielding Mexican villain. Stereotypes fall apart as the men merge in their mutual fear and vulnerability. "Thus the Kid was able to understand swiftly that they were all human beings." This vision of the Mexican becomes all the more significant when we remember that Crane's stories mark the first appearance of Mexico and Mexicans in serious American fiction.

During such moments of awareness in Crane's Westerns the dude often becomes "like a creature allowed a glimpse of another world." As action, the showdown in "The Five White Mice" is rightly defined by the last line of the story, "Nothing had happened." But as internal drama, everything was happening to the Kid. A shift in point of view, as Crane said in another story, could be like a blow in the chest. The tone of the remark, "Nothing had happened," and the calm response of the Kid's "Let's go home," underscore the attitude the Kids achieve in "The Wise Men," where they accept the consequences of events and learn to mock them or view them with detachment. Laughter is the great equalizer, and all the put-downs, practical jokes, put-ons, and hoaxes of Western humor serve to deflate an individual sense of self-importance. Nothing should be taken too seriously, and as we see in a tall tale used in both "In a Park Row Restaurant" and "London Impressions," everything—even matters of life and death—can be smiled at. It is this lesson—"Nothing had happened"—that the mountains and deserts of the West can teach, as we see in "A Man and Some Others."

> Finally, when the great moon climbed the heavens and cast its ghastly radiance upon the bushes, it made a new and more brilliant crimson of the camp-fire, where the flames capered merrily through its mesquit branches, filling the silence with the fire chorus, an ancient melody which surely bears a message of the inconsequence of individual tragedy—a message that is in the boom of the sea, the sliver of the wind through the grass-blades, the silken clash of hemlock boughs.
>
> No figures moved in the rosy space of the camp, and the search of the moonbeams failed to disclose a living thing in the bushes. There was no owl-faced clock to chant the weariness of the long silence that brooded upon the plain.

Because human fate becomes so inconsequential before such a point of view, nature usually assumes the force of character, if not the chief character, in much Western writing. In Crane's fiction, the most crucial difference between the Western stories written before and after his trip is that the early stories, like the initial Western drawings of Frederic Remington, were devoid of particular landscapes, while the later ones achieved much of their power through details evoking the country and its weather. John Berryman, in his important critical biography of Crane, suggests that along with Crane's run for life from Mexican bandits, the most significant experience of his trip was his encounter with a different kind of nature than he had known before. As if anticipating the importance of the Western landscape to his work, two of the desires Crane expressed before heading West, according to Thomas Beer, were to see the Mississippi and to be on the plains in a blizzard, and both desires were satisfied. After crossing the Mississippi, Crane was caught in a Nebraskan blizzard whose journalistic re-creation as man's "pitiless enemy" provided much of the force to his moving report of

"Nebraska's Bitter Fight for Life." Another view of nature came when Crane took the train from San Antonio through the volcanic colors of desert and cactus and climbed into the mountains where "beyond a plain arose the peak of Nevado de Toluca for 15,000 feet. . . . And no one feels like talking in the presence of these mountains that stand like gods on the world, for fear they might hear." The personification of this awesome mountain, like that of the hostile Nebraskan blizzard, dramatized extremes of nature that Crane never experienced before, but it was probably during quieter times, on the open plains when a man might crave mountains, that Crane perhaps knew most deeply that nature was not interested in man, even as an enemy. "They wanted mountains. They clamored for mountains. 'How soon, conductor, will we see any mountains?' The conductor indicated a long shadow in the pallor of the afterglow. Faint, delicate, it resembled the light rain-clouds of a faraway shower." At such a moment or among smaller mountains, "wrinkled, crumpled, bare of everything save sagebrush," one might feel "the world was declared to be a desert and unpeopled." It is against a backdrop of such a landscape that a tiny figure on horseback achieves cinematic power in a Crane story. Instead of fear or awe, one might then experience a loneliness that cowboy artist John Noble claimed could be a fatal disease. To a man unaccustomed to the plains, looking out over seemingly endless rises and swells of land and grass, expecting to see something different on the next rise and finding nothing but desolate distances, the effect, says Noble, can be appalling. " 'He's got loneliness,' we would say of such a man." It was perhaps a similar sense of isolation among an alien people and landscape that found Francis Parkman in *The Oregon Trail* staring into the cold ashes of a mountaineer's dead campfire: "it perplexed me a good deal to understand why I should look with so much interest on the ashes of his fire, when between him and me there was no other bond of sympathy than the slender and precarious one of a kindred race." Perhaps, as has been suggested, Parkman was longing not only for civilization but for the idea of civilization itself. Similarly, years later, Elizabeth Shepley Sergeant reports that Willa Cather, after spending two months in New Mexico, was sitting on the banks of the Rio Grande when "suddenly a bitter wind seemed to arise from the peaks and she saw, written before her in the dust, a sentence from Balzac she had long forgotten:

" 'Dans le désert, voyez-vous, il y a tout et il n'y a rien—
Dieu, sans les hommes.'

"Everything and nothing—God without men! . . .

"Panic seized her—it said the West is consuming you,
make tracks for home." Nothing or no one in the desert,
"certainly not the Indians, could replace a civilization, her
civilization. *Her own*." What similar estrangements Crane
may have experienced in the desert and mountains may be
hidden in the silences and conventional images of a letter ex-
plaining his sudden departure from Mexico.

> I was in southern Mexico last winter for a sufficient time
> to have my face turn the color of a brick side-walk.
> There was nothing American about me save a large Smith
> and Wesson revolver and I saw only Indians whom
> I suspected of loading their tomales [*sic*] with dog. In
> this state of mind and this physical condition, I arrived
> one day in the city of Puebla and there I saw an Ameri-
> can girl. There was a party of tourists in town and she
> was of their contingent. I only saw her four times—one
> in the hotel corridor and three in the street. I had been
> so long in the mountains and was such an outcast, that
> the sight of this American girl in a new spring gown
> nearly caused me to drop dead. She of course never
> looked in my direction. I never met her. Nevertheless I
> gained one of those peculiar thrills which a man only ac-
> knowledges upon occasion. I ran to the railroad office. I
> cried: "What is the shortest route to New York." I left
> Mexico.

No matter that the girl in Puebla "who startled me out of
my mountaineer senses" reminded Crane of Nellie Crouse of
Akron, Ohio. What matters more is the gulf he felt separating
his world from hers at the end of the Western trip. Changes
in his sense of self and point of view, as his letter allows, suggest the distance he may have traveled in an alien land. Only
his opaque references to his "mountaineer senses," his view of
himself as "an outcast," and his "state of mind" after being
so long in the mountains suggest what he was to reveal in
other writings.

During the year following his trip, while Crane vacillated
between the extremes of his imagination, swinging from the
irony of "A Texas Legend" to the sentimental tenderness of
"The Veteran," there emerged a point of view that would al-

ter his treatment of the Western hero. The landscape of the Western stories that lets us see the inconsequence of human tragedy also shapes a vision where the habits, values, customs, and codes by which we live and make sense of our world become arbitrary. In his earlier novel, *The Red Badge of Courage*, the ideal of courage lingers in the background as Crane tests certain traditional virtues against the actions of his boy soldier, but in the first story Crane wrote after his Western trip, "A Mystery of Heroism," the very conceptions of courage and heroism evaporate into mystery. In this war story we see all we can of the luck, will, chance, personality, thought, and everything else that make up an event, but we cannot reduce that event to any moral category. It is impossible to say whether the soldier in "A Mystery of Heroism" is a hero or a fool. In "Above All Things," a significant journalistic piece about the Indians of Mexico, Crane acknowledges that "the scheme of nature" does not exclusively support any man's particular moral view. This attitude became most firmly defined in "The Open Boat," the story Crane wrote after his own experience in January, 1897, when, two years after his Western trip, he was shipwrecked off the coast of Florida and spent thirty hours adrift at sea in a small lifeboat. With the writing of "The Open Boat," Crane mastered the vision that informed his best Western writing and culminated in his later stories, "The Bride Comes to Yellow Sky" and "The Blue Hotel."

As we have seen in "The Bride Comes to Yellow Sky," printed in 1898, Crane reached the point where he could treat the Wild West both comically and seriously, and he could test the legendary qualities of the West without the marring intrusions of his first Westerns. He could also create a Westerner of heroic stature without fully accepting or rejecting him as a Western hero. The increasingly complex world of his fiction eluded the conventional orderings of reason and morality that are often reduced in horse operas to simplistic notions of manliness and self-reliance. In Mexico Crane had written that along with attempts at moral judgment, "a man must not devote himself for a time to attempts at psychological perception. He can be sure of two things, form and color. Let him then see all he can and let him not sit in literary judgment on this or that matter of the people." In "A Man and Some Others," sheepherder Bill is certainly not a hero in any conventional sense. He is cruel, hotheaded, and a murderer, but he earns from the Eastern dude "a deep form of idolatry" during a gun battle in southwestern Texas. A new way of seeing and judging is called for, and it is dependent on vision rather than virtue. We respond with the dude as we see Bill, wounded and dying, "upreared like a great and bloody spirit of vengeance, his face lighted with the blaze of his last passion." In the beauty given off in the flush of dying, Bill enters a new realm where, in Robert Warshow's words, "a hero is one who looks like a hero."

The Westerner who in the twentieth century came to look like a hero to many Americans was the cowboy. His presence now defines a Western, but his potential as a folk hero did not emerge significantly until his real world was coming to an end. The droughts and blizzards of 1885–86, along with barbed wire, new strains of cattle stock, new markets, and collapsing prices, began the demise of the open range and the long drives from Texas. It was at this time that the first cowboy memoirs, Charlie Siringo's *A Texas Cow Boy or, Fifteen Years on the Hurricane Deck of a Spanish Pony*, appeared—in 1886, the same year that Frederic Remington's drawings of cowboys first appeared on the cover of America's most popular magazine, *Harper's Weekly*. In 1887 the cowboy became a dime-novel hero in Prentiss Ingraham's *Buck Taylor, King of the Cowboys*, and the following year Theodore Roosevelt began his glorification of the cowboy in articles for *The Century Magazine*. Four years later Owen Wister published a story in *Harper's Monthly* that became in 1897 the opening chapter of a novel about cowboy Lin McLean, the prototype of the mythical Virginian. In 1897 the cowboy also appeared in hard-cover works by Alfred Henry Lewis and Emerson Hough, two writers along with Wister normally considered responsible for the origin of the cowboy as a fictional hero. It was in that same significant year of 1897 that another creator of the cowboy, Frederic Remington, illustrated Crane's "A Man and Some Others" for *The Century*. At a time when the cowboy was just emerging as a subject for novels, Crane presented him as both a yokel and a hero. In one of his last Westerns, "Twelve O'Clock" he outlined characteristics that would define the cowboy in much early twentieth-century fiction and film.

From the street sounded a quick scudding of pony hoofs, and a party of cowboys swept past the door. One man, however, was seen to draw rein and dismount. He came clanking into the store. "Mornin', gentlemen," he said civilly.

"Mornin'," they answered in subdued voices.

He stepped to the counter and said, "Give me a paper of fine cut, please." The group of citizens contemplated him in silence. He certainly did not look threatening. He appeared to be a young man of twenty-five years, with a tan from wind and sun, with a remarkably clear eye from perhaps a period of enforced temperance, a quiet young man who wanted to buy some tobacco. A six-shooter swung low on his hip, but at the moment it looked more decorative than warlike; it seemed merely a part of his odd gala dress—his sombrero with its band of rattlesnake skin, his great flaming neckerchief, his belt of embroidered Mexican leather, his high-heeled boots, his huge spurs. And, above all, his hair had been watered and brushed until it lay as close to his head as the fur to a wet cat. Paying for his tobacco, he withdrew.

Ben Roddle resumed his harangue. "Well, there you are! Looks like a calm man now, but in less'n half an hour he'll be as drunk as three bucks an' a squaw, an' then. . . . excuse *me!*"

The cowboys in Crane's late stories are rowdy, sometimes stupid, quick to laugh and test the equanimity of others through practical jokes, but most important, "they would fight for nothing—yes—they often fought for nothing—but they would not fight for this dark something." The cowboy of legend, as Warshow demonstrates in his essay, "The Western-er," does not fight primarily for things like virtue or justice or order, but rather for nothing more substantial than the purity of his own image, his honor and dignity. "Dignity, however," as Lionel Trilling has said, "is not a moral quality—it is a quality of appearance, of style or manner." An aesthetic of harmonious appearance was certainly at the base of Crane's third wish before heading West when he expressed a desire to see a cowboy ride. Appearance or style does not preclude substance, especially in the West, where, J.B. Priestley observed, a cowboy does things that "cannot be faked, as politicians and professional men and directors of companies so often fake things. He cannot pretend to be able to ride and rope, and get away with it." Of all the possible meanings of the American West as the land of adventure or the land of self-reliance or the land of regeneration or manliness or riches or freedom, the most important to Crane seemed to be the West as the land of honesty. What mattered to him was "the atmosphere of the west which really is frank and honest." Good "form" to him was a person's simple truthfulness to who he was, and the real barbarian or savage was one who hid behind the artifice of social roles and affectations. "I fell in love with the straight out and out, sometimes hideous, often braggart westerners because I thought them to be the truer men. . . .

"And yet—

"[Hamlin] Garland will wring every westerner by the hand and hail him as a frank honest man. I won't. No, sir."

Crane's "No, sir" attests to his discovery of the snake in the garden. Even in the West, as seen in the greatest of Crane's Western stories, "The Blue Hotel," things are not always honest, and what seems to be real may be only another set of arbitrary conventions. "The Blue Hotel" reflects a deep cynicism that accompanies the discovery that everything is a game and nothing is certain—even in the supposedly frank and candid West. As the values of the Old West collapse, dread is loosed, and all the comforting conventions of the Western get turned inside out. "The Blue Hotel" can be read as a nightmare Western where the dude who is to be initiated into the ways of Western life does everything right and gets everything wrong.

According to Thomas Beer, Crane himself experienced a similar moment in a saloon in Lincoln, Nebraska, on February 13, 1895, when he tried to stop a lopsided fist fight between a big man and a much smaller one. "But then I offended a local custom," Crane says. "These men fought each other every night. Their friends expected it and I was a damned nuisance with my Eastern scruples and all that. So first everybody cursed me fully and then they took me off to a judge who told me that I was an imbecile and let me go; it was very saddening. Whenever I try to do right, it don't." Instead of confronting what is basic and elemental in the West, Crane found another code of social conduct, no more or less arbitrary than in the East. The curious ceremonial quality of Western violence Crane discovered became institutionalized in the ritualistic gunfights between Marshal Potter and Scratchy Wilson in "The Bride Comes to Yellow Sky." Unaware of the social rules in this ritual between her husband and Scratchy, the bride becomes a slave to some hideous rite and sees the apparitional snake. The aesthetic importance of stylized walkdowns becomes apparent in "A Texas Legend" and "Twelve O'Clock," where violence without its ceremonial characteristic stuns us. These stories provide truer views of Western gunfights than do the face-offs of horse operas. Seeds for the showdowns that grew from Wister's invention might be found in the shoot-outs of nineteenth-century Wild West Shows and dime novels, but there is no evidence that the quickdraws of TV Westerns had anything to do with historical fact until after their initial appearance in fiction. In "The Blue Hotel" Western ceremonies keep breaking down, and no code of conduct remains dependable. When the hotelkeeper slaps the Swede on the shoulder, he performs a gesture of welcome into the ways of Western life, but when the Swede later returns the slap to the hotelkeeper's shoulder, the meaning has changed, and the slap breeds resentment rather than good fellowship. In the saloon the meaning of the gesture is completely reversed when the Swede merely touches the shoulder of the gambler in what becomes an act of hostility culminating in the Swede's death. In such a world of shifting meanings, there can be no certain understanding or moral judgment. The position held by the cowboy that the Swede brought his death on himself is as limited as the Easterner's "fog of mysterious theory" which finds "from a dozen to forty women really involved in every murder."

Because "The Blue Hotel" fails to fit the stock formula of the horse opera, many readers do not see it as a Western at all. They are right, of course, in the strict sense that the Western must follow the recognizable patterns of cow fiction. In Crane's time, however, the formula had not hardened, and "The Blue Hotel" offered later writers a pattern that was as Western as the showdown of "The Bride Comes to Yellow Sky." In neglecting the underside of the Western myth presented in "The Blue Hotel," perhaps the Western missed a chance of becoming a genre of serious fiction. Like Yellow Sky, the town of Fort Romper in "The Blue Hotel" fits the role required by the setting of Western formula by being on the edge of civilization but not quite there. It is important to see that the things representative of Eastern urbanity and social order mentioned by the hotelkeeper have not yet arrived in Fort Romper. This junction town is clearly in a more primitive state than its boosters would like others to believe, but it is still a community, and the Swede, like the Indians and outlaws of other Westerns, is the outsider who comes to town and disturbs the fragile harmony of the community. A vast, distancing landscape provides a traditional backdrop for this Western drama. The image of a strangely painted light blue hotel makes this town seem particularly vulnerable and artificial in contrast to the surrounding plains whose comment on human tragedy is accentuated by the long cry of a blizzard.

The irony of the Swede's role is double. He represents savagery, but in aspiring to become like the Western hero, he also represents noble values. Yet he releases violence, not from savages outside Fort Romper or from a harsh, pitiless nature, but from the heart of the town's communal forms—the saloon and the hotel—where human nature, like the stove in the hotel, "was humming with godlike violence." Into this world the Swede comes, believing that the harsh landscape strips social artifice from the basic, honest, natural man of the West. Out West a man learns that he must be as tough as the land he lives in. The country soon brings out the strengths and weaknesses of character, and the Swede, appropriately, tests himself against the blizzard and says, "Yes, I like this weather. I like it. It suits me." As he grows confident in his manliness, he talks more and more like a man of the West, telling his host, "Well, old boy, that was a good square meal," and finally twanging out during a card game, "You are cheatin'!" Unlike the cowboy in this story whose bovine stupidity and lack of dignity make him a comic reversal of the heroic cowboy, the Swede in a way becomes the traditional Western hero. Unlike the obtuse cowboy who cannot understand why the Swede should fight when no money is involved, the Swede, like the heroic cowboy, fights for his honor: "Yes, fight! I'll show you what kind of a man I am!" Victorious in his fight with the cheater, the Swede achieves briefly in the eyes of the observing Easterner the dignity and isolation of a Western hero. Out of violence comes his moment of self-transcendence.

> There was a splendor of isolation in his situation at this time which the Easterner felt once when, lifting his eyes from the man on the ground, he beheld that mysterious and lonely figure, waiting.

The triumph of the Swede is short-lived, and in the saloon, we see that he is not the heroic savior of the community at all, but rather the savage threat that must be eliminated by the town's true hero, the gambler. There simply is no place in the community for the atavistic values of the Old West as adopted by the Swede. The individualism and self-sufficiency learned from nature destroy social values and breed isolation, narcissism, and violence. The Swede becomes a joke in the world of the saloon where people are interdependent rather than independent. Like the hero of the Old West he replaces, the gambler takes the traditional position between the community and this savage representing unrestrained passions and ignorance. As the man in the middle, the gambler lives on the fringes of society. He has a real wife and two real children in a suburb, but the town will not allow him the social recognition of belonging to the newly formed Pollywog Club. Like Owen Wister's heroic Virginian, this laconic gambler has a "quiet dignity," he speaks to the Swede in a tone of "heroic patronage," he acts according to a code of honor, he restrains himself from responding to the Swede's provocations until the Swede violently attacks him, then with efficient, frightening grace, he sticks the Swede and kills him. As the gambler calmly "wiped his knife on one of the towels that hung beneath the bar rail," he addressed the bartender: "You tell 'em where to find me. I'll be home, waiting for 'em." Then he vanished. The Virginian would respond similarly after shooting Trampas when Wister's novel would appear a few years later: "If anybody wants me about this," he said, "I will be at the hotel."

The horror behind this vision of the triumphant hero is what Crane finally unveils in "The Blue Hotel" and what subsequent Westerns have chosen to ignore. In stories like "The Five White Mice" and "The Bride Comes to Yellow Sky," we see the panic and chaos lingering behind the ceremonies of the Western showdown. In "A Man and Some Others," we feel a deep idolatry for a man who becomes heroic through the dignity of last defeat, but then we become like the dude when he looked down at this dead man and "all at once he made a gesture of fright and looked wildly about him." In "The Blue Hotel," we finally look into the living eyes of a self-composed, triumphant Western hero, and we become like the bartender in the saloon, who "found himself hanging limply to the arm of a chair and gazing into the eyes of a murderer." America's favorite heroes have been its killers, but a gesture of fright becomes our own as we look blankly at this man's violence so often disguised and even justified by the rituals of the showdown and the pleasant aesthetics of the quickdraw.

In "The Blue Hotel" we are awed by the grace of a knife's movement but appalled by the death that follows it. Out of such moments of violence, the precision of Crane's truthtelling glows with disturbing beauty.

Vassar College

FRANK BERGON

A Note on the Text

The text of this edition of Stephen Crane's Western stories, sketches, and reports is based on *The University of Virginia Edition of The Works of Stephen Crane*, edited by Fredson Bowers, Volume V, *Tales of Adventure*, with an introduction by J. C. Levenson, 1970, and Volume VIII, *Tales, Sketches, and Reports*, with an introduction by Edwin H. Cady, 1973. Variant titles have been used for some selections: "A Texas Legend" appears in the Virginia edition as "A Freight Car Incident," "Billy Atkins Went to Omaha" as "An Excursion Ticket," " 'Mid Cactus and Mesquite" as "Stephen Crane in Mexico (II)," and "Above All Things" as "The Mexican Lower Classes." Excerpts from Stephen Crane's letters are reprinted from *Stephen Crane: Letters*, edited by R. W. Stallman and Lillian Gilkes, New York University Press, 1960.

WESTERN STORIES

One Dash—Horses

Richardson pulled up his horse and looked back over the trail where the crimson serape of his servant flamed amid the dusk of the mesquite. The hills in the west were carved into peaks, and were painted the most profound blue. Above them, the sky was of that marvelous tone of green—like still, sun-shot water—which people denounce in pictures.

José was muffled deep in his blanket, and his great toppling sombrero was drawn low over his brow. He shadowed his master along the dimming trail in the fashion of an assassin. A cold wind of the impending night swept over the wilderness of mesquite.

"Man," said Richardson in lame Mexican as the servant drew near, "I want eat! I want sleep! Understand—no? Quickly! Understand?" "Si, señor," said José, nodding. He stretched one arm out of his blanket and pointed a yellow finger into the gloom. "Over there, small village! Si, señor."

They rode forward again. Once the American's horse shied and breathed quiveringly at something which he saw or imagined in the darkness, and the rider drew a steady, patient rein, and leaned over to speak tenderly as if he were addressing a frightened woman. The sky had faded to white over the mountains and the plain was a vast, pointless ocean of black.

Suddenly some low houses appeared squatting amid the bushes. The horsemen rode into a hollow until the houses rose against the sombre sundown sky, and then up a small hillock, causing these habitations to sink like boats in the sea of shadow.

A beam of red firelight fell across the trail. Richardson sat sleepily on his horse while the servant quarreled with somebody—a mere voice in the gloom—over the price of bed and board. The houses about him were for the most part like tombs in their whiteness and silence, but there were scudding black figures that seemed interested in his arrival.

31

José came at last to the horses' heads, and the American slid stiffly from his seat. He muttered a greeting, as with his spurred feet he clicked into the adobe house that confronted him. The brown stolid face of a woman shone in the light of the fire. He seated himself on the earthen floor and blinked drowsily at the blaze. He was aware that the woman was clinking earthenware and hieing here and everywhere in the maneuvers of the housewife. From a dark corner of the room there came the sound of two or three snores twining together.

The woman handed him a bowl of tortillas. She was a submissive creature, timid and large-eyed. She gazed at his enormous silver spurs, his large and impressive revolver, with the interest and admiration of the highly privileged cat of the adage. When he ate, she seemed transfixed off there in the gloom, her white teeth shining.

José entered, staggering under two Mexican saddles, large enough for building sites. Richardson decided to smoke a cigarette, and then changed his mind. It would be much finer to go to sleep. His blanket hung over his left shoulder furled into a long pipe of cloth, according to a Mexican fashion. By doffing his sombrero, unfastening his spurs and his revolver belt, he made himself ready for the slow blissful twist into the blanket. Like a cautious man he lay close to the wall, and all his property was very near his hand.

The mesquite brush burned long. José threw two gigantic wings of shadow as he flapped his blanket about him—first across his chest under his arms, and then around his neck and across his chest again—this time over his arms, with the end tossed on his right shoulder. A Mexican thus snugly enveloped can nevertheless free his fighting arm in a beautifully brisk way, merely shrugging his shoulder as he grabs for the weapon at his belt. (They always wear their serapes in this manner.)

The firelight smothered the rays which, streaming from a moon as large as a drum head, were struggling at the open door. Richardson heard from the plain the fine, rhythmical trample of the hoofs of hurried horses. He went to sleep wondering who rode so fast and so late. And in the deep silence the pale rays of the moon must have prevailed against the red spears of the fire until the room was slowly flooded to its middle with a rectangle of silver light.

Richardson was awakened by the sound of a guitar. It was badly played—in this land of Mexico, from which the romance of the instrument ascends to us like a perfume. The guitar was groaning and whining like a badgered soul. A noise of scuffling feet accompanied the music. Sometimes laughter arose, and often the voices of men saying bitter things to each other, but always the guitar cried on, the treble sounding as if some one were beating iron, and the bass humming like bees. "Damn it—they're having a dance," muttered Richardson, fretfully. He heard two men quarreling in short, sharp words, like pistol shots; they were calling each other worse names than common people know in other countries. He wondered why the noise was so loud. Raising his head from his saddle pillow, he saw, with the help of the valiant moonbeams, a blanket hanging flat against the wall at the further end of the room. Being of the opinion that it concealed a door, and remembering that Mexican drink made men very drunk, he pulled his revolver closer to him and prepared for sudden disaster.

Richardson was dreaming of his far and beloved North.

"Well, I would kill him, then!"

"No, you must not!"

"Yes, I will kill him! Listen! I will ask this American beast for his beautiful pistol and spurs and money and saddle, and if he will not give them—you will see!"

"But these Americans—they are a strange people. Look out, señor."

Then twenty voices took part in the discussion. They rose in quavering shrillness, as from men badly drunk. Richardson felt the skin draw tight around his mouth, and his knee-joints turned to bread. He slowly came to a sitting posture, glaring at the motionless blanket at the far end of the room. This stiff and mechanical movement, accomplished entirely by the muscles of the waist, must have looked like the rising of a corpse in the wan moonlight which gave everything a hue of the grave.

My friend, take my advice and never be executed by a hangman who doesn't talk the English language. It, or anything that resembles it, is the most difficult of deaths. The tumultuous emotions of Richardson's terror destroyed that slow and careful process of thought by means of which he understood Mexican. Then he used his instinctive comprehension of the first and universal language, which is tone. Still it is disheartening not to be able to understand the detail of threats against the blood of your body.

Suddenly the clamor of voices ceased. There was a silence—a silence of decision. The blanket was flung aside, and the red light of a torch flared into the room. It was held high by a fat, round-faced Mexican, whose little snake-like mustache was as black as his eyes, and whose eyes were black as jet. He was insane with the wild rage of a man whose liquor is dully burning at his brain. Five or six of his fellows crowded after him. The guitar, which had been thrummed doggedly during the time of the high words, now suddenly stopped. They contemplated each other. Richardson sat very straight and still, his right hand lost in the folds of his blanket. The Mexicans jostled in the light of the torch, their eyes blinking and glittering.

The fat one posed in the manner of a grandee. Presently his hand dropped to his belt, and from his lips there spun an epithet—a hideous word which often foreshadows knife-blows, a word peculiarly of Mexico, where people have to dig deep to find an insult that has not lost its savor. The American did not move. He was staring at the fat Mexican with a strange fixedness of gaze, not fearful, not dauntless, not anything that could be interpreted. He simply stared.

The fat Mexican must have been disconcerted, for he continued to pose as a grandee, with more and more sublimity, until it would have been easy for him to have fallen over backward. His companions were swaying in a very drunken manner. They still blinked their little beady eyes at Richardson. Ah, well, sirs, here was a mystery. At the approach of their menacing company, why did not this American cry out and turn pale, or run, or pray them mercy? The animal merely sat still, and stared, and waited for them to begin. Well, evidently he was a great fighter; or perhaps he was an idiot. Indeed, this was an embarrassing situation, for who was going forward to discover whether he was a great fighter or an idiot?

To Richardson, whose nerves were tingling and twitching like live wires and whose heart jolted inside him, this pause was a long horror; and for these men who could so frighten him there began to swell in him a fierce hatred—a hatred that made him long to be capable of fighting all of them, a hatred that made him capable of fighting all of them. A 44-caliber revolver can make a hole large enough for little boys to shoot marbles through, and there was a certain fat Mexican with a mustache like a snake who came extremely near to have eaten his last tamale merely because he frightened a man too much.

José had slept the first part of the night in his fashion, his body hunched into a heap, his legs crooked, his head touching his knees. Shadows had obscured him from the sight of the invaders. At this point he arose, and began to prowl quakingly over toward Richardson, as if he meant to hide behind him.

Of a sudden the fat Mexican gave a howl of glee. José had come within the torch's circle of light. With roars of ferocity the whole group of Mexicans pounced on the American's servant. He shrank shuddering away from them, beseeching by every device of word and gesture. They pushed him this way and that. They beat him with their fists. They stung him with their curses. As he groveled on his knees, the fat Mexican took him by the throat and said: "I am going to kill you!" And continually they turned their eyes to see if they were to succeed in causing the initial demonstration by the American. Richardson looked on impassively. Under the blanket, however, his fingers were clinched as rigidly as iron up on the handle of his revolver.

Here suddenly two brilliant clashing chords from the guitar were heard, and a woman's voice, full of laughter and confidence, cried from without: "Hello! Hello! Where are you?" The lurching company of Mexicans instantly paused and looked at the ground. One said, as he stood with his legs wide apart in order to balance himself: "It is the girls. They have come!" He screamed in answer to the question of the woman: "Here!" And without waiting he started on a pilgrimage toward the blanket-covered door. One could now hear a number of female voices giggling and chattering.

Two other Mexicans said: "Yes, it is the girls! Yes!" They also started quietly away. Even the fat Mexican's ferocity seemed to be affected. He looked uncertainly at the still-immovable American. Two of his friends grasped him gayly: "Come, the girls are here! Come!" He cast another glower at Richardson. "But this—," he began. Laughing, his comrades hustled him toward the door. On its threshold and holding back the blanket with one hand, he turned his yellow face with a last challenging glare toward the American. José, bewailing his state in little sobs of utter despair and woe, crept to Richardson and huddled near his knee. Then the cries of the Mexicans meeting the girls were heard, and the guitar burst out in joyous humming.

The moon clouded, and but a faint square of light fell through the open main door of the house. The coals of the fire were silent save for occasional sputters. Richardson did not change his position. He remained staring at the blanket which hid the strategic door in the far end. At his knees José was arguing, in a low, aggrieved tone, with the saints. Without the Mexicans laughed and danced, and—it would appear from the sound—drank more.

In the stillness and night Richardson sat wondering if some serpent-like Mexican was sliding toward him in the darkness, and if the first thing he knew of it would be the deadly sting of the knife. "Sssh," he whispered, to José. He drew his revolver from under the blanket and held it on his leg. The blanket over the door fascinated him. It was a vague form, black and unmoving. Through the opening it shielded was to come, probably, threats, death. Sometimes he thought he saw it move. As grim white sheets, the black and silver of coffins, all the panoply of death, affect us because of that which they hide, so this blanket, dangling before a hole in an adobe wall, was to Richardson a horrible emblem, and a horrible thing in itself. In his present mood Richardson could not have been brought to touch it with his finger.

The celebrating Mexicans occasionally howled in song. The guitarist played with speed and enthusiasm. Richardson longed to run. But in this vibrating and threatening gloom his terror convinced him that a move on his part would be a signal for the pounce of death. José, crouching abjectly, occasionally mumbled. Slowly and ponderous as stars the minutes went.

Suddenly Richardson thrilled and started. His breath, for a moment, left him. In sleep his nerveless fingers had allowed his revolver to fall and clang upon the hard floor. He grabbed it up hastily, and his glance swept apprehensively over the room. A chill blue light of dawn was in the place. Every outline was slowly growing; detail was following detail. The dread blanket did not move. The riotous company had gone or become silent. Richardson felt in his blood the effect of this cold dawn. The candor of breaking day brought his nerve. He touched José. "Come," he said. His servant lifted his lined yellow face, and comprehended. Richardson buckled on his spurs and strode up; José obediently lifted the two great saddles. Richardson held two bridles and a blanket on his left arm; in his right hand he held his revolver. They sneaked toward the door.

The man who said that spurs jingled was insane. Spurs have a mellow clash—clash—clash. Walking in spurs—notably Mexican spurs—you remind yourself vaguely of a telegraphic lineman. Richardson was inexpressibly shocked when he came to walk. He sounded to himself like a pair of cymbals. He would have known of this if he had reflected; but then he was escaping, not reflecting. He made a gesture of despair and from under the two saddles José tried to make one of hopeless horror. Richardson stooped, and with shaking fingers unfastened the spurs. Taking them in his left hand, he picked up his revolver and they slunk on toward the door. On the threshold Richardson looked back. In a corner, he saw, watching him with large eyes, the Indian man and woman who had been his hosts. Throughout the night they had made no sign, and now they neither spoke nor moved. Yet Richardson thought he detected meek satisfaction at his departure.

The street was still and deserted. In the eastern sky there was a lemon-colored patch. José had picketed the horses at the side of the house. As the two men came around the corner, Richardson's animal set up a whinny of welcome. The little horse had evidently heard them coming. He stood facing them, his ears cocked forward, his eyes bright with welcome.

Richardson made a frantic gesture, but the horse in his happiness at the appearance of his friends whinnied with enthusiasm. The American felt at this time that he could have strangled his well-beloved steed. Upon the threshold of safety, he was being betrayed by his horse, his friend. He felt the same hate for the horse that he would have felt for a dragon. And yet, as he glanced wildly about him, he could see nothing stirring in the street, nor at the doors of the tomb-like houses.

José had his own saddle girth and both bridles buckled in a moment. He curled the picket ropes with a few sweeps of his arm. The fingers of Richardson, however, were shaking so that he could hardly buckle the girth. His hands were in invisible mittens. He was wondering, calculating, hoping about his horse. He knew the little animal's willingness and courage under all circumstances up to this time, but then—here it was different. Who could tell if some wretched instance of equine perversity was not about to develop. Maybe the little fellow would not feel like smoking over the plain at express speed this morning, and so he would rebel and kick and be wicked. Maybe he would be without feeling of interest, and run listlessly. All men who have had to hurry in the saddle know what it is to be on a horse who does not understand the dramatic situation. Riding a lame sheep is bliss to it. Richardson, fumbling furiously at the girth, thought of these things.

Presently he had it fastened. He swung into the saddle, and as he did so his horse made a mad jump forward. The spurs of José scratched and tore the flanks of his great black animal, and side by side the two horses raced down the village street. The American heard his horse breathe a quivering sigh of excitement. Those four feet skimmed. They were as light as fairy puff balls. The houses of the village glided past in a moment, and the great, clear, silent plain appeared like a pale blue sea of mist and wet bushes. Above the mountains the colors of the sunlight were like the first tones, the opening chords of the mighty hymn of the morning.

The American looked down at his horse. He felt in his heart the first thrill of confidence. The little animal, unurged and quite tranquil, moving his ears this way and that way with an air of interest in the scenery, was nevertheless bounding into the eye of the breaking day with the speed of a frightened antelope. Richardson, looking down, saw the long, fine reach of forelimb, as steady as steel machinery. As the ground reeled past, the long, dried grasses hissed, and cactus plants were dull blurs. A wind whirled the horse's mane over his rider's bridle hand.

José's profile was lined against the pale sky. It was as that of a man who swims alone in an ocean. His eyes glinted like metal, fastened on some unknown point ahead of him, some fabulous place of safety. Occasionally his mouth puckered in a little unheard cry; and his legs, bended back, worked spasmodically as his spurred heels sliced the flanks of his charger.

Richardson consulted the gloom in the west for signs of a hard-riding, yelling cavalcade. He knew that whereas his friends the enemy had not attacked him when he had sat still and with apparent calmness confronted them, they would certainly take furiously after him now that he had run from them—now that he had confessed to them that he was the weaker. Their valor would grow like weeds in the spring, and upon discovering his escape they would ride forth dauntless warriors. Sometimes he was sure he saw them. Sometimes he was sure he heard them. Continually looking backward over his shoulder, he studied the purple expanses where the night was marching away. José rolled and shuddered in his saddle, persistently disturbing the stride of the black horse, fretting and worrying him until the white foam flew, and the great shoulders shone like satin from the sweat.

At last, Richardson drew his horse carefully down to a walk. José wished to rush insanely on, but the American spoke to him sternly. As the two paced forward side by side, Richardson's little horse thrust over his soft nose and inquired into the black's condition.

Riding with José was like riding with a corpse. His face resembled a cast in lead. Sometimes he swung forward and almost pitched from his seat. Richardson was too frightened himself to do anything but hate this man for his fear. Finally, he issued a mandate which nearly caused José's eyes to slide out of his head and fall to the ground like two coins. "Ride behind me—about fifty paces."

"Señor——" stuttered the servant. "Go," cried the American, furiously. He glared at the other and laid his hand on his revolver. José looked at his master wildly. He made a piteous gesture. Then slowly he fell back, watching the hard face of the American for a sign of mercy. Richardson had resolved in his rage that at any rate he was going to use the eyes and ears of extreme fear to detect the approach of danger; and so he established his servant as a sort of an outpost.

As they proceeded he was obliged to watch sharply to see that the servant did not slink forward and join him. When José made beseeching circles in the air with his arm he replied by menacingly gripping his revolver. José had a revolver, too; nevertheless it was very clear in his mind that the revolver was distinctly an American weapon. He had been educated in the Rio Grande country.

Richardson lost the trail once. He was recalled to it by the loud sobs of his servant.

Then at last José came clattering forward, gesticulating and wailing. The little horse sprang to the shoulder of the black. They were off.

Richardson, again looking backward, could see a slanting flare of dust on the whitening plain. He thought that he could detect small moving figures in it.

José's moans and cries amounted to a university course in theology. They broke continually from his quivering lips. His spurs were as motors. They forced the black horse over the plain in great headlong leaps. But under Richardson there was a little insignificant rat-colored beast who was running apparently with almost as much effort as it requires for a bronze statue to stand still. As a matter of truth, the ground seemed merely something to be touched from time to time with hoofs that were as light as blown leaves. Occasionally Richardson lay back and pulled stoutly at his bridle to keep from abandoning his servant. José harried at his horse's mouth, flopped around in the saddle and made his two heels beat like flails. The black ran like a horse in despair.

Crimson serapes in the distance resembled drops of blood on the great cloth of plain. Richardson began to dream of all possible chances. Although quite a humane man, he did not once think of his servant. José being a Mexican, it was natural that he should be killed in Mexico; but for himself, a New Yorker—— He remembered all the tales of such races for life, and he thought them badly written.

The great black horse was growing indifferent. The jabs of José's spurs no longer caused him to bound forward in wild leaps of pain. José had at last succeeded in teaching him that spurring was to be expected, speed or no speed, and now he took the pain of it dully and stolidly, as an animal who finds that doing his best gains him no respite. José was turned into a raving maniac. He bellowed and screamed, working his arms and his heels like one in a fit. He resembled a man on a sinking ship, who appeals to the ship. Richardson, too, cried madly to the black horse. The spirit of the horse responded to these calls, and quivering and breathing heavily he made a great effort, a sort of a final rush, not for himself apparently, but because he understood that his life's sacrifice, perhaps, had been invoked by these two men who cried to him in the universal tongue. Richardson had no sense of appreciation at this time—he was too frightened—but often now he remembers a certain black horse.

From the rear could be heard a yelling, and once a shot was fired—in the air, evidently. Richardson moaned as he looked back. He kept his hand on his revolver. He tried to imagine the brief tumult of his capture—the flurry of dust from the hoofs of horses pulled suddenly to their haunches, the shrill, biting curses of the men, the ring of the shots, his own last contortion. He wondered, too, if he could not somehow manage to pelt that fat Mexican, just to cure his abominable egotism.

It was José, the terror-stricken, who at last discovered safety. Suddenly he gave a howl of delight and astonished his horse into a new burst of speed. They were on a little ridge at the time, and the American at the top of it saw his servant gallop down the slope and into the arms, so to speak, of a small column of horsemen in gray and silver clothes. In the dim light of the early morning they were as vague as shadows, but Richardson knew them at once for a detachment of rurales, that crack cavalry corps of the Mexican army which polices the plain so zealously, being of themselves the law and the arm of it—a fierce and swift-moving body that knows little of prevention but much of vengeance. They drew up suddenly, and the rows of great silver-trimmed sombreros bobbed in surprise.

Richardson saw José throw himself from his horse and begin to jabber at the leader of the party. When he arrived he found that his servant had already outlined the entire situation, and was then engaged in describing him, Richardson, as an American señor of vast wealth who was the friend of almost every governmental potentate within two hundred miles. This seemed to profoundly impress the officer. He bowed gravely to Richardson and smiled significantly at his men, who unslung their carbines.

The little ridge hid the pursuers from view, but the rapid thud of their horses' feet could be heard. Occasionally they yelled and called to each other. Then at last they swept over the brow of the hill, a wild mob of almost fifty drunken horsemen. When they discerned the pale-uniformed rurales, they were sailing down the slope at top speed.

If toboggans half way down a hill should suddenly make up their minds to turn around and go back, there would be an effect somewhat like that now produced by the drunken horsemen. Richardson saw the rurales serenely swing their carbines forward, and, peculiar-minded person that he was, felt his heart leap into his throat at the prospective volley. But the officer rode forward alone.

It appeared that the man who owned the best horse in this astonished company was the fat Mexican with the snaky mustache, and, in consequence, this gentleman was quite a distance in the van. He tried to pull up, wheel his horse and scuttle back over the hill as some of his companions had done, but the officer called to him in a voice harsh with rage. "—!" howled the officer. "This señor is my friend, the friend of my friends. Do you dare pursue him, —? —! —! —! —!" These lines represent terrible names, all different, used by the officer.

The fat Mexican simply groveled on his horse's neck. His face was green; it could be seen that he expected death. The officer stormed with magnificent intensity: "—! —! —!" Finally he sprang from his saddle, and, running to the fat Mexican's side, yelled: "Go—" and kicked the horse in the belly with all his might. The animal gave a mighty leap into the air, and the fat Mexican, with one wretched glance at the contemplative rurales, aimed his steed for the top of the ridge. Richardson again gulped in expectation of a volley, for—it is said—this is one of the favorite methods of the rurales for disposing of objectionable people. The fat, green Mexican also evidently thought that he was to be killed while on the run, from the miserable look he cast at the troops. Nevertheless, he was allowed to vanish in a cloud of yellow dust at the ridge-top.

José was exultant, defiant, and, oh, bristling with courage. The black horse was drooping sadly, his nose to the ground. Richardson's little animal, with his ears bent forward, was staring at the horses of the rurales as if in an intense study. Richardson longed for speech, but he could only bend forward and pat the shining, silken shoulders. The little horse turned his head and looked back gravely.

The Wise Men:
A Detail of American Life in Mexico

They were youths of subtle mind. They were very wicked according to report, and yet they managed to have it reflect credit upon them. They often had the well-informed and the great talkers of the American colony engaged in reciting their misdeeds, and facts relating to their sins were usually told with a flourish of awe and fine admiration.

One was from San Francisco and one was from New York, but they resembled each other in appearance. This is an idiosyncrasy of geography.

They were never apart in the City of Mexico, at any rate, excepting perhaps when one had retired to his hotel for a respite, and then the other was usually camped down at the office sending up servants with clamorous messages. "Oh, get up and come on down."

They were two lads—they were called the Kids—and far from their mothers. Occasionally some wise man pitied them, but he usually was alone in his wisdom. The other folk frankly were transfixed at the splendor of the audacity and endurance of these Kids. "When do those two boys ever sleep?" murmured a man as he viewed them entering a café about eight o'clock one morning. Their smooth infantile faces looked bright and fresh enough, at any rate. "Jim told me he saw them still at it about four-thirty this morning."

"Sleep!" ejaculated a companion in a glowing voice. "They never sleep! They go to bed once in every two weeks." His boast of it seemed almost a personal pride.

"They'll end with a crash, though, if they keep it up at this pace," said a gloomy voice from behind a newspaper.

The Café Colorado has a front of white and gold, in which is set larger plate-glass windows than are commonly to be found in Mexico. Two little wings of willow flip-flapping incessantly serve as doors. Under them small stray dogs go furtively into the café, and are shied into the street again by the waiters. On the sidewalk there is always a decorative ef-

43

fect in loungers, ranging from the newly-arrived and superior tourist to the old veteran of the silver mines bronzed by violent suns. They contemplate with various shades of interest the show of the street—the red, purple, dusty white, glaring forth against the walls in the furious sunshine.

One afternoon the Kids strolled into the Café Colorado. A half-dozen of the men who sat smoking and reading with a sort of Parisian effect at the little tables which lined two sides of the room, looked up and bowed smiling, and although this coming of the Kids was anything but an unusual event, at least a dozen men wheeled in their seats to stare after them. Three waiters polished tables, and moved chairs noisily, and appeared to be eager. Distinctly these Kids were of importance.

Behind the distant bar, the tall form of old Pop himself awaited them smiling with broad geniality. "Well, my boys, how are you?" he cried in a voice of profound solicitude. He allowed five or six of his customers to languish in the care of Mexican bar-tenders, while he himself gave his eloquent attention to the Kids, lending all the dignity of a great event to their arrival. "How are the boys to-day, eh?"

"You're a smooth old guy," said one, eyeing him. "Are you giving us this welcome so we won't notice it when you push your worst whisky at us?"

Pop turned in appeal from one Kid to the other Kid. "There, now, hear that, will you?" He assumed an oratorical pose. "Why, my boys, you always get the best—the very best—that this house has got."

"Yes, we do!" The Kids laughed. "Well, bring it out, anyhow, and if it's the same you sold us last night, we'll grab your cash register and run."

Pop whirled a bottle along the bar and then gazed at it with a rapt expression. "Fine as silk," he murmured. "Now just taste that, and if it isn't the finest whisky you ever put in your face, why I'm a liar, that's all."

The Kids surveyed him with scorn, and poured out their allowances. Then they stood for a time insulting Pop about his whisky. "Usually it tastes exactly like new parlor furniture," said the San Francisco Kid. "Well, here goes, and you want to look out for your cash register."

"Your health, gentlemen," said Pop with a grand air, and as he wiped his bristling grey moustache he wagged his head with reference to the cash register question. "I could catch you before you got very far."

"Why, are you a runner?" said one derisively.

"You just bank on me, my boy," said Pop, with deep emphasis. "I'm a flier."

The Kids set down their glasses suddenly and looked at him. "You must be," they said. Pop was tall and graceful and magnificent in manner, but he did not display those qualities of form which mean speed in the animal. His hair was grey; his face was round and fat from much living. The buttons of his glittering white vest formed a fine curve, so that if the concave surface of a piece of barrel-hoop had been laid against Pop it would have touched each button. "You must be," observed the Kids again.

"Well, you can laugh all you like, but—no jolly now, boys, I tell you I'm a winner. Why, I bet you I can skin anything in this town on a square go. When I kept my place in Eagle Pass there wasn't anybody who could touch me. One of these sure things came down from San Anton'. Oh, he was a runner he was. One of these people with wings. Well, I skinned 'im. What? Certainly I did. Never touched me."

The Kids had been regarding him in grave silence, but at this moment they grinned, and said quite in chorus: "Oh, you old liar!"

Pop's voice took on a whining tone of earnestness. "Boys, I'm telling it to you straight. I'm a flier."

One of the Kids had had a dreamy cloud in his eye and he cried out suddenly. "Say, what a joke to play this on Freddie."

The other jumped ecstatically. "Oh, wouldn't it be, though. Say he wouldn't do a thing but howl! He'd go crazy."

They looked at Pop as if they longed to be certain that he was, after all, a runner. "Say, now, Pop, on the level," said one of them wistfully, "can you run?"

"Boys," swore Pop, "I'm a peach! On the dead level, I'm a peach."

"By golly, I believe the old Indian can run," said one to the other, as if they were alone in conference.

"That's what I can," cried Pop.

The Kids said: "Well, so long, old man." They went to a table and sat down. They ordered a salad. They were always ordering salads. This was because one Kid had a wild passion for salads, and the other didn't care much. So at any hour of the day or night they might be seen ordering a salad. When this one came they went into a sort of executive session. It was a very long consultation. Some of the men noted it; they said there was deviltry afoot. Occasionally the Kids laughed in supreme enjoyment of something unknown. The low rumble of wheels came from the street. Often could be heard the parrot-like cries of distant vendors. The sunlight streamed through the green curtains, and made some little amber-colored flitterings on the marble floor. High up among the severe decorations of the ceiling—reminiscent of the days when the great building was a palace—a small white butterfly was wending through the cool air spaces. The long billiard hall stretched back to a vague gloom. The balls were always clicking, and one could see endless elbows crooking. Beggars slunk through the wicker doors, and were ejected by the nearest waiter. At last the Kids called Pop to them.

"Sit down, Pop. Have a drink." They scanned him carefully. "Say now, Pop, on your solemn oath, can you run?"

"Boys," said Pop piously, and raising his hand, "I can run like a rabbit."

"On your oath?"

"On my oath."

"Can you beat Freddie?"

Pop appeared to look at the matter from all sides. "Well, boys, I'll tell you. No man is cock-sure of anything in this world, and I don't want to say that I can best any man, but I've seen Freddie run, and I'm ready to swear I can beat 'im. In a hundred yards I'd just about skin 'im neat—you understand—just about neat. Freddie is a good average runner, but I—you understand—I'm just—a little—bit—better." The Kids had been listening with the utmost attention. Pop spoke the latter part slowly and meaningly. They thought he intended them to see his great confidence.

One said: "Pop, if you throw us in this thing, we'll come here and drink for two weeks without paying. We'll back you and work a josh on Freddie! But oh!—if you throw us!"

To this menace Pop cried: "Boys, I'll make the run of my life! On my oath!"

The salad having vanished, the Kids arose. "All right, now," they warned him. "If you play us for duffers, we'll get square. Don't you forget it."

"Boys, I'll give you a race for your money. Bank on that. I may lose—understand, I may lose—no man can help meeting a better man. But I think I can skin 'im, and I'll give you a run for your money, you bet."

"All right, then. But, look here," they told him, "you keep

your face closed. Nobody but us gets in on this. Understand?"

"Not a soul," Pop declared. They left him, gesturing a last warning from the wicker doors.

In the street they saw Benson, his cane gripped in the middle, strolling among the white-clothed jabbering natives on the shady side. They semaphored to him eagerly, their faces ashine with a plot. He came across cautiously, like a man who ventures into dangerous company.

"We're going to get up a race. Pop and Fred. Pop swears he can skin 'im. This is a tip. Keep it dark, now. Say, won't Freddie be hot!"

Benson looked as if he had been compelled to endure these exhibitions of insanity for a century. "Oh, you fellows are off. Pop can't beat Freddie. He's an old bat. Why, it's impossible. Pop can't beat Freddie."

"Can't he? Want to bet he can't?" said the Kids. "There now, let's see—you're talking so large."

"Well, you——"

"Oh, bet. Bet or else close your trap. That's the way."

"How do you know you can pull off the race. Seen Freddie?"

"No, but——"

"Well, see him then. Can't bet now with no race arranged. I'll bet with you all right—all right. I'll give you fellows a tip though—you're a pair of asses. Pop can't run any faster than a brick school-house."

The Kids scowled at him and defiantly said: "Can't he?" They left him and went to the Casa Verde. Freddie, beautiful in his white jacket, was holding one of his innumerable conversations across the bar. He smiled when he saw them. "Where you boys been?" he demanded, in a paternal tone. Almost all the proprietors of American cafés in the city used to adopt a paternal tone when they spoke to the Kids.

"Oh, been 'round," they replied.

"Have a drink?" said the proprietor of the Casa Verde, forgetting his other social obligations. During the course of this ceremony one of the Kids remarked: "Freddie, Pop says he can beat you running."

"Does he?" observed Freddie without excitement. He was used to various snares of the Kids.

"That's what. He says he can leave you at the wire and not see you again."

"Well, he lies," replied Freddie placidly.

"And I'll bet you a bottle of wine that he can do it, too."

"Rats!" said Freddie.

"Oh, that's all right," pursued a Kid. "You can throw bluffs all you like, but he can lose you in a hundred yard dash, you bet."

Freddie drank his whisky, and then settled his elbows on the bar. "Say, now, what do you boys keep coming in here with some pipe-story all the time for? You can't josh me. Do you think you can scare me about Pop? Why, I know I can beat 'im. He's an old man. He can't run with me. Certainly not. Why, you fellows are just jollying me."

"Are we though?" said the Kids. "You daresn't bet the bottle of wine."

"Oh, of course I can bet you a bottle of wine," said Freddie disdainfully. "Nobody cares about a bottle of wine, but——"

"Well, make it five then," advised one of the Kids.

Freddie hunched his shoulders. "Why, certainly I will. Make it ten if you like, but——"

"We do," they said.

"Ten, is it? All right; that goes." A look of weariness came over Freddie's face. "But you boys are foolish. I tell you Pop is an old man. How can you expect him to run? Of course, I'm no great runner, but then I'm young and healthy and—and a pretty smooth runner, too. Pop is old and fat, and then he doesn't do a thing but tank all day. It's a cinch."

The kids looked at him and laughed rapturously. They waved their fingers at him. "Ah, there!" they cried. They meant they had made a victim of him.

But Freddie continued to expostulate. "I tell you he couldn't win—an old man like him. You're crazy. Of course, I know you don't care about ten bottles of wine, but, then— to make such bets as that. You're twisted."

"Are we, though?" cried the Kids in mockery. They had precipitated Freddie into a long and thoughtful treatise on every possible chance of the thing as he saw it. They disputed with him from time to time, and jeered at him. He labored on through his argument. Their childish faces were bright with glee.

In the midst of it Wilburson entered. Wilburson worked; not too much, though. He had hold of the Mexican end of a great importing house of New York, and as he was a junior partner he worked. But not too much, though. "What's the howl?" he said.

The Kids giggled. "We've got Freddie rattled."

"Why," said Freddie, turning to him, "these two Indians are trying to tell me that Pop can beat me running."

"Like the devil," said Wilburson, incredulously.

"Well, can't he?" demanded a Kid.

"Why, certainly not," said Wilburson, dismissing every possibility of it with a gesture. "That old bat? Certainly not. I'll bet fifty dollars that Freddie——"

"Take you," said a Kid.

"What?" said Wilburson, "that Freddie won't beat Pop?"

The Kid that had spoken now nodded his head.

"That Freddie won't beat Pop?" repeated Wilburson.

"Yes. It's a go?"

"Why, certainly," retorted Wilburson. "Fifty? All right."

"Bet you five bottles on the side," ventured the other Kid.

"Why, certainly," exploded Wilburson wrathfully. "You fellows must take me for something easy. I'll take all those kind of bets I can get. Cer—tain—ly."

They settled the details. The course was to be paced off on the asphalt of one of the adjacent side-streets, and then, at about eleven o'clock in the evening, the match would be run. Usually in Mexico the streets of a city grow lonely and dark but a little time after nine o'clock. There are occasional lurking figures, perhaps, but no crowds, lights, noise. The course would doubtless be undisturbed. As for the policemen in the vicinity, they—well, they were conditionally amiable.

The Kids went to see Pop; they told him of the arrangements, and then in deep tones they said: "Oh, Pop, if you throw us!"

Pop appeared to be a trifle shaken by the weight of responsibility thrust upon him, but he spoke out bravely. "Boys, I'll pinch that race. Now you watch me. I'll pinch it."

The Kids went then on some business of their own, for they were not seen again until evening. When they returned to the neighborhood of the Café Colorado the usual evening stream of carriages was whirling along the *calle*. The wheels hummed on the asphalt, and the coachmen towered in their great sombreros. On the sidewalk a gazing crowd sauntered, the better class self-satisfied and proud, in their derby hats and cutaway coats, the lower classes muffling their dark faces in their blankets, slipping along in leather sandals. An electric light sputtered and fumed over the throng. The afternoon shower had left the pave wet and glittering. The air was still laden with the odor of rain on flowers, grass, leaves.

In the Café Colorado a cosmopolitan crowd ate, drank, played billiards, gossiped, or read in the glaring yellow light. When the Kids entered a large circle of men that had been gesticulating near the bar greeted them with a roar.

"Here they are now!"

"Oh, you pair of peaches!"

"Say, got any more money to bet with?"

The Kids smiled complacently. Old Colonel Hammigan, grinning, pushed his way to them. "Say, boys, we'll all have a drink on you now because you won't have any money after eleven o'clock. You'll be going down the back stairs in your stocking feet."

Although the Kids remained unnaturally serene and quiet, argument in the Café Colorado became tumultuous. Here and there a man who did not intend to bet ventured meekly that perchance Pop might win, and the others swarmed upon him in a whirlwind of angry denial and ridicule.

Pop, enthroned behind the bar, looked over at this storm with a shadow of anxiety upon his face. This widespread flouting affected him, but the Kids looked blissfully satisfied with the tumult they had stirred.

Blanco, honest man, ever worrying for his friends, came to them. "Say, you fellows, you aren't betting too much? This thing looks kind of shaky, don't it?"

The faces of the Kids grew sober, and after consideration one said: "No, I guess we've got a good thing, Blanco. Pop is going to surprise them, I think."

"Well, don't——"

"All right, old boy. We'll watch out."

From time to time the Kids had much business with certain orange, red, blue, purple, and green bills. They were making little memoranda on the back of visiting cards. Pop watched them closely, the shadow still upon his face. Once he called to them, and when they came he leaned over the bar and said intensely: "Say, boys, remember, now—I might lose this race. Nobody can ever say for sure, and if I do, why——"

"Oh, that's all right, Pop," said the Kids, reassuringly. "Don't mind it. Do your derndest and let it go at that."

When they had left him, however, they went to a corner to consult. "Say, this is getting interesting. Are you in deep?" asked one anxiously of his friend.

"Yes, pretty deep," said the other stolidly. "Are you?"

"Deep as the devil," replied the other in the same tone.

They looked at each other stonily and went back to the crowd. Benson had just entered the café. He approached them with a gloating smile of victory. "Well, where's all that money you were going to bet?"

"Right here," said the Kids, thrusting into their vest pockets.

At eleven o'clock a curious thing was learned. When Pop and Freddie, the Kids and all, came to the little side street, it was thick with people. It seems that the news of this great race had spread like the wind among the Americans, and they had come to witness the event. In the darkness the crowd moved, gesticulating and mumbling in argument.

The principals, the Kids, and those with them, surveyed this scene with some dismay. "Say—here's a go." Even then a policeman might be seen approaching, the light from his little lantern flickering on his white cap, gloves, brass buttons, and on the butt of the old-fashioned Colt's revolver which hung at his belt. He addressed Freddie in swift Mexican. Freddie listened, nodding from time to time. Finally Freddie turned to the others to translate. "He says he'll get into trouble if he allows this race when all this crowd is here."

There was a murmur of discontent. The policeman looked at them with an expression of anxiety on his broad brown face.

"Oh, come on. We'll go hold it on some other fellow's beat," said one of the Kids. The group moved slowly away debating. Suddenly the other Kid cried: "I know! The Paseo!"

"By jiminy," said Freddie, "just the thing. We'll get a cab and go out to the Paseo. S-s-sh! Keep it quiet; we don't want all this mob."

Later they tumbled into a cab—Pop, Freddie, the Kids, old Colonel Hammigan and Benson. They whispered to the men who had wagered: "The Paseo." The cab whirled away up the black street. There was occasional grunts and groans, cries of "Oh, get off me feet," and of "Quit! you're killing me." Six people do not have fun in one cab. The principals spoke to each other with the respect and friendliness which comes to good men at such times. Once a Kid put his head out of the window and looked backward. He pulled it in again and cried: "Great Scott! Look at that, would you!" The others struggled to do as they were bid, and afterward shouted: "Holy smoke! Well, I'll be blowed! Thunder and turf!"

Galloping after them came innumerable other cabs, their lights twinkling, streaming in a great procession through the night. "The street is full of them," ejaculated the old colonel.

The Paseo de la Reforma is the famous drive of the City of Mexico, leading to the Castle of Chapultepec, which last ought to be well known in the United States.

It is a broad fine avenue of macadam with a much greater quality of dignity than anything of the kind we possess in our own land. It seems of the Old World, where to the beauty of the thing itself is added the solemnity of tradition and history, the knowledge that feet in buskins trod the same stones, that cavalcades of steel thundered there before the coming of carriages.

When the Americans tumbled out of their cabs the giant bronzes of Aztec and Spaniard loomed dimly above them like towers. The four rows of poplar trees rustled weirdly off there in the darkness. Pop took out his watch and struck a match. "Well, hurry up this thing. It's almost midnight."

The other cabs came swarming, the drivers lashing their horses, for these Americans, who did all manner of strange things, nevertheless always paid well for it. There was a mighty hubbub then in the darkness. Five or six men began to pace off the distance and quarrel. Others knotted their handkerchiefs together to make a tape. Men were swearing over bets, fussing and fuming about the odds. Benson came to the Kids swaggering. "You're a pair of asses." The cabs waited in a solid block down the avenue. Above the crowd the tall statues hid their visages in the night.

At last a voice floated through the darkness. "Are you ready there?" Everybody yelled excitedly. The men at the tape pulled it out straight. "Hold it higher, Jim, you fool!" A silence fell then upon the throng. Men bended down trying to pierce the darkness with their eyes. From out at the starting point came muffled voices. The crowd swayed and jostled.

The racers did not come. The crowd began to fret, its nerves burning. "Oh, hurry up," shrilled some one.

The voice called again: "Ready there?" Everybody replied: "Yes, all ready. Hurry up!"

There was more muffled discussion at the starting point. In the crowd a man began to make a proposition. "I'll bet twenty——" but the throng interrupted with a howl. "Here they come!" The thickly packed body of men swung as if the ground had moved. The men at the tape shouldered madly at their fellows, bawling: "Keep back! Keep back!"

From the profound gloom came the noise of feet pattering furiously. Vague forms flashed into view for an instant. A hoarse roar broke from the crowd. Men bended and swayed and fought. The Kids back near the tape exchanged another stolid look. A white form shone forth. It grew like a spectre. Always could be heard the wild patter. A barbaric scream broke from the crowd. "By Gawd, it's Pop! Pop! Pop's ahead!"

The old man spun toward the tape like a madman, his chin thrown back, his grey hair flying. His legs moved like maniac machinery. And as he shot forward a howl as from forty cages of wild animals went toward the imperturbable chieftains in bronze. The crowd flung themselves forward. "Oh, you old Indian! You savage! You cuss, you! Dern my buttons, did you ever see such running?"

"Ain't he a peach! Well!"

"Say, this beats anything!"

"Where's the Kids? H-e-y, Kids!"

"Look at 'im, would you? Did you ever think?" These cries flew in the air blended in a vast shout of astonishment and laughter.

For an instant the whole great tragedy was in view. Freddie, desperate, his teeth shining, his face contorted, whirling along in deadly effort, was twenty feet behind the tall form of old Pop, who, dressed only in his—only in his underclothes—gained with each stride. One grand insane moment, and then Pop had hurled himself against the tape—victor!

Freddie, falling into the arms of some men, struggled with his breath, and at last managed to stammer: "Say, can't—can't that old—old man run!"

Pop, puffing and heaving, could only gasp: "Where's my shoes? Who's got my shoes?" Later Freddie scrambled panting through the crowd, and held out his hand. "Good man, Pop!" And then he looked up and down the tall, stout form. "Hell! who would think you could run like that."

The Kids were surrounded by a crowd, laughing tempestuously.

"How did you know he could run?"

"Why didn't you give me a line on him?"

"Say—great snakes!—you fellows had a nerve to bet on Pop."

"Why, I was cock-sure he couldn't win."

"Oh, you fellows must have seen him run before."

"Who would ever think it?"

Benson came by, filling the midnight air with curses. They turned to jeer him. "What's the matter, Benson?"

"Somebody pinched my handkerchief. I tied it up in that string. Damn it."

The Kids laughed blithely. "Why, hollo, Benson!" they said.

There was a great rush for cabs. Shouting, laughing, wondering, the crowd hustled into their conveyances, and the drivers flogged their horses toward the city again.

"Won't Freddie be crazy! Say, he'll be guyed about this for years."

"But who would ever think that old tank could run so?"

One cab had to wait while Pop and Freddie resumed various parts of their clothing.

As they drove home, Freddie said: "Well, Pop, you beat me."

Pop said: "That's all right, old man."

The Kids, grinning, said: "How much did you lose, Benson?"

Benson said defiantly: "Oh, not so much. How much did you win?"

"Oh, not so much."

Old Colonel Hammigan, squeezed down in a corner, had apparently been reviewing the event in his mind, for he suddenly remarked: "Well, I'm damned!"

They were late in reaching the Café Colorado, but when they did, the bottles were on the bar as thick as pickets on a fence.

The Five White Mice

Freddie was mixing a cocktail. His hand with the long spoon was whirling swiftly and the ice in the glass hummed and rattled like a cheap watch. Over by the window, a gambler, a millionaire, a railway conductor and the agent of a vast American syndicate were playing seven-up. Freddie surveyed them with the ironical glance of a man who is mixing a cocktail.

From time to time a swarthy Mexican waiter came with his tray from the rooms at the rear and called his orders across the bar. The sounds of the indolent stir of the city, awakening from its siesta, floated over the screens which barred the sun and the inquisitive eye. From the faraway kitchen could be heard the roar of the old French chef, driving, herding and abusing his Mexican helpers.

A string of men came suddenly in from the street. They stormed up to the bar. There were impatient shouts. "Come, now, Freddie, don't stand there like a portrait of yourself. Wiggle!" Drinks of many kinds and colors, amber, green, mahogany, strong and mild, began to swarm upon the bar with all the attendants of lemon, sugar, mint and ice. Freddie, with Mexican support, worked like a sailor in the provision of them, sometimes talking with that scorn for drink and admiration for those who drink which is the attribute of a good-bar-keeper.

At last a man was afflicted with a stroke of dice-shaking. A herculean discussion was waging and he was deeply engaged in it but at the same time he lazily flirted the dice. Occasionally he made great combinations. "Look at that, would you?" he cried proudly. The others paid little heed. Then violently the craving took them. It went along the line like an epidemic and involved them all. In a moment they had arranged a carnival of dice-shaking with money penalties and liquid prizes. They clamorously made it a point of honor with Freddie that he too should play and take his chance of sometimes providing this large group with free refreshment. With bended heads like foot-ball players they surged over the tinkling dice, jostling, cheering and bitterly arguing. One of the quiet company playing seven-up at the corner table said profanely that the row reminded him of a bowling contest at a picnic.

After the regular shower, many carriages rolled over the smooth *calle* and sent a musical thunder through the Casa Verde. The shop-windows became aglow with light and the walks were crowded with youths, callow and ogling, dressed vainly according to supposititious fashions. The policemen had muffled themselves in their gnome-like cloaks and placed their lanterns as obstacles for the carriages in the middle of the street. The City of Mexico gave forth the deep mellow organ-tones of its evening resurrection.

But still the group at the bar of the Casa Verde were shaking dice. They had passed beyond shaking for drinks for the crowd, for Mexican dollars, for dinner, for the wine at dinner. They had even gone to the trouble of separating the cigars and cigarettes from the dinner's bill and causing a distinct man to be responsible for them. Finally they were aghast. Nothing remained within sight of their minds which even remotely suggested further gambling. There was a pause for deep consideration.

"Well——"

"Well——"

A man called out in the exuberance of creation. "I know! Let's shake for a box tonight at the circus! A box at the circus!" The group was profoundly edified. "That's it! That's it! Come on now! Box at the circus!" A dominating voice cried: "Three dashes—high man out!" An American, tall and with a face of copper red from the rays that flash among the Sierra Madres and burn on the cactus deserts, took the little leathern cup and spun the dice out upon the polished wood. A fascinated assemblage hung upon the bar-rail. Three kings turned their pink faces upward. The tall man flourished the cup, burlesquing, and flung the two other dice. From them he ultimately extracted one more pink king. "There," he said. "Now, let's see! Four kings!" He began to swagger in a sort of provisional way.

The next man took the cup and blew softly in the top of it. Poising it in his hand, he then surveyed the company with a stony eye and paused. They knew perfectly well that he was applying the magic of deliberation and ostentatious indifference but they could not wait in tranquility during the performances of all these rites. They began to call out impatiently. "Come now—hurry up." At last the man, with a gesture that was singularly impressive, threw the dice. The others set up a howl of joy. "Not a pair!" There was another solemn pause. The men moved restlessly. "Come, now, go ahead!" In the end the man, induced and abused, achieved something that was nothing in the presence of four kings. The tall man climbed on the foot-rail and leaned hazardously forward. "Four kings! My four kings are good to go out," he bellowed into the middle of the mob and although in a moment he did pass into the radiant region of exemption he continued to bawl advice and scorn.

The mirrors and oiled woods of the Casa Verde were now dancing with blue flashes from a great buzzing electric lamp. A host of quiet members of the Anglo-Saxon colony had come in for their pre-dinner cocktails. An amiable person was exhibiting to some tourists this popular American saloon. It was a very sober and respectable time of day. Freddie reproved courageously the dice-shaking brawlers and, in return, he received the choicest advice in a tumult of seven combined vocabularies. He laughed; he had been compelled to retire from the game but he was keeping an interested, if furtive, eye upon it.

Down at the end of the line, there was a youth at whom everybody railed for his flaming ill-luck. At each disaster, Freddie swore from behind the bar in a sort of affectionate contempt. "Why this Kid has had no luck for two days. Did you ever see such throwin'."

The contest narrowed eventually to the New York Kid and an individual who swung about placidly on legs that moved in nefarious circles. He had a grin that resembled a bit of carving. He was obliged to lean down and blink rapidly to ascertain the facts of his venture but fate presented him with five queens. His smile did not change but he puffed gently like a man who has been running.

The others, having emerged scatheless from this part of the conflict, waxed hilarious with the Kid. They smote him on either shoulder. "We've got you stuck for it, Kid! You can't beat that game! Five queens!"

Up to this time, the Kid had displayed only the temper of the gambler but the cheerful hoots of the players supplemented now by a ring of guying non-combatants caused him to feel profoundly that it would be fine to beat the five queens. He addressed a gambler's slogan to the interior of the cup.

"Oh, five white mice of chance,
Shirts of wool and corduroy pants,
Gold and wine, women and sin,
All for you if you let me come in—
Into the house of chance."

Flashing the dice sardonically out upon the bar, he displayed three aces. From two dice in the next throw, he achieved one more ace. For his last throw, he rattled the single dice for a long time. He already had four aces; if he accomplished another one, the five queens were vanquished and the box at the circus came from the drunken man's pocket. All of the Kid's movements were slow and elaborate. For his last throw he planted the cup bottom-up on the bar with the one dice hidden under it. Then he turned and faced the crowd with the air of a conjuror or a cheat. "Oh, maybe it's an ace," he said in boastful calm. "Maybe it's an ace." Instantly he was presiding over a little drama in which every man was absorbed. The Kid leaned with his back against the bar-rail and with his elbows upon it. "Maybe it's an ace," he repeated.

A jeering voice in the background said: "Yes, maybe it is, Kid!"

The Kid's eyes searched for a moment among the men. "I'll bet fifty dollars it is an ace," he said.

Another voice asked: "American money?"

"Yes," answered the Kid.

"Oh!" There was a genial laugh at this discomfiture. However no one came forward at the Kid's challenge and presently he turned to the cup. "Now, I'll show you." With the manner of a mayor unveiling a statue, he lifted the cup. There was revealed naught but a ten-spot. In the roar which arose could be heard each man ridiculing the cowardice of his neighbor and above all the din rang the voice of Freddie berating everyone. "Why, there isn't one liver to every five men in the outfit. That was the greatest cold bluff I ever saw worked. He wouldn't know how to cheat with dice if he wanted to. Don't know the first thing about it. I could hardly keep from laughin' when I seen him drillin' you around. Why, I tell you, I had that fifty dollars right in my pocket if I wanted to be a chump. You're an easy lot——"

Nevertheless the group who had won in the circus-box game did not relinquish their triumph. They burst like a storm about the head of the Kid, swinging at him with their fists. " 'Five white mice'!" they quoted choking. " 'Five white mice'!"

"Oh, they are not so bad," said the Kid.

Afterward it often occurred that a man would suddenly jeer a finger at the Kid and derisively say: " 'Five white mice'."

On the route from the dinner to the circus, others of the party often asked the Kid if he had really intended to make his appeal to mice. They suggested other animals—rabbits, dogs, hedgehogs, snakes, opossums. To this banter the Kid replied with a serious expression of his belief in the fidelity and wisdom of the five white mice. He presented a most eloquent case, decorated with fine language and insults, in which he proved that if one was going to believe in anything at all, one might as well choose the five white mice. His companions however at once and unanimously pointed out to him that his recent exploit did not place him in the light of a convincing advocate.

The Kid discerned two figures in the street. They were making imperious signs at him. He waited for them to approach, for he recognized one as the other Kid—the 'Frisco Kid—there were two Kids. With the 'Frisco Kid was Benson. They arrived almost breathless. "Where you been?" cried the 'Frisco Kid. It was an arrangement that upon a meeting the one that could first ask this question was entitled to use a tone of limitless injury. "What you been doing? Where you going? Come on with us. Benson and I have got a little scheme."

The New York Kid pulled his arm from the grapple of the other. "I can't. I've got to take these sutlers to the circus. They stuck me for it shaking dice at Freddie's. I can't, I tell you."

The two did not at first attend to his remarks. "Come on! We've got a little scheme."

"I can't. They stuck me. I've got to take'm to the circus."

At this time it did not suit the men with the scheme to recognize these objections as important. "Oh, take'm some other time. Well, can't you take'm some other time? Let 'em go. Damn the circus. Get cold feet. What did you get stuck for? Get cold feet."

But despite their fighting, the New York Kid broke away from them. "I can't, I tell you. They stuck me." As he left them, they yelled with rage. "Well, meet us, now, do you hear? In the Casa Verde as soon as the circus quits! Hear?" They threw maledictions after him.

In the City of Mexico, a man goes to the circus without descending in any way to infant amusements because the Circo Teatro Orrin is one of the best in the world and too easily surpasses anything of the kind in the United States where it is merely a matter of a number of rings, if possible, and a great professional agreement to lie to the public. Moreover the American clown who in the Mexican arena prances and gabbles is the clown to whom writers refer as the delight of their childhood and lament that he is dead. At this circus the Kid was not debased by the sight of mournful prisoner elephants and caged animals forlorn and sickly. He sat in his box until late and laughed and swore when past laughing at the comic, foolish, wise clown.

When he returned to the Casa Verde there was no display of the 'Frisco Kid and Benson. Freddie was leaning upon the bar listening to four men terribly discuss a question that was not plain. There was a card-game in the corner, of course. Sounds of revelry pealed from the rear rooms.

When the Kid asked Freddie if he had seen his friend and Benson, Freddie looked bored. "Oh, yes, they were in here just a minute ago but I don't know where they went. They've got their skates on. Where've they been? Came in here rolling across the floor like two little gilt gods. They wobbled around for a time and then 'Frisco wanted me to send six bottles of wine around to Benson's rooms, but I didn't have anybody to send this time of night and so they got mad and went out. Where did they get their loads?"

In the first deep gloom of the street, the Kid paused a moment debating. But presently he heard quavering voices. "Oh, Kid! Kid! Comere!" Peering, he recognized two vague figures against the opposite wall. He crossed the street and they said: "Hellokid."

"Say, where did you get it?" he demanded sternly. "You Indians better go home. What did you want to get scragged for?" His face was luminous with virtue.

As they swung to and fro, they made angry denials. "We ain' load'. We ain' load.' Big chump. Comonangetadrink." The sober youth turned then to his friend. "Hadn't you better go home, Kid? Come on, it's late. You'd better break away."

The 'Frisco Kid wagged his head decisively. "Got take Benson home first. He'll be wallowing 'round in a minute. Don't mind me. I'm all right."

"Cer'ly, he's all right," said Benson arousing from deep thought. "He's all right. But better take'm home, though. That's ri-right. He's load'. But he's all right. No need go home any more'n you. But better take'm home. He's load'." He looked at his companion with compassion. "Kid, you're load'."

The sober Kid spoke abruptly to his friend from San Francisco. "Kid, pull yourself together, now. Don't fool. We've got to brace this ass of a Benson all the way home. Get hold of his other arm."

The 'Frisco Kid immediately obeyed his comrade without a word or a glower. He seized Benson and came to attention like a soldier. Later, indeed, he meekly ventured: "Can't we take cab?" But when the New York Kid snapped out that there were no convenient cabs he subsided to an impassive silence. He seemed to be reflecting upon his state without astonishment, dismay or any particular emotion. He submitted himself woodenly to the direction of his friend.

Benson had protested when they had grasped his arms. "Washa doing?" he said in a new and guttural voice. "Washa doing? I ain' load'. Comonangetadrink. I——"

"Oh, come along, you idiot," said the New York Kid. The 'Frisco Kid merely presented the mien of a stoic to the appeal of Benson and in silence dragged away at one of his arms. Benson's feet came from that particular spot on the pavement with the reluctance of roots and also with the ultimate suddenness of roots. The three of them lurched out into the street in the abandon of tumbling chimneys. Benson was meanwhile noisily challenging the others to produce any reasons for his being taken home. His toes clashed into the kerb when they reached the other side of the *calle* and for a moment the Kids hauled him along with the points of his shoes scraping musically on the pavement. He balked formidably as they were about to pass the Casa Verde. "No! No! Leshavanothdrink! Anothdrink! Onemore!"

But the 'Frisco Kid obeyed the voice of his partner in a manner that was blind but absolute and they scummed Benson on past the door. Locked together the three swung into a dark street. The sober Kid's flank was continually careering ahead of the other wing. He harshly admonished the 'Frisco child and the latter promptly improved in the same manner of unthinking complete obedience. Benson began to recite the tale of a love affair, a tale that didn't even have a middle.

Occasionally the New York Kid swore. They toppled on their way like three comedians playing at it on the stage.

At midnight a little Mexican street burrowing among the walls of the city is as dark as a whale's throat at deep sea. Upon this occasion heavy clouds hung over the capital and the sky was a pall. The projecting balconies could make no shadows.

"Shay," said Benson breaking away from his escort suddenly, "what want gome for? I ain' load'. You got reg'lar spool-fact'ry in your head—you N' York Kid there. Thish oth' Kid, he's mos' proper, mos' proper shober. He's drunk but—but he's shober."

"Ah, shut up, Benson," said the New York Kid. "Come along now. We can't stay here all night." Benson refused to be corralled but spread his legs and twirled like a dervish, meanwhile under the evident impression that he was conducting himself most handsomely. It was not long before he gained the opinion that he was laughing at the others. "Eight purple dogsh—dogs! Eight purple dogs. Thas what Kid'll see in the morn'. Look ou' for 'em. They——"

As Benson, describing the canine phenomena, swung wildly across the sidewalk, it chanced that three other pedestrians were passing in shadowy rank. Benson's shoulder jostled one of them.

A Mexican wheeled upon the instant. His hand flashed to his hip. There was a moment of silence during which Benson's voice was not heard raised in apology. Then an indescribable comment, one burning word, came from between the Mexican's teeth.

Benson, rolling about in a semi-detached manner, stared vacantly at the Mexican who thrust his lean yellow face forward while his fingers played nervously at his hip. The New York Kid could not follow Spanish well but he understood when the Mexican breathed softly: "Does the señor want fight?"

Benson simply gazed in gentle surprise. The woman next to him at dinner had said something inventive. His tailor had presented his bill. Something had occurred which was mildly out of the ordinary and his surcharged brain refused to cope with it. He displayed only the agitation of a smoker temporarily without a light.

The New York Kid had almost instantly grasped Benson's arm and was about to jerk him away when the other Kid who up to this time had been an automaton suddenly projected himself forward, thrust the rubber Benson aside and said: "Yes!"

There was no sound nor light in the world. The wall at the left happened to be of the common prison-like construction—no door, no window, no opening at all. Humanity was enclosed and asleep. Into the mouth of the sober Kid came a wretched bitter taste as if it had filled with blood. He was transfixed as if he was already seeing the lightning ripples on the knife-blade.

But the Mexican's hand did not move at that time. His face went still further forward and he whispered: "So?" The sober Kid saw this face as if he and it were alone in space—a yellow mask smiling in eager cruelty, in satisfaction, and above all it was lit with sinister decision. As for the features they were reminiscent of an unplaced, a forgotten type which really resembled with precision those of a man who had shaved him three times in Boston in 1888. But the expression burned his mind as sealing-wax burns the palm and fascinated, stupefied, he actually watched the progress of the man's thought toward the point where a knife would be wrenched from its sheath. The emotion, a sort of mechanical fury, a breeze made by electric fans, a rage made by vanity, smote the dark countenance in wave after wave.

Then the New York Kid took a sudden step forward. His hand was also at his hip. He was gripping there a revolver of robust size. He recalled that upon its black handle was stamped a hunting scene in which a sportsman in fine leggings and a peaked cap was taking aim at a stag less than one eighth of an inch away.

His pace forward caused instant movement of the Mexicans. One immediately took two steps to face him squarely. There was a general adjustment, pair and pair. This opponent of the New York Kid was a tall man and quite stout. His sombrero was drawn low over his eyes. His serape was flung on his left shoulder. His back was bended in the supposed manner of a Spanish grandee. This concave gentleman cut a fine and terrible figure. The lad, moved by the spirits of his modest and perpendicular ancestors, had time to feel his blood roar at sight of the pose.

He was aware that the third Mexican was over on the left fronting Benson and he was aware that Benson was leaning against the wall sleepily and peacefully eyeing the convention. So it happened that these six men stood, side fronting side, five of them with their right hands at their hips and with their bodies lifted nervously while the central pair exchanged a crescendo of provocations. The meaning of their words rose and rose. They were travelling in a straight line toward collision.

The New York Kid contemplated his Spanish grandee. He drew his revolver upward until the hammer was surely free of the holster. He waited immovable and watchful while the garrulous 'Frisco Kid expended two and a half lexicons on the middle Mexican.

The Eastern lad suddenly decided that he was going to be killed. His mind leaped forward and studied the aftermath. The story would be a marvel of brevity when first it reached the far New York home, written in a careful hand on a bit of cheap paper topped and footed and backed by the printed fortifications of the cable company. But they are often as stones flung into mirrors, these bits of paper upon which are laconically written all the most terrible chronicles of the times. He witnessed the uprising of his mother and sister and the invincible calm of his hard-mouthed old father who would probably shut himself in his library and smoke alone. Then his father would come and they would bring him here and say: "This is the place." Then, very likely, each would remove his hat. They would stand quietly with their hats in their hands for a decent minute. He pitied his old financing father, unyielding and millioned, a man who commonly spoke twenty-two words a year to his beloved son. The Kid understood it at this time. If his fate was not impregnable, he might have turned out to be a man and have been liked by his father.

The other Kid would mourn his death. He would be preternaturally correct for some weeks and recite the tale without swearing. But it would not bore him. For the sake of his dead comrade he would be glad to be preternaturally correct and to recite the tale without swearing.

These views were perfectly stereopticon, flashing in and away from his thoughts with an inconceivable rapidity until after all they were simply one quick dismal impression. And now here is the unreal real: into this Kid's nostrils, at the expectant moment of slaughter, had come the scent of new-mown hay, a fragrance from a field of prostrate grass, a fragrance which contained the sunshine, the bees, the peace of meadows and the wonder of a distant crooning stream. It had no right to be supreme but it was supreme and he breathed it as he waited for pain and a sight of the unknown.

But in the same instant, it may be, his thought flew to the 'Frisco Kid and it came upon him like a flicker of lightning that the 'Frisco Kid was not going to be there to perform, for instance, the extraordinary office of respectable mourner. The other Kid's head was muddled, his hand was unsteady, his agility was gone. This other Kid was facing the determined and most ferocious gentleman of the enemy. The New York Kid became convinced that his friend was lost. There was going to be a screaming murder. He was so certain of it that he wanted to shield his eyes from sight of the leaping arm and the knife. It was sickening, utterly sickening. The New York Kid might have been taking his first sea-voyage. A combination of honorable manhood and inability prevented him from running away.

He suddenly knew that it was possible to draw his own revolver and by a swift manoeuver face down all three Mexicans. If he was quick enough he would probably be victor. If any hitch occurred in the draw he would undoubtedly be dead with his friends. It was a new game; he had never been obliged to face a situation of this kind in the Beacon Club in New York. In this test, the lungs of the Kid still continued to perform their duty.

"Oh, five white mice of chance.
Shirts of wool and corduroy pants,
Gold and wine, women and sin,
All for you if you let me come in—
Into the house of chance."

He thought of the weight and size of his revolver and dismay pierced him. He feared that in his hands it would be as unwieldy as a sewing-machine for this quick work. He imagined, too, that some singular providence might cause him to lose his grip as he raised his weapon. Or it might get fatally entangled in the tails of his coat. Some of the eels of despair lay wet and cold against his back.

But at the supreme moment the revolver came forth as if it were greased and it arose like a feather. This somnolent machine, after months of repose, was finally looking at the breasts of men.

Perhaps in this one series of movements, the Kid had unconsciously used nervous force sufficient to raise a bale of hay. Before he comprehended it he was standing behind his revolver glaring over the barrel at the Mexicans menacing first one and then another. His finger was tremoring on the trigger. The revolver gleamed in the darkness with a fine silver light.

The fulsome grandee sprang backward with a low cry. The man who had been facing the 'Frisco Kid took a quick step away. The beautiful array of Mexicans was suddenly disorganized.

The cry and the backward steps revealed something of great importance to the New York Kid. He had never dreamed that he did not have a complete monopoly of all possible trepidations. The cry of the grandee was that of a man who suddenly sees a poisonous snake. Thus the Kid was able to understand swiftly that they were all human beings. They were unanimous in not wishing for too bloody combat. There was a sudden expression of the equality. He had vaguely believed that they were not going to evince much consideration for his dramatic development as an active factor. They even might be exasperated into an onslaught by it. Instead, they had respected his movement with a respect as great even as an ejaculation of fear and backward steps. Upon the instant he pounced forward and began to swear, unreeling great English oaths as thick as ropes and lashing the faces of the Mexicans with them. He was bursting with rage because these men had not previously confided to him that they were vulnerable. The whole thing had been an absurd imposition. He had been seduced into respectful alarm by the concave attitude of the grandee. And after all there had been an equality of emotion, an equality: he was furious. He wanted to take the serape of the grandee and swaddle him in it.

The Mexicans slunk back, their eyes burning wistfully. The Kid took aim first at one and then at another. After they had achieved a certain distance they paused and drew up in a rank. They then resumed some of their old splendor of manner. A voice hailed him in a tone of cynical bravado as if it had come from between high lips of smiling mockery. "Well, señor, it is finished?"

The Kid scowled into the darkness, his revolver drooping at his side. After a moment he answered: "I am willing." He found it strange that he should be able to speak after this silence of years.

"Good night, señor."

"Good night."

When he turned to look at the 'Frisco Kid he found him in

his original position, his hand upon his hip. He was blinking in perplexity at the point from whence the Mexicans had vanished.

"Well," said the sober Kid crossly, "are you ready to go home now?"

The 'Frisco Kid said: "Where they gone?" His voice was undisturbed but inquisitive.

Benson suddenly propelled himself from his dreamful position against the wall. "Frishco Kid's all right. He's drunk's fool and he's all right. But you New York Kid, you're sho-ber." He passed into a state of profound investigation. "Kid shober 'cause didn't go with us. Didn't go with us 'cause went to damn circus. Went to damn circus 'cause lose shakin' dice. Lose shakin' dice 'cause—what make lose shakin' dice, Kid?"

The New York Kid eyed the senile youth. "I don't know. The five white mice, maybe."

Benson puzzled so over this reply that he had to be held erect by his friends. Finally the 'Frisco Kid said: "Let's go home."

Nothing had happened.

A Texas Legend

"Remember that time, Major?" said the railroad man.

"You bet I do," rejoined the major.

"Go ahead and tell it," said the others.

The major lifted his glass and carefully scrutinized the bright liquid. "Well, Tom's line you see, was just being put through the interior of the State at that time, and one day he asked me to go out with him to some little town which he was going to open with an auction sale of lots and free beer and sandwiches for the people, and all that, you know. Well, I went along, and there was a big freight car loaded down with kegs and provisions. Everybody was having a great time. Tom got ill during the sale, so he went into a little shanty to lie down, while I went over to the freight car to get some ice to put on his head. I was in the car scouting around after ice when, all of a sudden, some one slammed the door to, and made the inside of the car as dark as pitch. Then somebody in the darkness began to swear like a pirate, and I heard him swing his revolver loose. I began to see the game then. It seems that there was a fellow around there that a good many people wanted to kill, and they said they were going to kill him that day at the sale, too. Somebody had pointed him out to me during the morning, and I had heard him brag, so I recognized this voice in the darkness. I think he decided that they had slammed the door on him so that when he opened it to come out they could get a good fair chance to make a sieve of him. The way that man swore was positively frightful.

"He wasn't very good company, either. I stood still so long that I felt the bones in my legs creak like old timbers, and I didn't breathe any harder than a canary bird. He went on swearing at a great rate.

"I began to think of Tom and his pain, wishing he had died rather than I had come for that ice.

"At last I found that I had got to move. There was no help

68

for it. My legs refused to support me in this position any longer. My head was growing dizzy, and if I didn't change my attitude I would fall down. I hadn't remained motionless for so very long either, but in a darkness where a man can't tell whether he is standing on his feet or his ears, the faculty of balance isn't much to be counted on. My heart stopped short when I felt myself sway, but I shifted one foot quickly, and there I was again. But that accursed foot had made a squeak.

"The fellow listened for a moment, and then he yelled: 'Who th' hell is in here?'

"I didn't say a word, but just dropped down to the floor as easy as a sack of oats.

"He listened for a time, and then bellowed out again: 'Who's in here?' I supposed he figured that it wasn't one of his enemies, or they would have got him while he was swearing to himself over in the corner.

" 'Who's in here, by Gawd! Come along now, galoot, an' speak up er I'll begin t' bore leetle holes in yeh! Who er yeh, anyhow! Whistle some now, by Gawd, er I'll fair eat ye!'

"He was beginning to get mad as a wildcat. I could fairly hear that fellow lashing himself into a rage, and getting more crazy every minute. All the kegs were up in his corner, and when I felt around with one hand I couldn't find a thing to get behind. Every second I expected to hear him begin to work his gun, and if you have ever lain in the darkness and wondered at what precise spot the impending bullet would strike, you know how I felt. So when he yelled out again, 'Who er you?' I spoke up and said, 'It's only me.'

" 'Thunder,' cried he, in a roar like a bull. 'Who's me! Give yer hull damn name an' pedigree, mister, if yeh ain't fond of reg'lar howling, helling row!'

" 'I'm from Houston,' said I.

" 'Houston,' said he, with a snort. 'An' what er yeh doin' here, stranger?'

" 'I came out to the sale,' I told him.

" 'Hum,' said he; and then he remained still for some time over in his end of the car.

"I was congratulating myself that I ran no more chance of trouble with this fiend, and that the whole thing was now a mere matter of waiting for some merciful fate to let me out, when suddenly the fellow said: 'Mister!'

" 'Sir?' said I.

" 'Open that there door!'

" 'Er—what?'

" 'Open that there door!'

" 'Er—the door to the car?'

"He began to froth at the mouth, I think. 'Sure,' he roared. 'Th' door t' th' car! There hain't fifty doors here, be ther! Slid 'er open or else, mister, you be a goner sure!' And then he cursed my ancestors for fifteen generations.

" 'Well—but—look here,' said I. 'Ain't—look here—ain't they going to shoot as soon as anybody opens that door. It—'

" 'None 'a yer damned business, stranger,' the fellow howled. 'Open that there door, er I'll everlastin'ly make er ventilator of yeh. Come on, now! Step up!' He began to prowl over in my direction. 'Where are yeh? Come on now, galoot! Where are yeh? Oh, just lemme lay my ol' gun ag'in yeh an' I'll fin' out! Step up!'

"This cat-like approach in the darkness was too much for me. 'Hold on,' said I, 'I'll open the door.'

"He gave a grunt and paused. I got up and went over to the door. 'Now, stranger,' the fellow said, 'es soon as yeh open th' door, jest step erside an' watch Luke Burnham peel th' skin off er them skunks.'

" 'But, look here—' said I.

" 'Stranger, this hain't no time t' arger! Open th' door!'

"I put my hand on the door and prepared to slide my body along with it. I had hoped to find it locked, but unfortunately it was not. When I gave it a preliminary shake, it rattled easily, and I could see that there was going to be no trouble in opening the door.

"I turned toward the interior of the car for one last remonstrance. 'Say, I haven't got anything to do with this thing. I'm just up here from Houston to go to the sale——'

"But the fellow howled again: 'Stranger, er you makin' a damn' fool 'a me? By the——'

" 'Hold on,' said I. 'I'll open the door.'

"I got all prepared, and then turned my head. 'Are you ready?'

" 'Let 'er go!'

"He was standing back in the car. I could see the dull glint of the revolvers in each hand.

" 'Let 'er go!' he said again.

"I braced myself, and put one hand out to reach the end of the door, then with a groan, I pulled. The door slid open, and I fell on my hands and knees in the end of the car.

" 'Hell,' said the fellow. I turned my head. There was nothing to be seen but blue sky and green prairie, and the little group of yellow board shanties with a red auction flag and a crowd of people in front of one of them.

"The fellow swore and flung himself out of the car. He went prowling off toward the crowd with his guns held barrels down and with his nervous fingers on the triggers. I followed him at a respectful distance.

"As he came near to them he began to walk like a cat on wet pavements, lifting each leg away up. 'Where is he? Where is th' white-livered skunk what slammed thet door on me? Where is he? Where is he? Let 'im show hisself! He dassent! Where is he? Where is he?'

"He went among them, bellowing in his bull fashion, and not a man moved. 'Where's all these galoots what was goin' t' shoot at me? Where be they? Let 'em come! Let 'em show theirselves! Let 'em come at me! Oh, there's them here as has got guns hangin' to 'em, but let 'em pull 'em! Let 'em pull 'em onct! Jest let 'em tap 'em with their fingers, an' I'll drive a stove-hole through every last one 'a their low-down hides! Lessee a man pull a gun! Lessee! An' lessee th' man what slammed th' door on me. Let 'im projuce hisself, th'——,' and he cursed this unknown individual in language that was like black smoke.

"But the men with guns remained silent and grave. The crowd for the most part gave him room enough to pitch a circus tent. When the train left he was still roaring around after the man who had slammed the door."

"And so they didn't kill him after all," said some one at the end of the narrative.

"Oh, yes, they got him that night," said the major. "In a saloon somewhere. They got him all right."

A Man and Some Others

I

Dark mesquit spread from horizon to horizon. There was no house or horseman from which a mind could evolve a city or a crowd. The world was declared to be a desert and unpeopled. Sometimes, however, on days when no heat-mist arose, a blue shape, dim, of the substance of a specter's veil, appeared in the southwest, and a pondering sheep-herder might remember that there were mountains.

In the silence of these plains the sudden and childish banging of a tin pan could have made an iron-nerved man leap into the air. The sky was ever flawless; the manœuvering of clouds was an unknown pageant; but at times a sheep-herder could see, miles away, the long, white streamers of dust rising from the feet of another's flock, and the interest became intense.

Bill was arduously cooking his dinner, bending over the fire, and toiling like a blacksmith. A movement, a flash of strange color, perhaps, off in the bushes, caused him suddenly to turn his head. Presently he arose, and, shading his eyes with his hand, stood motionless and gazing. He perceived at last a Mexican sheep-herder winding through the brush toward his camp.

"Hello!" shouted Bill.

The Mexican made no answer, but came steadily forward until he was within some twenty yards. There he paused, and, folding his arms, drew himself up in the manner affected by the villain in the play. His serape muffled the lower part of his face, and his great sombrero shaded his brow. Being unexpected and also silent, he had something of the quality of an apparition; moreover, it was clearly his intention to be mysterious and devilish.

The American's pipe, sticking carelessly in the corner of his mouth, was twisted until the wrong side was uppermost,

72

and he held his frying-pan poised in the air. He surveyed with evident surprise this apparition in the mesquit. "Hello, José!" he said; "what's the matter?"

The Mexican spoke with the solemnity of funeral tollings: "Beel, you mus' geet off range. We want you geet off range. We no like. Un'erstan'? We no like."

"What you talking about?" said Bill. "No like what?"

"We no like you here. Un'erstan'? Too mooch. You mus' geet out. We no like. Un'erstan'?"

"Understand? No; I don't know what the blazes you're gittin' at." Bill's eyes wavered in bewilderment, and his jaw fell. "I must git out? I must git off the range? What you givin' us?"

The Mexican unfolded his serape with his small yellow hand. Upon his face was then to be seen a smile that was gently, almost caressingly murderous. "Beel," he said, "geet out!"

Bill's arm dropped until the frying-pan was at his knee. Finally he turned again toward the fire. "Go on, you dog-gone little yaller rat!" he said over his shoulder. "You fellers can't chase me off this range. I got as much right here as anybody."

"Beel," answered the other in a vibrant tone, thrusting his head forward and moving one foot, "you geet out or we keel you."

"Who will?" said Bill.

"I—and the others." The Mexican tapped his breast gracefully.

Bill reflected for a time, and then he said: "You ain't got no manner of license to warn me off'n this range, and I won't move a rod. Understand? I've got rights, and I suppose if I don't see 'em through, no one is likely to give me a good hand and help me lick you fellers, since I'm the only white man in half a day's ride. Now, look; if you fellers try to rush this camp, I'm goin' to plug about fifty per cent of the gentlemen present, sure. I'm goin' in for trouble, an' I'll git a lot of you. 'Nuther thing: if I was a fine valuable caballero like you, I'd stay in the rear till the shootin' was done, because I'm goin' to make a particular p'int of shootin' you through the chest." He grinned affably, and made a gesture of dismissal.

As for the Mexican, he waved his hands in a consummate expression of indifference. "Oh, all right," he said. Then, in a tone of deep menace and glee, he added: "We will keel you eef you no geet. They have decide'."

"They have, have they?" said Bill. "Well, you tell them to go to the devil!"

II

Bill had been a mine-owner in Wyoming, a great man, an aristocrat, one who possessed unlimited credit in the saloons down the gulch. He had the social weight that could interrupt a lynching or advise a bad man of the particular merits of a remote geographical point. However, the fates exploded the toy balloon with which they had amused Bill, and on the evening of the same day he was a professional gambler with ill fortune dealing him unspeakable irritation in the shape of three big cards whenever another fellow stood pat. It is well here to inform the world that Bill considered his calamities of life all dwarfs in comparison with the excitement of one particular evening, when three kings came to him with criminal regularity against a man who always filled a straight. Later he became a cow-boy, more weirdly abandoned than if he had never been an aristocrat. By this time all that remained of his former splendor was his pride, or his vanity, which was one thing which need not have remained. He killed the foreman of the ranch over an inconsequent matter as to which of them was a liar, and the midnight train carried him eastward. He became a brakeman on the Union Pacific, and really gained high honors in the hobo war that for many years has devastated the beautiful railroads of our country. A creature of ill fortune himself, he practised all the ordinary cruelties upon these other creatures of ill fortune. He was of so fierce a mien that tramps usually surrendered at once whatever coin or tobacco they had in their possession; and if afterward he kicked them from the train, it was only because this was a recognized treachery of the war upon the hoboes. In a famous battle fought in Nebraska in 1879, he would have achieved a lasting distinction if it had not been for a deserter from the United States army. He was at the head of a heroic and sweeping charge, which really broke the power of the hoboes in that county for three months; he had already worsted four tramps with his own coupling-stick, when a stone thrown by the ex-third baseman of F Troop's nine laid him flat on the prairie, and later enforced a stay in the hospital in Omaha. After his recovery he engaged with other railroads, and shuffled cars in countless yards. An order to strike came upon him in Michigan, and afterward the vengeance of the railroad pursued him until he assumed a name. This mask is like the darkness in which the burglar chooses to move. It destroys many of the healthy fears. It is a small thing, but it eats that which we call our conscience. The conductor of No. 419 stood in the caboose within two feet of Bill's nose, and called him a liar. Bill requested him to use a milder term. He had not bored the foreman of Tin Can Ranch with any such request, but had killed him with expedition. The conductor seemed to insist, and so Bill let the matter drop.

He became the bouncer of a saloon on the Bowery in New York. Here most of his fights were as successful as had been his brushes with the hoboes in the West. He gained the complete admiration of the four clean bartenders who stood behind the great and glittering bar. He was an honored man. He nearly killed Bad Hennessy, who, as a matter of fact, had more reputation than ability, and his fame moved up the Bowery and down the Bowery.

But let a man adopt fighting as his business, and the thought grows constantly within him that it is his business to fight. These phrases became mixed in Bill's mind precisely as they are here mixed; and let a man get this idea in his mind, and defeat begins to move toward him over the unknown ways of circumstances. One summer night three sailors from the U.S.S. *Seattle* sat in the saloon drinking and attending to other people's affairs in an amiable fashion. Bill was a proud man since he had thrashed so many citizens, and it suddenly occurred to him that the loud talk of the sailors was very offensive. So he swaggered upon their attention, and warned them that the saloon was the flowery abode of peace and gentle silence. They glanced at him in surprise, and without a moment's pause consigned him to a worse place than any stoker of them knew. Whereupon he flung one of them through the side door before the others could prevent it. On the sidewalk there was a short struggle, with many hoarse epithets in the air, and then Bill slid into the saloon again. A frown of false rage was upon his brow, and he strutted like a savage king. He took a long yellow night-stick from behind the lunch-counter, and started importantly toward the main doors to see that the incensed seamen did not again enter.

The ways of sailormen are without speech, and, together in the street, the three sailors exchanged no word, but they moved at once. Landsmen would have required two years of discussion to gain such unanimity. In silence, and immediately, they seized a long piece of scantling that lay handily. With one forward to guide the battering-ram, and with two behind him to furnish the power, they made a beautiful curve, and came down like the Assyrians on the front door of that saloon.

Strange and still strange are the laws of fate. Bill, with his kingly frown and his long night-stick, appeared at precisely that moment in the doorway. He stood like a statue of victory; his pride was at its zenith; and in the same second this atrocious piece of scantling punched him in the bulwarks of his stomach, and he vanished like a mist. Opinions differed as to where the end of the scantling landed him, but it was ultimately clear that it landed him in southwestern Texas, where he became a sheep-herder.

The sailors charged three times upon the plate-glass front of the saloon, and when they had finished, it looked as if it had been the victim of a rural fire company's success in saving it from the flames. As the proprietor of the place surveyed the ruins, he remarked that Bill was a very zealous guardian of property. As the ambulance surgeon surveyed Bill, he remarked that the wound was really an excavation.

III

As his Mexican friend tripped blithely away, Bill turned with a thoughtful face to his frying-pan and his fire. After dinner he drew his revolver from its scarred old holster, and examined every part of it. It was the revolver that had dealt death to the foreman, and it had also been in free fights in which it had dealt death to several or none. Bill loved it because its allegiance was more than that of man, horse, or dog. It questioned neither social nor moral position; it obeyed alike the saint and the assassin. It was the claw of the eagle, the tooth of the lion, the poison of the snake; and when he swept it from its holster, this minion smote where he listed, even to the battering of a far penny. Wherefore it was his dearest possession, and was not to be exchanged in southwestern Texas for a handful of rubies, nor even the shame and homage of the conductor of No. 419.

During the afternoon he moved through his monotony of work and leisure with the same air of deep meditation. The smoke of his supper-time fire was curling across the shadowy sea of mesquit when the instinct of the plainsman warned him that the stillness, the desolation, was again invaded. He saw a motionless horseman in black outline against the pallid sky. The silhouette displayed serape and sombrero, and even the Mexican spurs as large as pies. When this black figure began to move toward the camp, Bill's hand dropped to his revolver.

The horseman approached until Bill was enabled to see pronounced American features, and a skin too red to grow on a Mexican face. Bill released his grip on his revolver.

"Hello!" called the horseman.

"Hello!" answered Bill.

The horseman cantered forward. "Good evening," he said, as he again drew rein.

"Good evenin'," answered Bill, without committing himself by too much courtesy.

For a moment the two men scanned each other in a way that is not ill-mannered on the plains, where one is in danger of meeting horse-thieves or tourists.

Bill saw a type which did not belong in the mesquit. The young fellow had invested in some Mexican trappings of an expensive kind. Bill's eyes searched the outfit for some sign of craft, but there was none. Even with his local regalia, it was clear that the young man was of a far, black Northern city. He had discarded the enormous stirrups of his Mexican saddle; he used the small English stirrup, and his feet were thrust forward until the steel tightly gripped his ankles. As Bill's eyes traveled over the stranger, they lighted suddenly upon the stirrups and the thrust feet, and immediately he smiled in a friendly way. No dark purpose could dwell in the innocent heart of a man who rode thus on the plains.

As for the stranger, he saw a tattered individual with a tangle of hair and beard, and with a complexion turned brick-color from the sun and whisky. He saw a pair of eyes that at first looked at him as the wolf looks at the wolf, and then became childlike, almost timid, in their glance. Here was evidently a man who had often stormed the iron walls of the city of success, and who now sometimes valued himself as the rabbit values his prowess.

The stranger smiled genially, and sprang from his horse. "Well, sir, I suppose you will let me camp here with you tonight?"

"Eh?" said Bill.

"I suppose you will let me camp here with you to-night?"

Bill for a time seemed too astonished for words.

"Well,"—he answered, scowling in inhospitable annoyance— "well, I don't believe this here is a good place to camp to-night, mister."

The stranger turned quickly from his saddle-girth.

"What?" he said in surprise. "You don't want me here? You don't want me to camp here?"

Bill's feet scuffled awkwardly, and he looked steadily at a cactus-plant. "Well, you see, mister," he said, "I'd like your company well enough, but—you see, some of these here greasers are goin' to chase me off the range to-night; and while I might like a man's company all right, I couldn't let him in for no such game when he ain't got nothin' to do with the trouble."

"Going to chase you off the range?" cried the stranger.

"Well, they said they were goin' to do it," said Bill.

"And—great heavens! will they kill you, do you think?"

"Don't know. Can't tell till afterwards. You see, they take some feller that's alone like me, and then they rush his camp when he ain't quite ready for 'em, and ginerally plug 'im with a sawed-off shot-gun load before he has a chance to git at 'em. They lay around and wait for their chance, and it comes soon enough. Of course a feller alone like me has got to let up watching some time. Maybe they ketch 'im asleep. Maybe the feller gits tired waiting, and goes out in broad day, and kills two or three just to make the whole crowd pile on him and settle the thing. I heard of a case like that once. It's awful hard on a man's mind—to git a gang after him."

"And so they're going to rush your camp to-night?" cried the stranger. "How do you know? Who told you?"

"Feller come and told me."

"And what are you going to do? Fight?"

"Don't see nothin' else to do," answered Bill, gloomily, still staring at the cactus-plant.

There was a silence. Finally the stranger burst out in an amazed cry. "Well, I never heard of such a thing in my life! How many of them are there?"

"Eight," answered Bill. "And now look-a-here; you ain't got no manner of business foolin' around here just now, and you might better lope off before dark. I don't ask no help in this here row. I know your happening along here just now don't give me no call on you, and you better hit the trail."

"Well, why in the name of wonder don't you go get the sheriff?" cried the stranger.

"Oh, h——!" said Bill.

IV

Long, smoldering clouds spread in the western sky, and to the east silver mists lay on the purple gloom of the wilderness.

Finally, when the great moon climbed the heavens and cast its ghastly radiance upon the bushes, it made a new and more brilliant crimson of the camp-fire, where the flames capered merrily through its mesquit branches, filling the silence with the fire chorus, an ancient melody which surely bears a message of the inconsequence of individual tragedy—a message that is in the boom of the sea, the sliver of the wind through the grassblades, the silken clash of hemlock boughs.

No figures moved in the rosy space of the camp, and the search of the moonbeams failed to disclose a living thing in the bushes. There was no owl-faced clock to chant the weariness of the long silence that brooded upon the plain.

The dew gave the darkness under the mesquit a velvet quality that made air seem nearer to water, and no eye could have seen through it the black things that moved like monster lizards toward the camp. The branches, the leaves, that are fain to cry out when death approaches in the wilds, were frustrated by these uncanny bodies gliding with the finesse of the escaping serpent. They crept forward to the last point where assuredly no frantic attempt of the fire could discover them, and there they paused to locate the prey. A romance relates the tale of the black cell hidden deep in the earth, where, upon entering, one sees only the little eyes of snakes fixing him in menaces. If a man could have approached a certain spot in the bushes, he would not have found it romantically necessary to have his hair rise. There would have been a sufficient expression of horror in the feeling of the death-hand at the nape of his neck and in his rubber knee-joints.

Two of these bodies finally moved toward each other until for each there grew out of the darkness a face placidly smiling with tender dreams of assassination. "The fool is asleep by the fire, God be praised!" The lips of the other widened in a grin of affectionate appreciation of the fool and his plight. There was some signaling in the gloom, and then began a series of subtle rustlings, interjected often with pauses, during which no sound arose but the sound of faint breathing.

A bush stood like a rock in the stream of firelight, sending

its long shadow backward. With painful caution the little
company traveled along this shadow, and finally arrived at
the rear of the bush. Through its branches they surveyed for
a moment of comfortable satisfaction a form in a gray blanket extended on the ground near the fire. The smile of joyful
anticipation fled quickly, to give place to a quiet air of
business. Two men lifted shot-guns with much of the barrels
gone, and sighting these weapons through the branches,
pulled trigger together.

The noise of the explosions roared over the lonely mesquit
as if these guns wished to inform the entire world; and as the
gray smoke fled, the dodging company back of the bush saw
the blanketed form twitching. Whereupon they burst out in
chorus in a laugh, and arose as merry as a lot of banqueters.
They gleefully gestured congratulations, and strode bravely
into the light of the fire.

Then suddenly a new laugh rang from some unknown spot
in the darkness. It was a fearsome laugh of ridicule, hatred,
ferocity. It might have been demoniac. It smote them motionless in their gleeful prowl, as the stern voice from the sky
smites the legendary malefactor. They might have been a
weird group in wax, the light of the dying fire on their yellow
faces, and shining athwart their eyes turned toward the
darkness whence might come the unknown and the terrible.

The thing in the gray blanket no longer twitched; but if the
knives in their hands had been thrust toward it, each knife
was now drawn back, and its owner's elbow was thrown upward, as if he expected death from the clouds.

This laugh had so chained their reason that for a moment
they had no wit to flee. They were prisoners to their terror.
Then suddenly the belated decision arrived, and with bub-
bling cries they turned to run; but at that instant there was a
long flash of red in the darkness, and with the report one of
the men shouted a bitter shout, spun once, and tumbled headlong. The thick bushes failed to impede the rout of the others.

The silence returned to the wilderness. The tired flames
faintly illumined the blanketed thing and the flung corpse of
the marauder, and sang the fire chorus, the ancient melody
which bears the message of the inconsequence of human
tragedy.

V

"Now you are worse off than ever," said the young man, dry-voiced and awed.

"No, I ain't," said Bill, rebelliously. "I'm one ahead."

After reflection, the stranger remarked, "Well, there's seven more."

They were cautiously and slowly approaching the camp. The sun was flaring its first warming rays over the gray wilderness. Upreared twigs, prominent branches, shone with golden light, while the shadows under the mesquit were heavily blue.

Suddenly the stranger uttered a frightened cry. He had arrived at a point whence he had, through openings in the thicket, a clear view of a dead face.

"Gosh!" said Bill, who at the next instant had seen the thing: "I thought at first it was that there José. That would have been queer, after what I told 'im yesterday."

They continued their way, the stranger wincing in his walk, and Bill exhibiting considerable curiosity.

The yellow beams of the new sun were touching the grim hues of the dead Mexican's face, and creating there an inhuman effect, which made his countenance more like a mask of dulled brass. One hand, grown curiously thinner, had been flung out regardlessly to a cactus bush.

Bill walked forward and stood looking respectfully at the body. "I know that feller; his name is Miguel. He——"

The stranger's nerves might have been in that condition when there is no backbone to the body, only a long groove. "Good heavens!" he exclaimed, much agitated; "don't speak that way!"

"What way?" said Bill. "I only said his name was Miguel."

After a pause the stranger said:

"Oh, I know; but——" He waved his hand. "Lower your voice, or something. I don't know. This part of the business rattles me, don't you see?"

"Oh, all right," replied Bill, bowing to the other's mysterious mood. But in a moment he burst out violently and loud in the most extraordinary profanity, the oaths winging from him as the sparks go from the funnel.

He had been examining the contents of the bundled gray blanket, and he had brought forth, among other things, his frying-pan. It was now only a rim with a handle; the Mexican

volley had centered upon it. A Mexican shot-gun of the ab-
breviated description is ordinarily loaded with flat-irons, stove-
lids, lead pipe, old horseshoes, sections of chain, window
weights, railroad sleepers and spikes, dumb-bells, and any
other junk which may be at hand. When one of these loads
encounters a man vitally, it is likely to make an impression
upon him, and a cooking-utensil may be supposed to subside
before such an assault of curiosities.

Bill held high the desecrated frying-pan, turning it this way
and that way. He swore until he happened to note the absence of the stranger. A moment later he saw him leading his
horse from the bushes. In silence and sullenly the young man
went about saddling the animal. Bill said, "Well, goin' to pull
out?"

The stranger's hands fumbled uncertainly at the throat-
latch. Once he exclaimed irritably, blaming the buckle for the
trembling of his fingers. Once he turned to look at the dead
face with the light of the morning sun upon it. At last he
cried, "Oh, I know the whole thing was all square enough—
couldn't be squarer—but—somehow or other, that man there
takes the heart out of me." He turned his troubled face for
another look. "He seems to be all the time calling me a—he
makes me feel like a murderer."

"But," said Bill, puzzling, "you didn't shoot him, mister; I
shot him."

"I know; but I feel that way, somehow. I can't get rid of
it."

Bill considered for a time; then he said diffidently, "Mister,
you're a' eddycated man, ain't you?"

"What?"

"You're what they call a'—a' eddycated man, ain't you?"

The young man, perplexed, evidently had a question upon
his lips, when there was a roar of guns, bright flashes, and in
the air such hooting and whistling as would come from a
swift flock of steam-boilers. The stranger's horse gave a
mighty, convulsive spring, snorting wildly in its sudden anguish, fell upon its knees, scrambled afoot again, and was
away in the uncanny death run known to men who have seen
the finish of brave horses.

"This comes from discussin' things," cried Bill, angrily.

He had thrown himself flat on the ground facing the
thicket whence had come the firing. He could see the smoke
winding over the bush-tops. He lifted his revolver, and the
weapon came slowly up from the ground and poised like the

glittering crest of a snake. Somewhere on his face there was a kind of smile, cynical, wicked, deadly, of a ferocity which at the same time had brought a deep flush to his face, and had caused two upright lines to glow in his eyes.

"Hello, José!" he called, amiable for satire's sake. "Got your old blunderbusses loaded up again yet?"

The stillness had returned to the plain. The sun's brilliant rays swept over the sea of mesquit, painting the far mists of the west with faint rosy light, and high in the air some great bird fled toward the south.

"You come out here," called Bill, again addressing the landscape, "and I'll give you some shootin' lessons. That ain't the way to shoot." Receiving no reply, he began to invent epithets and yell them at the thicket. He was something of a master of insult, and, moreover, he dived into his memory to bring forth imprecations tarnished with age, unused since fluent Bowery days. The occupation amused him, and sometimes he laughed so that it was uncomfortable for his chest to be against the ground.

Finally the stranger, prostrate near him, said wearily, "Oh, they've gone."

"Don't you believe it," replied Bill, sobering swiftly. "They're there yet—every man of 'em."

"How do you know?"

"Because I do. They won't shake us so soon. Don't put your head up, or they'll get you, sure."

Bill's eyes, meanwhile, had not wavered from their scrutiny of the thicket in front. "They're there, all right; don't you forget it. Now you listen." So he called out: "José! Ojo, José! Speak up, *hombre*! I want have talk. Speak up, you yaller cuss, you!"

Whereupon a mocking voice from off in the bushes said, "Señor?"

"There," said Bill to his ally; "didn't I tell you? The whole batch." Again he lifted his voice. "José—look—ain't you gittin' kinder tired? You better go home, you fellers, and git some rest."

The answer was a sudden furious chatter of Spanish, eloquent with hatred, calling down upon Bill all the calamities which life holds. It was as if some one had suddenly enraged a cageful of wildcats. The spirits of all the revenges which they had imagined were loosened at this time, and filled the air.

"They're in a holler," said Bill, chuckling, "or there'd be shootin'."

Presently he began to grow angry. His hidden enemies called him nine kinds of coward, a man who could fight only in the dark, a baby who would run from the shadows of such noble Mexican gentlemen, a dog that sneaked. They described the affair of the previous night, and informed him of the base advantage he had taken of their friend. In fact, they in all sincerity endowed him with every quality which he no less earnestly believed them to possess. One could have seen the phrases bite him as he lay there on the ground fingering his revolver.

VI

It is sometimes taught that men do the furious and desperate thing from an emotion that is as even and placid as the thoughts of a village clergyman on Sunday afternoon. Usually, however, it is to be believed that a panther is at the time born in the heart, and that the subject does not resemble a man picking mulberries.

"B' G——!" said Bill, speaking as from a throat filled with dust, "I'll go after 'em in a minute."

"Don't you budge an inch!" cried the stranger, sternly. "Don't you budge!"

"Well," said Bill, glaring at the bushes—"well——"

"Put your head down!" suddenly screamed the stranger, in white alarm. As the guns roared, Bill uttered a loud grunt, and for a moment leaned panting on his elbow, while his arm shook like a twig. Then he upreared like a great and bloody spirit of vengeance, his face lighted with the blaze of his last passion. The Mexicans came swiftly and in silence.

The lightning action of the next few moments was of the fabric of dreams to the stranger. The muscular struggle may not be real to the drowning man. His mind may be fixed on the far, straight shadows back of the stars, and the terror of them. And so the fight, and his part in it, had to the stranger only the quality of a picture half drawn. The rush of feet, the spatter of shots, the cries, the swollen faces seen like masks on the smoke, resembled a happening of the night.

And yet afterward certain lines, forms, lived out so strongly from the incoherence that they were always in his memory.

He killed a man, and the thought went swiftly by him, like the feather on the gale, that it was easy to kill a man.

Moreover, he suddenly felt for Bill, this grimy sheep-herder, some deep form of idolatry. Bill was dying, and the dignity of last defeat, the superiority of him who stands in his grave, was in the pose of the lost sheep-herder.

The stranger sat on the ground idly mopping the sweat and powder-stain from his brow. He wore the gentle idiot smile of an aged beggar as he watched three Mexicans limping and staggering in the distance. He noted at this time that one who still possessed a serape had from it none of the grandeur of the cloaked Spaniard, but that against the sky the silhouette resembled a cornucopia of childhood's Christmas.

They turned to look at him, and he lifted his weary arm to menace them with his revolver. They stood for a moment banded together, and hooted curses at him.

Finally he arose, and, walking some paces, stooped to loosen Bill's gray hands from a throat. Swaying as if slightly drunk, he stood looking down into the still face.

Struck suddenly with a thought, he went about with dulled eyes on the ground, until he plucked his gaudy blanket from where it lay dirty from trampling feet. He dusted it carefully, and then returned and laid it over Bill's form. There he again stood motionless, his mouth just agape and the same stupid glance in his eyes, when all at once he made a gesture of fright and looked wildly about him.

He had almost reached the thicket when he stopped, smitten with alarm. A body contorted, with one arm stiff in the air, lay in his path. Slowly and warily he moved around it, and in a moment the bushes, nodding and whispering, their leaf-faces turned toward the scene behind him, swung and swung again into stillness and the peace of the wilderness.

The Bride Comes to Yellow Sky

I

The great Pullman was whirling onward with such dignity of motion that a glance from the window seemed simply to prove that the plains of Texas were pouring eastward. Vast flats of green grass, dull-hued spaces of mesquite and cactus, little groups of frame houses, woods of light and tender trees, all were sweeping into the east, sweeping over the horizon, a precipice.

A newly married pair had boarded this coach at San Antonio. The man's face was reddened from many days in the wind and sun, and a direct result of his new black clothes was that his brick-colored hands were constantly performing in a most conscious fashion. From time to time he looked down respectfully at his attire. He sat with a hand on each knee, like a man waiting in a barber's shop. The glances he devoted to other passengers were furtive and shy.

The bride was not pretty, nor was she very young. She wore a dress of blue cashmere, with small reservations of velvet here and there and with steel buttons abounding. She continually twisted her head to regard her puff sleeves, very stiff, straight, and high. They embarrassed her. It was quite apparent that she had cooked, and that she expected to cook, dutifully. The blushes caused by the careless scrutiny of some passengers as she had entered the car were strange to see upon this plain, under-class countenance, which was drawn in placid, almost emotionless lines.

They were evidently very happy. "Ever been in a parlor-car before?" he asked, smiling with delight.

"No," she answered. "I never was. It's fine, ain't it?"

"Great! And then after a while we'll go forward to the diner and get a big lay-out. Finest meal in the world. Charge a dollar."

"Oh, do they?" cried the bride. "Charge a dollar? Why, that's too much—for us—ain't it, Jack?"

"Not this trip, anyhow," he answered bravely. "We're going to go the whole thing."

Later, he explained to her about the trains. "You see, it's a thousand miles from one end of Texas to the other, and this train runs right across it and never stops but four times." He had the pride of an owner. He pointed out to her the dazzling fittings of the coach, and in truth her eyes opened wider as she contemplated the sea-green figured velvet, the shining brass, silver, and glass, the wood that gleamed as darkly brilliant as the surface of a pool of oil. At one end a bronze figure sturdily held a support for a separated chamber, and at convenient places on the ceiling were frescoes in olive and silver.

To the minds of the pair, their surroundings reflected the glory of their marriage that morning in San Antonio. This was the environment of their new estate, and the man's face in particular beamed with an elation that made him appear ridiculous to the negro porter. This individual at times surveyed them from afar with an amused and superior grin. On other occasions he bullied them with skill in ways that did not make it exactly plain to them that they were being bullied. He subtly used all the manners of the most unconquerable kind of snobbery. He oppressed them, but of this oppression they had small knowledge, and they speedily forgot that infrequently a number of travelers covered them with stares of derisive enjoyment. Historically there was supposed to be something infinitely humorous in their situation.

"We are due in Yellow Sky at 3.42," he said, looking tenderly into her eyes.

"Oh, are we?" she said, as if she had not been aware of it. To evince surprise at her husband's statement was part of her wifely amiability. She took from a pocket a little silver watch, and as she held it before her and stared at it with a frown of attention, the new husband's face shone.

"I bought it in San Anton' from a friend of mine," he told her gleefully.

"It's seventeen minutes past twelve," she said, looking up at him with a kind of shy and clumsy coquetry. A passenger, noting this play, grew excessively sardonic, and winked at himself in one of the numerous mirrors.

At last they went to the dining-car. Two rows of negro waiters in glowing white suits surveyed their entrance with the interest and also the equanimity of men who had been forewarned. The pair fell to the lot of a waiter who happened to feel pleasure in steering them through their meal. He viewed them with the manner of a fatherly pilot, his countenance radiant with benevolence. The patronage entwined with the ordinary deference was not plain to them. And yet as they returned to their coach they showed in their faces a sense of escape.

To the left, miles down a long purple slope, was a little ribbon of mist where moved the keening Rio Grande. The train was approaching it at an angle, and the apex was Yellow Sky. Presently it was apparent that as the distance from Yellow Sky grew shorter, the husband became commensurately restless. His brick-red hands were more insistent in their prominence. Occasionally he was even rather absent-minded and far-away when the bride leaned forward and addressed him.

As a matter of truth, Jack Potter was beginning to find the shadow of a deed weigh upon him like a leaden slab. He, the town marshal of Yellow Sky, a man known, liked, and feared in his corner, a prominent person, had gone to San Antonio to meet a girl he believed he loved, and there, after the usual prayers, had actually induced her to marry him, without consulting Yellow Sky for any part of the transaction. He was now bringing his bride before an innocent and unsuspecting community.

Of course, people in Yellow Sky married as it pleased them in accordance with a general custom; but such was Potter's thought of his duty to his friends, or of their idea of his duty, or of an unspoken form which does not control men in these matters, that he felt he was heinous. He had committed an extraordinary crime. Face to face with this girl in San Antonio, and spurred by his sharp impulse, he had gone headlong over all the social hedges. At San Antonio he was like a man hidden in the dark. A knife to sever any friendly duty, any form, was easy to his hand in that remote city. But the hour of Yellow Sky, the hour of daylight, was approaching.

He knew full well that his marriage was an important thing to his town. It could only be exceeded by the burning of the new hotel. His friends would not forgive him. Frequently he had reflected on the advisability of telling them by telegraph, but a new cowardice had been upon him. He feared to do it. And now the train was hurrying him toward a scene of amazement, glee, reproach. He glanced out of the window at the line of haze swinging slowly in toward the train.

Yellow Sky had a kind of brass band which played painfully to the delight of the populace. He laughed without heart as he thought of it. If the citizens could dream of his prospective arrival with his bride, they would parade the band at the station and escort them, amid cheers and laughing congratulations, to his adobe home.

He resolved that he would use all the devices of speed and plains-craft in making the journey from the station to his house. Once within that safe citadel, he could issue some sort of a vocal bulletin, and then not go among the citizens until they had time to wear off a little of their enthusiasm.

The bride looked anxiously at him. "What's worrying you, Jack?"

He laughed again. "I'm not worrying, girl. I'm only thinking of Yellow Sky."

She flushed in comprehension.

A sense of mutual guilt invaded their minds and developed a finer tenderness. They looked at each other with eyes softly aglow. But Potter often laughed the same nervous laugh. The flush upon the bride's face seemed quite permanent.

The traitor to the feelings of Yellow Sky narrowly watched the speeding landscape. "We're nearly there," he said.

Presently the porter came and announced the proximity of Potter's home. He held a brush in his hand and, with all his airy superiority gone, he brushed Potter's new clothes as the latter slowly turned this way and that way. Potter fumbled out a coin and gave it to the porter as he had seen others do. It was a heavy and muscle-bound business, as that of a man shoeing his first horse.

The porter took their bag, and as the train began to slow they moved forward to the hooded platform of the car. Presently the two engines and their long string of coaches rushed into the station of Yellow Sky.

"They have to take water here," said Potter, from a constricted throat and in mournful cadence as one announcing death. Before the train stopped his eye had swept the length of the platform, and he was glad and astonished to see there was none upon it but the station-agent, who, with a slightly hurried and anxious air, was walking toward the water-tanks. When the train had halted, the porter alighted first and placed in position a little temporary step.

"Come on, girl," said Potter hoarsely. As he helped her down they each laughed on a false note. He took the bag from the negro, and bade his wife cling to his arm. As they slunk rapidly away, his hang-dog glance perceived that they were unloading the two trunks, and also that the station-agent far ahead near the baggage-car had turned and was running toward him, making gestures. He laughed, and groaned as he laughed, when he noted the first effect of his marital bliss upon Yellow Sky. He gripped his wife's arm firmly to his side, and they fled. Behind them the porter stood chuckling fatuously.

II

The California Express on the Southern Railway was due at Yellow Sky in twenty-one minutes. There were six men at the bar of the Weary Gentleman saloon. One was a drummer who talked a great deal and rapidly; three were Texans who did not care to talk at that time; and two were Mexican sheep-herders who did not talk as a general practice in the Weary Gentleman saloon. The bar-keeper's dog lay on the board-walk that crossed in front of the door. His head was on his paws, and he glanced drowsily here and there with the constant vigilance of a dog that is kicked on occasion. Across the sandy street were some vivid green grass plots, so wonderful in appearance amid the sands that burned near them in a blazing sun that they caused a doubt in the mind. They exactly resembled the grass mats used to represent lawns on the stage. At the cooler end of the railway station a man without a coat sat in a tilted chair and smoked his pipe. The fresh-cut bank of the Rio Grande circled near the town, and there could be seen beyond it a great plum-colored plain of mesquite.

Save for the busy drummer and his companions in the saloon, Yellow Sky was dozing. The new-comer leaned gracefully upon the bar, and recited many tales with the confidence of a bard who has come upon a new field.

"—and at the moment that the old man fell down stairs with the bureau in his arms, the old woman was coming up with two scuttles of coal, and, of course——"

The drummer's tale was interrupted by a young man who suddenly appeared in the open door. He cried: "Scratchy Wilson's drunk, and has turned loose with both hands." The two Mexicans at once set down their glasses and faded out of the rear entrance of the saloon.

The drummer, innocent and jocular, answered: "All right, old man. S'pose he has. Come in and have a drink, anyhow."

But the information had made such an obvious cleft in every skull in the room that the drummer was obliged to see its importance. All had become instantly morose. "Say," said he, mystified, "what is this?" His three companions made the introductory gesture of eloquent speech, but the young man at the door forestalled them.

"It means, my friend," he answered, as he came into the saloon, "that for the next two hours this town won't be a health resort."

The bar-keeper went to the door and locked and barred it. Reaching out of the window, he pulled in heavy wooden shutters and barred them. Immediately a solemn, chapel-like gloom was upon the place. The drummer was looking from one to another.

"But say," he cried, "what is this, anyhow? You don't mean there is going to be a gun-fight?"

"Don't know whether there'll be a fight or not," answered one man grimly. "But there'll be some shootin'—some good shootin'."

The young man who had warned them waved his hand. "Oh, there'll be a fight fast enough, if anyone wants it. Anybody can get a fight out there in the street. There's a fight just waiting."

The drummer seemed to be swayed between the interest of a foreigner and a perception of personal danger.

"What did you say his name was?" he asked.

"Scratchy Wilson," they answered in chorus.

"And will he kill anybody? What are you going to do? Does this happen often? Does he rampage around like this once a week or so? Can he break in that door?"

"No, he can't break down that door," replied the bar-keeper. "He's tried it three times. But when he comes you'd better lay down on the floor, stranger. He's dead sure to shoot at it, and a bullet may come through."

Thereafter the drummer kept a strict eye upon the door. The time had not yet been called for him to hug the floor, but as a minor precaution he sidled near to the wall. "Will he kill anybody?" he said again.

The men laughed low and scornfully at the question.

"He's out to shoot, and he's out for trouble. Don't see any good in experimentin' with him."

"But what do you do in a case like this? What do you do?"

A man responded: "Why, he and Jack Potter——"

But, in chorus, the other men interrupted: "Jack Potter's in San Anton'."

"Well, who is he? What's he got to do with it?"

"Oh, he's the town marshal. He goes out and fights Scratchy when he gets on one of these tears."

"Wow," said the drummer, mopping his brow. "Nice job he's got."

The voices had toned away to mere whisperings. The drummer wished to ask further questions which were born of the increasing anxiety and bewilderment; but when he attempted them, the men merely looked at him in irritation and motioned him to remain silent. A tense waiting hush was upon them. In the deep shadows of the room their eyes shone as they listened for sounds from the street. One man made three gestures at the bar-keeper, and the latter, moving like a ghost, handed him a glass and a bottle. The man poured a full glass of whisky, and set down the bottle noiselessly. He gulped the whisky in a swallow, and turned again toward the door in immovable silence. The drummer saw that the bar-keeper, without a sound, had taken a Winchester from beneath the bar. Later he saw this individual beckoning to him, so he tiptoed across the room.

"You better come with me back of the bar."

"No thanks," said the drummer, perspiring. "I'd rather be where I can make a break for the back door."

Whereupon the man of bottles made a kindly but peremptory gesture. The drummer obeyed it, and finding himself seated on a box with his head below the level of the bar, balm was laid upon his soul at sight of various zinc and copper fittings that bore a resemblance to armor-plate. The bar-keeper took a seat comfortably upon an adjacent box.

"You see," he whispered, "this here Scratchy Wilson is a wonder with a gun—a perfect wonder—and when he goes on the war trail, we hunt our holes—naturally. He's about the last one of the old gang that used to hang out along the river here. He's a terror when he's drunk. When he's sober he's all right—kind of simple—wouldn't hurt a fly—nicest fellow in town. But when he's drunk—whoo!"

There were periods of stillness. "I wish Jack Potter was back from San Anton'," said the bar-keeper. "He shot Wilson up once—in the leg—and he would sail in and pull out the kinks in this thing."

Presently they heard from a distance the sound of a shot, followed by three wild yowls. It instantly removed a bond from the men in the darkened saloon. There was a shuffling of feet. They looked at each other. "Here he comes," they said.

III

A man in a maroon-colored flannel shirt, which had been purchased for purposes of decoration and made, principally, by some Jewish women on the east side of New York, rounded a corner and walked into the middle of the main street of Yellow Sky. In either hand the man held a long, heavy blue-black revolver. Often he yelled, and these cries rang through a semblance of a deserted village, shrilly flying over the roofs in a volume that seemed to have no relation to the ordinary vocal strength of a man. It was as if the surrounding stillness formed the arch of a tomb over him. These cries of ferocious challenge rang against walls of silence. And his boots had red tops with gilded imprints, of the kind beloved in winter by little sledding boys on the hillsides of New England.

The man's face flamed in a rage begot of whisky. His eyes, rolling and yet keen for ambush, hunted the still door-ways and windows. He walked with the creeping movement of the midnight cat. As it occurred to him, he roared menacing information. The long revolvers in his hands were as easy as straws; they were moved with an electric swiftness. The little fingers of each hand played sometimes in a musician's way. Plain from the low collar of the shirt, the cords of his neck straightened and sank, straightened and sank, as passion moved him. The only sounds were his terrible invitations. The calm adobes preserved their demeanor at the passing of this small thing in the middle of the street.

There was no offer of fight; no offer of fight. The man called to the sky. There were no attractions. He bellowed and fumed and swayed his revolvers here and everywhere.

The dog of the bar-keeper of the Weary Gentleman saloon had not appreciated the advance of events. He yet lay dozing in front of his master's door. At sight of the dog, the man paused and raised his revolver humorously. At sight of the man, the dog sprang up and walked diagonally away, with a sullen head and growling. The man yelled, and the dog broke into a gallop. As it was about to enter an alley, there was a loud noise, a whistling, and something spat the ground directly before it. The dog screamed, and, wheeling in terror, galloped headlong in a new direction. Again there was a noise, a whistling, and sand was kicked viciously before it.

Fear-stricken, the dog turned and flurried like an animal in a pen. The man stood laughing, his weapons at his hips.

Ultimately the man was attracted by the closed door of the Weary Gentleman saloon. He went to it, and hammering with a revolver, demanded drink.

The door remaining imperturbable, he picked a bit of paper from the walk and nailed it to the framework with a knife. He then turned his back contemptuously upon this popular resort, and walking to the opposite side of the street, and spinning there on his heel quickly and lithely, fired at the bit of paper. He missed it by a half inch. He swore at himself, and went away. Later, he comfortably fusilladed the windows of his most intimate friend. The man was playing with this town. It was a toy for him.

But still there was no offer of fight. The name of Jack Potter, his ancient antagonist, entered his mind, and he concluded that it would be a glad thing if he should go to Potter's house and by bombardment induce him to come out and fight. He moved in the direction of his desire, chanting Apache scalp-music.

When he arrived at it, Potter's house presented the same still, calm front as had the other adobes. Taking up a strategic position, the man howled a challenge. But this house regarded him as might a great stone god. It gave no sign. After a decent wait, the man howled further challenges, mingling with them wonderful epithets.

Presently there came the spectacle of a man churning himself into deepest rage over the immobility of a house. He fumed at it as the winter wind attacks a prairie cabin in the North. To the distance there should have gone the sound of a tumult like the fighting of two hundred Mexicans. As necessity bade him, he paused for breath or to reload his revolvers.

IV

Potter and his bride walked sheepishly and with speed. Sometimes they laughed together shamefacedly and low.

"Next corner, dear," he said finally.

They put forth the efforts of a pair walking bowed against a strong wind. Potter was about to raise a finger to point the first appearance of the new home when, as they circled the corner, they came face to face with a man in a maroon-colored shirt was feverishly pushing cartridges into a large revolver. Upon the instant the man dropped this revolver to the ground, and, like lightning, whipped another from its holster. The second weapon was aimed at the bridegroom's chest.

There was a silence. Potter's mouth seemed to be merely a grave for his tongue. He exhibited an instinct to at once loosen his arm from the woman's grip, and he dropped the bag to the sand. As for the bride, her face had gone as yellow as old cloth. She was a slave to hideous rites gazing at the apparitional snake.

The two men faced each other at a distance of three paces. He of the revolver smiled with a new and quiet ferocity. "Tried to sneak up on me," he said. "Tried to sneak up on me!" His eyes grew more baleful. As Potter made a slight movement, the man thrust his revolver venomously forward. "No, don't you do it, Jack Potter. Don't you move a finger toward a gun just yet. Don't you move an eyelash. The time has come for me to settle with you, and I'm goin' to do it my own way and loaf along with no interferin'. So if you don't want a gun bent on you, just mind what I tell you."

Potter looked at his enemy. "I ain't got a gun on me, Scratchy," he said. "Honest, I ain't." He was stiffening and steadying, but yet somewhere at the back of his mind a vision of the Pullman floated, the sea-green figured velvet, the shining brass, silver, and glass, the wood that gleamed as darkly brilliant as the surface of a pool of oil—all the glory of the marriage, the environment of the new estate. "You know I fight when it comes to fighting, Scratchy Wilson, but I ain't got a gun on me. You'll have to do all the shootin' yourself."

His enemy's face went livid. He stepped forward and lashed his weapon to and fro before Potter's chest. "Don't you tell me you ain't got no gun on you, you whelp. Don't tell me no lie like that. There ain't a man in Texas ever seen you without no gun. Don't take me for no kid." His eyes blazed with light, and his throat worked like a pump.

"I ain't takin' you for no kid," answered Potter. His heels had not moved an inch backward. "I'm takin' you for a—— fool. I tell you I ain't got a gun, and I ain't. If you're goin' to shoot me up, you better begin now. You'll never get a chance like this again."

So much enforced reasoning had told on Wilson's rage. He was calmer. "If you ain't got a gun, why ain't you got a gun?" he sneered. "Been to Sunday-school?"

"I ain't got a gun because I've just come from San Anton' with my wife. I'm married," said Potter. "And if I'd thought there was going to be any galoots like you prowling around when I brought my wife home, I'd had a gun, and don't you forget it."

"Married!" said Scratchy, not at all comprehending.

"Yes, married. I'm married," said Potter distinctly.

"Married?" said Scratchy. Seemingly for the first time he saw the drooping drowning woman at the other man's side. "No!" he said. He was like a creature allowed a glimpse of another world. He moved a pace backward, and his arm with the revolver dropped to his side. "Is this—is this the lady?" he asked.

"Yes, this is the lady," answered Potter.

There was another period of silence.

"Well," said Wilson at last, slowly, "I s'pose it's all off now."

"It's all off if you say so, Scratchy. You know I didn't make the trouble." Potter lifted his valise.

"Well, I 'low it's off, Jack," said Wilson. He was looking at the ground. "Married!" He was not a student of chivalry; it was merely that in the presence of this foreign condition he was a simple child of the earlier plains. He picked up his starboard revolver, and placing both weapons in their holsters, he went away. His feet made funnel-shaped tracks in the heavy sand.

The Blue Hotel

I

The Palace Hotel at Fort Romper was painted a light blue, a shade that is on the legs of a kind of heron, causing the bird to declare its position against any background. The Palace Hotel, then, was always screaming and howling in a way that made the dazzling winter landscape of Nebraska seem only a gray swampish hush. It stood alone on the prairie, and when the snow was falling the town two hundred yards away was not visible. But when the traveler alighted at the railway station he was obliged to pass the Palace Hotel before he could come upon the company of low clap-board houses which composed Fort Romper, and it was not to be thought that any traveler could pass the Palace Hotel without looking at it. Pat Scully, the proprietor, had proved himself a master of strategy when he chose his paints. It is true that on clear days, when the great trans-continental expresses, long lines of swaying Pullmans, swept through Fort Romper, passengers were overcome at the sight, and the cult that knows the brown-reds and the subdivisions of the dark greens of the East expressed shame, pity, horror, in a laugh. But to the citizens of this prairie town, and to the people who would naturally stop there, Pat Scully had performed a feat. With this opulence and splendor, these creeds, classes, egotisms, that streamed through Romper on the rails day after day, they had no color in common.

As if the displayed delights of such a blue hotel were not sufficiently enticing, it was Scully's habit to go every morning and evening to meet the leisurely trains that stopped at Romper and work his seductions upon any man that he might see wavering, gripsack in hand.

One morning, when a snow-crusted engine dragged its long string of freight cars and its one passenger coach to the station, Scully performed the marvel of catching three men. One was a shaky and quick-eyed Swede, with a great shining cheap valise; one was a tall bronzed cowboy, who was on his way to a ranch near the Dakota line; one was a little silent man from the East, who didn't look it, and didn't announce it. Scully practically made them prisoners. He was so nimble and merry and kindly that each probably felt it would be the height of brutality to try to escape. They trudged off over the creaking board sidewalks in the wake of the eager little Irishman. He wore a heavy fur cap squeezed tightly down on his head. It caused his two red ears to stick out stiffly, as if they were made of tin.

At last, Scully, elaborately, with boisterous hospitality, conducted them through the portals of the blue hotel. The room which they entered was small. It seemed to be merely a proper temple for an enormous stove, which, in the center, was humming with god-like violence. At various points on its surface the iron had become luminous and glowed yellow from the heat. Beside the stove Scully's son Johnnie was playing High-Five with an old farmer who had whiskers both gray and sandy. They were quarreling. Frequently the old farmer turned his face toward a box of sawdust—colored brown from tobacco juice—that was behind the stove, and spat with an air of great impatience and irritation. With a loud flourish of words Scully destroyed the game of cards, and bustled his son upstairs with part of the baggage of the new guests. He himself conducted them to three basins of the coldest water in the world. The cowboy and the Easterner burnished themselves fiery red with this water, until it seemed to be some kind of metal polish. The Swede, however, merely dipped his fingers gingerly and with trepidation. It was notable that throughout this series of small ceremonies the three travelers were made to feel that Scully was very benevolent. He was conferring great favors upon them. He handed the towel from one to the other with an air of philanthropic impulse.

Afterward they went to the first room, and, sitting about the stove, listened to Scully's officious clamor at his daughters, who were preparing the midday meal. They reflected in the silence of experienced men who tread carefully amid new people. Nevertheless, the old farmer, stationary, invincible in his chair near the warmest part of the stove, turned his face from the sawdust box frequently and addressed a glowing commonplace to the strangers. Usually he was answered in short but adequate sentences by either the cowboy or the Easterner. The Swede said nothing. He seemed to be occupied in making furtive estimates of each man in the room. One might have thought that he had the sense of silly suspicion which comes to guilt. He resembled a badly frightened man.

Later, at dinner, he spoke a little, addressing his conversation entirely to Scully. He volunteered that he had come from New York, where for ten years he had worked as a tailor. These facts seemed to strike Scully as fascinating, and afterward he volunteered that he had lived at Romper for fourteen years. The Swede asked about the crops and the price of labor. He seemed barely to listen to Scully's extended replies. His eyes continued to rove from man to man.

Finally, with a laugh and a wink, he said that some of these Western communities were very dangerous; and after his statement he straightened his legs under the table, tilted his head, and laughed again, loudly. It was plain that the demonstration had no meaning to the others. They looked at him wondering and in silence.

II

As the men trooped heavily back into the front room, the two little windows presented views of a turmoiling sea of snow. The huge arms of the wind were making attempts—mighty, circular, futile—to embrace the flakes as they sped. A gate-post like a still man with a blanched face stood aghast amid this profligate fury. In a hearty voice Scully announced the presence of a blizzard. The guests of the blue hotel, lighting their pipes, assented with grunts of lazy masculine contentment. No island of the sea could be exempt in the degree of this little room with its humming stove. Johnnie, son of Scully, in a tone which defined his opinion of his ability as a card-player, challenged the old farmer of both gray and sandy whiskers to a game of High-Five. The farmer agreed with a contemptuous and bitter scoff. They sat close to the stove, and squared their knees under a wide board. The cowboy and the Easterner watched the game with interest. The Swede remained near the window, aloof, but with a countenance that showed signs of an inexplicable excitement.

The play of Johnnie and the gray-beard was suddenly ended by another quarrel. The old man arose while casting a look of heated scorn at his adversary. He slowly buttoned his coat, and then stalked with fabulous dignity from the room. In the discreet silence of all other men the Swede laughed.

His laughter rang somehow childish. Men by this time had begun to look at him askance, as if they wished to inquire what ailed him.

A new game was formed jocosely. The cowboy volunteered to become the partner of Johnnie, and they all then turned to ask the Swede to throw in his lot with the little Easterner. He asked some questions about the game, and learning that it wore many names, and that he had played it when it was under an alias, he accepted the invitation. He strode toward the men nervously, as if he expected to be assaulted. Finally, seated, he gazed from face to face and laughed shrilly. This laugh was so strange that the Easterner looked up quickly, the cowboy sat intent and with his mouth open, and Johnnie paused, holding the cards with still fingers.

Afterward there was a short silence. Then Johnnie said: "Well, let's get at it. Come on now!" They pulled their chairs forward until their knees were bunched under the board. They began to play, and their interest in the game caused the others to forget the manner of the Swede.

The cowboy was a board-whacker. Each time that he held superior cards he whanged them, one by one, with exceeding force, down upon the improvised table, and took the tricks with a glowing air of prowess and pride that sent thrills of indignation into the hearts of his opponents. A game with a board-whacker in it is sure to become intense. The countenances of the Easterner and the Swede were miserable whenever the cowboy thundered down his aces and kings, while Johnnie, his eyes gleaming with joy, chuckled and chuckled.

Because of the absorbing play none considered the strange ways of the Swede. They paid strict heed to the game. Finally, during a lull caused by a new deal, the Swede suddenly addressed Johnnie: "I suppose there have been a good many men killed in this room." The jaws of the others dropped and they looked at him.

"What in hell are you talking about?" said Johnnie.

The Swede laughed again his blatant laugh, full of a kind of false courage and defiance. "Oh, you know what I mean all right," he answered.

"I'm a liar if I do!" Johnnie protested. The card was halted, and the men stared at the Swede. Johnnie evidently felt that as the son of the proprietor he should make a direct inquiry. "Now, what might you be drivin' at, mister?" he asked. The Swede winked at him. It was a wink full of cunning. His fingers shook on the edge of the board. "Oh, maybe you think I have been to nowheres. Maybe you think I'm a tenderfoot?"

"I don't know nothin' about you," answered Johnnie, "and I don't give a damn where you've been. All I got to say is that I don't know what you're driving at. There hain't never been nobody killed in this room."

The cowboy, who had been steadily gazing at the Swede, then spoke. "What's wrong with you, mister?"

Apparently it seemed to the Swede that he was formidably menaced. He shivered and turned white near the corners of his mouth. He set an appealing glance in the direction of the little Easterner. During these moments he did not forget to wear his air of advanced pot-valor. "They say they don't know what I mean," he remarked mockingly to the Easterner.

The latter answered after prolonged and cautious reflection. "I don't understand you," he said, impassively.

The Swede made a movement then which announced that he thought he had encountered treachery from the only quarter where he had expected sympathy if not help. "Oh, I see you are all against me. I see——"

The cowboy was in a state of deep stupefaction. "Say," he cried, as he tumbled the deck violently down upon the board. "Say, what are you gittin' at, hey?"

The Swede sprang up with the celerity of a man escaping from a snake on the floor. "I don't want to fight!" he shouted. "I don't want to fight!"

The cowboy stretched his long legs indolently and deliberately. His hands were in his pockets. He spat into the sawdust box. "Well, who the hell thought you did?" he inquired.

The Swede backed rapidly toward a corner of the room. His hands were out protectingly in front of his chest, but he was making an obvious struggle to control his fright. "Gentlemen," he quavered, "I suppose I am going to be killed before I can leave this house! I suppose I am going to be killed before I can leave this house!" In his eyes was the dying swan look. Through the windows could be seen the snow turning blue in the shadow of dusk. The wind tore at the house and some loose thing beat regularly against the clap-boards like a spirit tapping.

A door opened, and Scully himself entered. He paused in surprise as he noted the tragic attitude of the Swede. Then he said: "What's the matter here?"

The Swede answered him swiftly and eagerly: "These men are going to kill me."

"Kill you!" ejaculated Scully. "Kill you! What are you talkin'?"

The Swede made the gesture of a martyr.

Scully wheeled sternly upon his son. "What is this, Johnnie?"

The lad had grown sullen. "Damned if I know," he answered. "I can't make no sense to it." He began to shuffle the cards, fluttering them together with an angry snap. "He says a good many men have been killed in this room, or something like that. And he says he's goin' to be killed here too. I don't know what ails him. He's crazy, I shouldn't wonder."

Scully then looked for explanation to the cowboy, but the cowboy simply shrugged his shoulders.

"Kill you?" said Scully again to the Swede. "Kill you? Man, you're off your nut."

"Oh, I know," burst out the Swede. "I know what will happen. Yes, I'm crazy—yes. Yes, of course, I'm crazy—yes. But I know one thing——" There was a sort of sweat of misery and terror upon his face. "I know I won't get out of here alive."

The cowboy drew a deep breath, as if his mind was passing into the last stages of dissolution. "Well, I'm dog-goned," he whispered to himself.

Scully wheeled suddenly and faced his son. "You've been troublin' this man!"

Johnnie's voice was loud with its burden of grievance. "Why, good Gawd, I ain't done nothin' to 'im."

The Swede broke in. "Gentlemen, do not disturb yourselves. I will leave this house. I will go 'way because——" He accused them dramatically with his glance. "Because I do not want to be killed."

Scully was furious with his son. "Will you tell me what is the matter, you young divil? What's the matter, anyhow? Speak out!"

"Blame it," cried Johnnie in despair, "don't I tell you I don't know. He—he says we want to kill him, and that's all I know. I can't tell what ails him."

The Swede continued to repeat: "Never mind, Mr. Scully, never mind. I will leave this house. I will go away, because I do not wish to be killed. Yes, of course, I am crazy—yes. But I know one thing! I will go away. I will leave this house. Never mind, Mr. Scully, never mind. I will go away."

"You will not go 'way,' said Scully. "You will not go 'way until I hear the reason of this business. If anybody has troubled you I will take care of him. This is my house. You are under my roof, and I will not allow any peaceable man to be troubled here." He cast a terrible eye upon Johnnie, the cowboy, and the Easterner.

"Never mind, Mr. Scully, never mind. I will go 'way. I do not wish to be killed." The Swede moved toward the door, which opened upon the stairs. It was evidently his intention to go at once for his baggage.

"No, no," shouted Scully peremptorily; but the white-faced man slid by him and disappeared. "Now," said Scully severely, "what does this mane?"

Johnnie and the cowboy cried together: "Why, we didn't do nothin' to 'im!"

Scully's eyes were cold. "No," he said, "you didn't?"

Johnnie swore a deep oath. "Why, this is the wildest loon I ever see. We didn't do nothin' at all. We were jest sittin' here playin' cards and he——"

The father suddenly spoke to the Easterner. "Mr. Blanc," he asked, "what has these boys been doin'?"

The Easterner reflected again. "I didn't see anything wrong at all," he said at last slowly.

Scully began to howl. "But what does it mane?" He stared ferociously at his son. "I have a mind to lather you for this, me boy."

Johnnie was frantic. "Well, what have I done?" he bawled at his father.

III

"I think you are tongue-tied," said Scully finally to his son, the cowboy and the Easterner, and at the end of this scornful sentence he left the room.

Upstairs the Swede was swiftly fastening the straps of his great valise. Once his back happened to be half-turned toward the door, and hearing a noise there, he wheeled and sprang up, uttering a loud cry. Scully's wrinkled visage showed grimly in the light of the small lamp he carried. This yellow effulgence, streaming upward, colored only his prominent features, and left his eyes, for instance, in mysterious shadow. He resembled a murderer.

"Man, man!" he exclaimed, "have you gone daffy?"

"Oh, no! Oh, no!" rejoined the other. "There are people in

this world who know pretty nearly as much as you do—understand?"

For a moment they stood gazing at each other. Upon the Swede's deathly pale cheeks were two spots brightly crimson and sharply edged, as if they had been carefully painted. Scully placed the light on the table and sat himself on the edge of the bed. He spoke ruminatively. "By cracky, I never heard of such a thing in my life. It's a complete muddle. I can't for the soul of me think how you ever got this idea into your head." Presently he lifted his eyes and asked: "And did you sure think they were going to kill you?"

The Swede scanned the old man as if he wished to see into his mind. "I did," he said at last. He obviously suspected that this answer might precipitate an outbreak. As he pulled on a strap his whole arm shook, the elbow wavering like a bit of paper.

Scully banged his hand impressively on the footboard of the bed. "Why, man, we're goin' to have a line of ilictric street-cars in this town next spring."

" 'A line of electric street-cars,' " repeated the Swede stupidly.

"And," said Scully, "there's a new railroad goin' to be built down from Broken Arm to here. Not to mintion the four churches and the smashin' big brick school-house. Then there's the big factory, too. Why, in two years Romper'll be a met-tro-*pol*-is."

Having finished the preparation of his baggage, the Swede straightened himself. "Mr. Scully," he said with sudden hardihood, "how much do I owe you?"

"You don't owe me anythin'," said the old man angrily.

"Yes, I do," retorted the Swede. He took seventy-five cents from his pocket and tendered it to Scully; but the latter snapped his fingers in disdainful refusal. However, it happened that they both stood gazing in a strange fashion at three silver pieces on the Swede's open palm.

"I'll not take your money," said Scully at last. "Not after what's been goin' on here." Then a plan seemed to strike him. "Here," he cried, picking up his lamp and moving toward the door. "Here! Come with me a minute."

"No," said the Swede in overwhelming alarm.

"Yes," urged the old man. "Come on! I want you to come and see a picter—just across the hall—in my room."

The Swede must have concluded that his hour was come. His jaw dropped and his teeth showed like a dead man's. He ultimately followed Scully across the corridor, but he had the step of one hung in chains.

Scully flashed the light high on the wall of his own chamber. There was revealed a ridiculous photograph of a little girl. She was leaning against a balustrade of gorgeous decoration, and the formidable bang to her hair was prominent. The figure was as graceful as an upright sled-stake, and, withal, it was of the hue of lead. "There," said Scully tenderly. "That's the picter of my little girl that died. Her name was Carrie. She had the purtiest hair you ever saw! I was that fond of her, she——"

Turning then he saw that the Swede was not contemplating the picture at all, but, instead, was keeping keen watch on the gloom in the rear.

"Look, man!" shouted Scully heartily. "That's the picter of my little gal that died. Her name was Carrie. And then here's the picter of my oldest boy, Michael. He's a lawyer in Lincoln an' doin' well. I gave that boy a grand eddycation, and I'm glad for it now. He's a fine boy. Look at 'im now. Ain't he bold as blazes, him there in Lincoln, an honored an' respicted gintleman. An honored an' respicted gintleman," concluded Scully with a flourish. And so saying, he smote the Swede jovially on the back.

The Swede faintly smiled.

"Now," said the old man, "there's only one more thing." He dropped suddenly to the floor and thrust his head beneath the bed. The Swede could hear his muffled voice. "I'd keep it under me piller if it wasn't for that boy Johnnie. Then there's the old woman—— Where is it now? I never put it twice in the same place. Ah, now come out with you!"

Presently he backed clumsily from under the bed, dragging with him an old coat rolled into a bundle. "I've fetched him," he muttered. Kneeling on the floor he unrolled the coat and extracted from its heart a large yellow-brown whisky bottle.

His first maneuver was to hold the bottle up to the light. Reassured, apparently, that nobody had been tampering with it, he thrust it with a generous movement toward the Swede.

The weak-kneed Swede was about to eagerly clutch this element of strength, but he suddenly jerked his hand away and cast a look of horror upon Scully.

"Drink," said the old man affectionately. He had arisen to his feet, and now stood facing the Swede.

There was a silence. Then again Scully said: "Drink!"

The Swede laughed wildly. He grabbed the bottle, put it to

his mouth, and as his lips curled absurdly around the opening and his throat worked, he kept his glance burning with hatred upon the old man's face.

IV

After the departure of Scully the three men, with the cardboard still upon their knees, preserved for a long time an astounded silence. Then Johnnie said: "That's the dod-dangest Swede I ever see."

"He ain't no Swede," said the cowboy scornfully.

"Well, what is he then?" cried Johnnie. "What is he then?"

"It's my opinion," replied the cowboy deliberately, "he's some kind of a Dutchman." It was a venerable custom of the country to entitle as Swedes all light-haired men who spoke with a heavy tongue. In consequence the idea of the cowboy was not without its daring. "Yes, sir," he repeated. "It's my opinion this feller is some kind of a Dutchman."

"Well, he says he's a Swede, anyhow," muttered Johnnie sulkily. He turned to the Easterner: "What do you think, Mr. Blanc?"

"Oh, I don't know," replied the Easterner.

"Well, what do you think makes him act that way?" asked the cowboy.

"Why, he's frightened!" The Easterner knocked his pipe against a rim of the stove. "He's clear frightened out of his boots."

"What at?" cried Johnnie and cowboy together.

The Easterner reflected over his answer.

"What at?" cried the others again.

"Oh, I don't know, but it seems to me this man has been reading dime-novels, and he thinks he's right out in the middle of it—the shootin' and stabbin' and all."

"But," said the cowboy, deeply scandalized, "this ain't Wyoming, ner none of them places. This is Nebrasker."

"Yes," added Johnnie, "an' why don't he wait till he gits *out West?*"

The traveled Easterner laughed. "It isn't different there even—not in these days. But he thinks he's right in the middle of hell."

Johnnie and the cowboy mused long.

"It's awful funny," remarked Johnnie at last.

"Yes," said the cowboy. "This is a queer game. I hope we don't git snowed in, because then we'd have to stand this here man bein' around with us all the time. That wouldn't be no good."

"I wish pop would throw him out," said Johnnie.

Presently they heard a loud stamping on the stairs, accompanied by ringing jokes in the voice of old Scully, and laughter, evidently from the Swede. The men around the stove stared vacantly at each other. "Gosh," said the cowboy. The door flew open, and old Scully, flushed and anecdotal, came into the room. He was jabbering at the Swede, who followed him, laughing bravely. It was the entry of two roysterers from a banquet hall.

"Come now," said Scully sharply to the three seated men, "move up and give us a chance at the stove." The cowboy and the Easterner obediently sidled their chairs to make room for the newcomers. Johnnie, however, simply arranged himself in a more indolent attitude, and then remained motionless.

"Come! Git over, there," said Scully.

"Plenty of room on the other side of the stove," said Johnnie.

"Do you think we want to sit in the draught?" roared the father.

But the Swede here interposed with a grandeur of confidence. "No, no. Let the boy sit where he likes," he cried in a bullying voice to the father.

"All right! All right!" said Scully deferentially. The cowboy and the Easterner exchanged glances of wonder.

The five chairs were formed in a crescent about one side of the stove. The Swede began to talk; he talked arrogantly, profanely, angrily. Johnnie, the cowboy and the Easterner maintained a morose silence, while old Scully appeared to be receptive and eager, breaking in constantly with sympathetic ejaculations.

Finally the Swede announced that he was thirsty. He moved in his chair, and said that he would go for a drink of water.

"I'll git it for you," cried Scully at once.

"No," said the Swede contemptuously. "I'll get it for myself." He arose and stalked with the air of an owner off into the executive parts of the hotel.

As soon as the Swede was out of hearing Scully sprang to his feet and whispered intensely to the others. "Upstairs he thought I was tryin' to poison 'im."

"Say," said Johnnie, "this makes me sick. Why don't you throw 'im out in the snow?"

"Why, he's all right now," declared Scully. "It was only that he was from the East and he thought this was a tough place. That's all. He's all right now."

The cowboy looked with admiration upon the Easterner. "You were straight," he said. "You were on to that there Dutchman."

"Well," said Johnnie to his father, "he may be all right now, but I don't see it. Other time he was scared, and now he's too fresh."

Scully's speech was always a combination of Irish brogue and idiom, Western twang and idiom, and scraps of curiously formal diction taken from the story-books and newspapers. He now hurled a strange mass of language at the head of his son. "What do I keep? What do I keep? What do I keep?" he demanded in a voice of thunder. He slapped his knee impressively, to indicate that he himself was going to make reply, and that all should heed. "I keep a hotel," he shouted. "A hotel, do you mind? A guest under my roof has sacred privileges. He is to be intimidated by none. Not one word shall he hear that would prijudice him in favor of goin' away. I'll not have it. There's no place in this here town where they can say they iver took in a guest of mine because he was afraid to stay here." He wheeled suddenly upon the cowboy and the Easterner. "Am I right?"

"Yes, Mr. Scully," said the cowboy, "I think you're right."

"Yes, Mr. Scully," said the Easterner, "I think you're right."

V

At six-o'clock supper, the Swede fizzed like a fire-wheel. He sometimes seemed on the point of bursting into riotous song, and in all his madness he was encouraged by old Scully. The Easterner was incased in reserve; the cowboy sat in wide-mouthed amazement, forgetting to eat, while Johnnie wrathily demolished great plates of food. The daughters of the house when they were obliged to replenish the biscuits approached as warily as Indians, and, having succeeded in their purposes, fled with ill-concealed trepidation. The Swede domineered the whole feast, and he gave it the appearance of a cruel bacchanal. He seemed to have grown suddenly taller; he gazed, brutally disdainful, into every face. His voice rang through the room. Once when he jabbed out harpoon-fashion with his fork to pinion a biscuit the weapon nearly impaled the hand of the Easterner which had been stretched quietly out for the same biscuit.

After supper, as the men filed toward the other room, the Swede smote Scully ruthlessly on the shoulder. "Well, old boy, that was a good square meal." Johnnie looked hopefully at his father; he knew that shoulder was tender from an old fall; and indeed it appeared for a moment as if Scully was going to flame out over the matter, but in the end he smiled a sickly smile and remained silent. The others understood from his manner that he was admitting his responsibility for the Swede's new viewpoint.

Johnnie, however, addressed his parent in an aside. "Why don't you license somebody to kick you downstairs?" Scully scowled darkly by way of reply.

When they were gathered about the stove, the Swede insisted on another game of High-Five. Scully gently deprecated the plan at first, but the Swede turned a wolfish glare upon him. The old man subsided, and the Swede canvassed the others. In his tone there was always a great threat. The cowboy and the Easterner both remarked indifferently that they would play. Scully said that he would presently have to go to meet the 6.58 train, and so the Swede turned menacingly upon Johnnie. For a moment their glances crossed like blades, and then Johnnie smiled and said: "Yes, I'll play."

They formed a square with the little board on their knees. The Easterner and the Swede were again partners. As the play went on, it was noticeable that the cowboy was not board-whacking as usual. Meanwhile, Scully, near the lamp, had put on his spectacles and, with an appearance curiously like an old priest, was reading a newspaper. In time he went out to meet the 6.58 train, and, despite his precautions, a gust of polar wind whirled into the room as he opened the door. Besides scattering the cards, it chilled the players to the marrow. The Swede cursed frightfully. When Scully returned, his entrance disturbed a cozy and friendly scene. The Swede again cursed. But presently they were once more intent, their heads bent forward and their hands moving swiftly. The Swede had adopted the fashion of board-whacking.

Scully took up his paper and for a long time remained immersed in matters which were extraordinarily remote from him. The lamp burned badly, and once he stopped to adjust the wick. The newspaper as he turned from page to page rustled with a slow and comfortable sound. Then suddenly he heard three terrible words: "You are cheatin'!"

Such scenes often prove that there can be little of dramatic import in environment. Any room can present a tragic front; any room can be comic. This little den was now hideous as a torture-chamber. The new faces of the men themselves had changed it upon the instant. The Swede held a huge fist in front of Johnnie's face, while the latter looked steadily over it into the blazing orbs of his accuser. The Easterner had grown pallid; the cowboy's jaw had dropped in that expression of bovine amazement which was one of his important mannerisms. After the three words, the first sound in the room was made by Scully's paper as it floated forgotten to his feet. His spectacles had also fallen from his nose, but by a clutch he had saved them in air. His hand, grasping the spectacles, now remained poised awkwardly and near his shoulder. He stared at the card-players.

Probably the silence was while a second elapsed. Then, if the floor had been suddenly twitched out from under the men they could not have moved quicker. The five had projected themselves headlong toward a common point. It happened that Johnnie in rising to hurl himself upon the Swede had stumbled slightly because of his curiously instinctive care for the cards and the board. The loss of the moment allowed time for the arrival of Scully, and also allowed the cowboy time to give the Swede a great push which sent him staggering back. The men found tongue together, and hoarse shouts of rage, appeal or fear burst from every throat. The cowboy pushed and and jostled feverishly at the Swede, and the Easterner and Scully clung wildly to Johnnie; but, through the smoky air, above the swaying bodies of the peace-compellers, the eyes of the two warriors ever sought each other in glances of challenge that were at once hot and steely.

Of course the board had been overturned, and now the whole company of cards was scattered over the floor, where the boots of the men trampled the fat and painted kings and queens as they gazed with their silly eyes at the war that was waging above them.

Scully's voice was dominating the yells. "Stop now! Stop, I say! Stop, now——"

Johnnie, as he struggled to burst through the rank formed by Scully and the Easterner, was crying: "Well, he says I cheated! He says I cheated! I won't allow no man to say I cheated! If he says I cheated, he's a—— ——!"

The cowboy was telling the Swede: "Quit, now! Quit, d'ye hear——"

The screams of the Swede never ceased. "He did cheat! I saw him! I saw him——"

As for the Easterner, he was importuning in a voice that was not heeded. "Wait a moment, can't you? Oh, wait a moment. What's the good of a fight over a game of cards? Wait a moment——"

In this tumult no complete sentences were clear. "Cheat"—"Quit"—"He says"—These fragments pierced the uproar and rang out sharply. It was remarkable that whereas Scully undoubtedly made the most noise, he was the least heard of any of the riotous band.

Then suddenly there was a great cessation. It was as if each man had paused for breath, and although the room was still lighted with the anger of men, it could be seen that there was no danger of immediate conflict, and at once Johnnie, shouldering his way forward, almost succeeded in confronting the Swede. "What did you say I cheated for? What did you say I cheated for? I don't cheat and I won't let no man say I do!"

The Swede said: "I saw you! I saw you!"

"Well," cried Johnnie, "I'll fight any man what says I cheat!"

"No, you won't," said the cowboy. "Not here."

"Ah, be still, can't you?" said Scully, coming between them.

The quiet was sufficient to allow the Easterner's voice to be heard. He was repeating: "Oh, wait a moment, can't you? What's the good of a fight over a game of cards? Wait a moment."

Johnnie, his red face appearing above his father's shoulder, hailed the Swede again. "Did you say I cheated?"

The Swede showed his teeth. "Yes."

"Then," said Johnnie, "we must fight."

"Yes, fight," roared the Swede. He was like a demoniac. "Yes, fight! I'll show you what kind of a man I am! I'll show you who you want to fight! Maybe you think I can't fight! Maybe you think I can't! I'll show you, you skin, you card-sharp! Yes, you cheated! You cheated! You cheated!"

"Well, let's git at it, then, mister," said Johnnie coolly.

The cowboy's brow was beaded with sweat from his efforts in intercepting all sorts of raids. He turned in despair to Scully. "What are you goin' to do now?"

A change had come over the Celtic visage of the old man. He now seemed all eagerness; his eyes glowed.

"We'll let them fight," he answered stalwartly. "I can't put up with it any longer. I've stood this damned Swede till I'm sick. We'll let them fight."

VI

The men prepared to go out of doors. The Easterner was so nervous that he had great difficulty in getting his arms into the sleeves of his new leather-coat. As the cowboy drew his fur-cap down over his ears his hands trembled. In fact, Johnnie and old Scully were the only ones who displayed no agitation. These preliminaries were conducted without words.

Scully threw open the door. "Well, come on," he said. Instantly a terrific wind caused the flame of the lamp to struggle at its wick, while a puff of black smoke sprang from the chimney-top. The stove was in mid-current of the blast, and its voice swelled to equal the roar of the storm. Some of the scarred and bedabbled cards were caught up from the floor and dashed helplessly against the further wall. The men lowered their heads and plunged into the tempest as into a sea.

No snow was falling, but great whirls and clouds of flakes, swept up from the ground by the frantic winds, were streaming southward with the speed of bullets. The covered land was blue with the sheen of an unearthly satin, and there was no other hue save where at the low black railway station—which seemed incredibly distant—one light gleamed like a tiny jewel. As the men floundered into a thigh-deep drift, it was known that the Swede was bawling out something. Scully went to him, put a hand on his shoulder and projected an ear. "What's that you say?" he shouted.

"I say," bawled the Swede again. "I won't stand much show against this gang. I know you'll all pitch on me."

Scully smote him reproachfully on the arm. "Tut, man," he yelled. The wind tore the words from Scully's lips and scattered them far a-lee.

"You are all a gang of——" boomed the Swede, but the storm also seized the remainder of this sentence.

Immediately turning their backs upon the wind, the men had swung around a corner to the sheltered side of the hotel. It was the function of the little house to preserve here, amid this great devastation of snow, an irregular V-shape of heavily-incrusted grass, which crackled beneath the feet. One could imagine the great drifts piled against the windward side. When the party reached the comparative peace of this spot it was found that the Swede was still bellowing.

"Oh, I know what kind of a thing this is! I know you'll all pitch on me. I can't lick you all!"

Scully turned upon him panther-fashion. "You'll not have to whip all of us. You'll have to whip my son Johnnie. An' the man what troubles you durin' that time will have me to dale with."

The arrangements were swiftly made. The two men faced each other, obedient to the harsh commands of Scully, whose face, in the subtly luminous gloom, could be seen set in the austere impersonal lines that are pictured on the countenances of the Roman veterans. The Easterner's teeth were chattering, and he was hopping up and down like a mechanical toy. The cowboy stood rock-like.

The contestants had not stripped off any clothing. Each was in his ordinary attire. Their fists were up, and they eyed each other in a calm that had the elements of leonine cruelty in it.

During this pause, the Easterner's mind, like a film, took lasting impressions of three men—the iron-nerved master of the ceremony; the Swede, pale, motionless, terrible; and Johnnie, serene yet ferocious, brutish yet heroic. The entire prelude had in it a tragedy greater than the tragedy of action, and this aspect was accentuated by the long mellow cry of the blizzard, as it sped the tumbling and wailing flakes into the black abyss of the south.

"Now!" said Scully.

The two combatants leaped forward and crashed together like bullocks. There was heard the cushioned sound of blows, and of a curse squeezing out from between the tight teeth of one.

As for the spectators, the Easterner's pent-up breath exploded from him with a pop of relief, absolute relief from the tension of the preliminaries. The cowboy bounded into the air with a yowl. Scully was immovable as from supreme amazement and fear at the fury of the fight which he himself had permitted and arranged.

For a time the encounter in the darkness was such a perplexity of flying arms that it presented no more detail than would a swiftly-revolving wheel. Occasionally a face, as if illumined by a flash of light, would shine out, ghastly and marked with pink spots. A moment later, the men might have been known as shadows, if it were not for the involuntary utterance of oaths that came from them in whispers.

Suddenly a holocaust of warlike desire caught the cowboy, and he bolted forward with the speed of a broncho. "Go it, Johnnie; go it! Kill him! Kill him!"

Scully confronted him. "Kape back," he said; and by his glance the cowboy could tell that this man was Johnnie's father.

To the Easterner there was a monotony of unchangeable fighting that was an abomination. This confused mingling was eternal to his sense, which was concentrated in a longing for the end, the priceless end. Once the fighters lurched near him, and as he scrambled hastily backward, he heard them breathe like men on the rack.

"Kill him, Johnnie! Kill him! Kill him! Kill him!" The cowboy's face was contorted like one of those agony-masks in museums.

"Keep still," said Scully icily.

Then there was a sudden loud grunt, incomplete, cut-short, and Johnnie's body swung away from the Swede and fell with sickening heaviness to the grass. The cowboy was barely in time to prevent the mad Swede from flinging himself upon his prone adversary. "No, you don't," said the cowboy, interposing an arm. "Wait a second."

Scully was at his son's side. "Johnnie! Johnnie, me boy?" His voice had a quality of melancholy tenderness. "Johnnie? Can you go on with it?" He looked anxiously down into the bloody pulpy face of his son.

There was a moment of silence, and then Johnnie answered in his ordinary voice: "Yes, I—it—yes."

Assisted by his father he struggled to his feet. "Wait a bit now till you git your wind," said the old man.

A few paces away the cowboy was lecturing the Swede. "No, you don't! Wait a second!"

The Easterner was plucking at Scully's sleeve. "Oh, this is enough," he pleaded. "This is enough! Let it go as it stands. This is enough!"

"Bill," said Scully, "git out of the road." The cowboy stepped aside. "Now." The combatants were actuated by a new caution as they advanced toward collision. They glared at each other, and then the Swede aimed a lightning blow that carried with it his entire weight. Johnnie was evidently

Good Guys. Bad Guys.
Zane Grey knew both kinds and lived to tell about it.

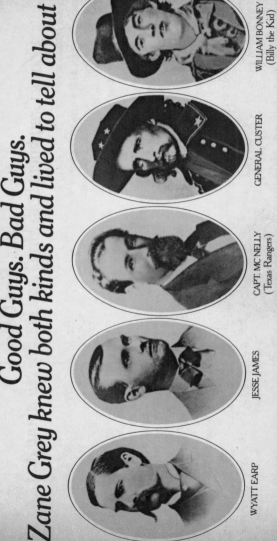

WYATT EARP

JESSE JAMES

CAPT. MC NELLY
(Texas Rangers)

GENERAL CUSTER

WILLIAM BONNEY
(Billy the Kid)

Zane Grey actually stood face-to-face with gunslingers, gamblers, and lawmen. He hunted mountain lions with Indians and outlaws with Texas Rangers.

Zane Grey sought out men who had known Wyatt Earp, Jesse James, Captain McNelly and General George Armstrong Custer. He would play poker with Arizona card sharks. Talk with the dance-hall girls and cowboys who had looked into the icy eyes of Billy the Kid. He got the facts about the most exciting episodes in the history of the West first-hand.

For example, his novel *The Border Legion* is based on eye witness accounts of how an outlaw army led by Henry Plummer and Boone Helm robbed, murdered and terrorized the town of Alder Gulch on the Idaho-

(Continued on other side)

Mail this card to get 4 Zane Grey books for $1.

Please enroll me as a subscriber and send me at once The Border Legion, Wild Horse Mesa, Riders of the Purple Sage and The Thundering Herd. I enclose no money now. After a week's examination, I will either keep my books and pay $1 (plus postage and handling) or return them.

Also reserve for me additional volumes in the Zane Grey Library series. As a subscriber, I will get advance descriptions of future volumes. For each volume I choose, I will pay $4.89 (plus postage and handling). I may return any book at the Library's expense for full credit and cancel my reservations at any time. *NOTE: Subscribers accepted in U.S.A. and Canada. Canadian subscribers will be serviced from Ontario; offer slightly different in Canada. (Canadians should enclose this card in an envelope and mail to address on the other side.)*

NAME _____ ZER
           (PLEASE PRINT PLAINLY)

STREET _____

                                     13-50B

CITY _____ STATE _____ ZIP _____

half-stupid from weakness, but he miraculously dodged, and his fist sent the over-balanced Swede sprawling.

The cowboy, Scully and the Easterner burst into a cheer that was like a chorus of triumphant soldiery, but before its conclusion the Swede had scuffled agilely to his feet and come in berserk abandon at his foe. There was another perplexity of flying arms, and Johnnie's body again swung away and fell, even as a bundle might fall from a roof. The Swede instantly staggered to a little wind-waved tree and leaned upon it, breathing like an engine, while his savage and flame-lit eyes roamed from face to face as the men bent over Johnnie. There was a splendor of isolation in his situation at this time which the Easterner felt once when, lifting his eyes from the man on the ground, he beheld that mysterious and lonely figure, waiting.

"Are you any good yet, Johnnie?" asked Scully in a broken voice.

The son gasped and opened his eyes languidly. After a moment he answered: "No—I ain't—any good—any—more." Then, from shame and bodily ill, he began to weep, the tears furrowing down through the blood-stains on his face. "He was too—too—too heavy for me."

Scully straightened and addressed the waiting figure. "Stranger," he said, evenly, "it's all up with our side." Then his voice changed into that vibrant huskiness which is commonly the tone of the most simple and deadly announcements. "Johnnie is whipped."

Without replying, the victor moved off on the route to front door of the hotel.

The cowboy was formulating new and unspellable blasphemies. The Easterner was startled to find that they were out in a wind that seemed to come direct from the shadowed arctic floes. He heard again the wail of the snow as it was flung to its grave in the south. He knew now that all this time the cold had been sinking into him deeper and deeper, and he wondered that he had not perished. He felt indifferent to the condition of the vanquished man.

"Johnnie, can you walk?" asked Scully.

"Did I hurt—hurt him any?" asked the son.

"Can you walk, boy? Can you walk?"

Johnnie's voice was suddenly strong. There was a robust impatience in it. "I asked you whether I hurt him any!"

"Yes, yes, Johnnie," answered the cowboy consolingly; "he's hurt a good deal."

They raised him from the ground, and as soon as he was on his feet he went tottering off, rebuffing all attempts at assistance. When the party rounded the corner they were fairly blinded by the pelting of the snow. It burned their faces like fire. The cowboy carried Johnnie through the drift to the door. As they entered some cards again rose from the floor and beat against the wall.

The Easterner rushed to the stove. He was so profoundly chilled that he almost dared to embrace the glowing iron. The Swede was not in the room. Johnnie sank into a chair, and folding his arms on his knees, buried his face in them. Scully, warming one foot and then the other at a rim of the stove, muttered to himself with Celtic mournfulness. The cowboy had removed his fur-cap, and with a dazed and rueful air he was now running one hand through his tousled locks. From overhead they could hear the creaking of boards, as the Swede tramped here and there in his room.

The sad quiet was broken by the sudden flinging open of a door that led toward the kitchen. It was instantly followed by an inrush of women. They precipitated themselves upon Johnnie amid a chorus of lamentation. Before they carried their prey off to the kitchen, there to be bathed and harangued with that mixture of sympathy and abuse which is a feat of their sex, the mother straightened herself and fixed old Scully with an eye of stern reproach. "Shame be upon you, Patrick Scully!" she cried. "Your own son, too. Shame be upon you!"

"There, now! Be quiet, now!" said the old man weakly.

"Shame be upon you, Patrick Scully!" The girls, rallying to this slogan, sniffed disdainfully in the direction of those trembling accomplices, the cowboy and the Easterner. Presently they bore Johnnie away, and left the three men to dismal reflection.

VII

"I'd like to fight this here Dutchman myself," said the cowboy, breaking a long silence.

Scully wagged his head sadly. "No, that wouldn't do. It wouldn't be right. It wouldn't be right."

"Well, why wouldn't it?" argued the cowboy. "I don't see no harm in it."

"No," answered Scully with mournful heroism. "It

wouldn't be right. It was Johnnie's fight, and now we mustn't whip the man just because he whipped Johnnie."

"Yes, that's true enough," said the cowboy; "but—he better not get fresh with me, because I couldn't stand no more of it."

"You'll not say a word to him," commanded Scully, and even then they heard the tread of the Swede on the stairs. His entrance was made theatric. He swept the door back with a bang and swaggered to the middle of the room. No one looked at him. "Well," he cried, insolently, at Scully, "I s'pose you'll tell me now how much I owe you?"

The old man remained stolid. "You don't owe me nothin'."

"Huh!" said the Swede, "huh! Don't owe 'im nothin'."

The cowboy addressed the Swede. "Stranger, I don't see how you come to be so gay around here."

Old Scully was instantly alert. "Stop!" he shouted, holding his hands forth, fingers upward. "Bill, you shut up!"

The cowboy spat carelessly into the sawdust box. "I didn't say a word, did I?" he asked.

"Mr. Scully," called the Swede, "how much do I owe you?" It was seen that he was attired for departure, and that he had his valise in his hand.

"You don't owe me nothin'," repeated Scully in his same imperturbable way.

"Huh!" said the Swede. "I guess you're right. I guess if it was any way at all, you'd owe me somethin'. That's what I guess." He turned to the cowboy. " 'Kill him! Kill him! Kill him!' " he mimicked, and then guffawed victoriously. " 'Kill him!' " He was convulsed with ironical humor.

But he might have been jeering with the dead. The three men were immovable and silent, staring with glassy eyes at the stove.

The Swede opened the door and passed into the storm, giving one derisive glance backward at the still group.

As soon as the door was closed, Scully and the cowboy leaped to their feet and began to curse. They trampled to and fro, waving their arms and smashing into the air with their fists. "Oh, but that was a hard minute!" wailed Scully. "That was a hard minute! Him there leerin' and scoffin'! One bang at his nose was worth forty dollars to me that minute! How did you stand it, Bill?"

"How did I stand it?" cried the cowboy in a quivering voice. "How did I stand it? Oh!"

The old man burst into sudden brogue. "I'd loike to take

that Swade," he wailed, "and hould 'im down on a shtone flure and bate 'im to a jelly wid a shtick!"

The cowboy groaned in sympathy. "I'd like to git him by the neck and ha-ammer him"——he brought his hand down on a chair with a noise like a pistol-shot——"hammer that there Dutchman until he couldn't tell himself from a dead coyote!"

"I'd bate 'im until he——"

"I'd show *him* some things——"

And then together they raised a yearning fanatic cry. "Oh-o-oh! If we only could——"

"Yes!"

"Yes!"

"And then I'd——"

"O-o-oh!"

VIII

The Swede, tightly gripping his valise, tacked across the face of the storm as if he carried sails. He was following a line of little naked gasping trees, which he knew must mark the way of the road. His face, fresh from the pounding of Johnnie's fists, felt more pleasure than pain in the wind and the driving snow. A number of square shapes loomed upon him finally, and he knew them as the houses of the main body of the town. He found a street and made travel along it, leaning heavily upon the wind whenever, at a corner, a terrific blast caught him.

He might have been in a deserted village. We picture the world as thick with conquering and elate humanity, but here, with the bugles of the tempest pealing, it was hard to imagine a peopled earth. One viewed the existence of man then as a marvel, and conceded a glamour of wonder to these lice which were caused to cling to a whirling, fire-smote, ice-locked, disease-stricken, space-lost bulb. The conceit of man was explained by this storm to be the very engine of life. One was a coxcomb not to die in it. However, the Swede found a saloon.

In front of it an indomitable red light was burning, and the snow-flakes were made blood-color as they flew through the circumscribed territory of the lamp's shining. The Swede pushed open the door of the saloon and entered. A sanded expanse was before him, and at the end of it four men sat about a table drinking. Down one side of the room extended a radiant bar, and its guardian was leaning upon his elbows listening to the talk of the men at the table. The Swede dropped his valise upon the floor, and smiling fraternally upon the barkeeper, said: "Gimme some whisky, will you?" The man placed a bottle, a whisky-glass, and a glass of ice-thick water upon the bar. The Swede poured himself an abnormal portion of whisky and drank it in three gulps. "Pretty bad night," remarked the bartender indifferently. He was making the pretension of blindness, which is usually a distinction of his class; but it could have been seen that he was furtively studying the half-erased blood-stains on the face of the Swede. "Bad night," he said again.

"Oh, it's good enough for me," replied the Swede, hardily, as he poured himself some more whisky. The barkeeper took his coin and maneuvered it through its reception by the highly-nickeled cash-machine. A bell rang; a card labeled "20 cts." had appeared.

"No," continued the Swede, "this isn't too bad weather. It's good enough for me."

"So?" murmured the barkeeper languidly.

The copious drams made the Swede's eyes swim, and he breathed a trifle heavier. "Yes, I like this weather. I like it. It suits me." It was apparently his design to impart a deep significance to these words.

"So?" murmured the bartender again. He turned to gaze dreamily at the scroll-like birds and bird-like scrolls which had been drawn with soap upon the mirrors back of the bar.

"Well, I guess I'll take another drink," said the Swede presently. "Have something?"

"No, thanks; I'm not drinkin'," answered the bartender. Afterward he asked: "How did you hurt your face?"

The Swede immediately began to boast loudly. "Why, in a fight. I thumped the soul out of a man down here at Scully's hotel."

The interest of the four men at the table was at last aroused.

"Who was it?" said one.

"Johnnie Scully," blustered the Swede. "Son of the man what runs it. He will be pretty near dead for some weeks, I can tell you. I made a nice thing of him, I did. He couldn't get up. They carried him in the house. Have a drink?"

Instantly the men in some subtle way incased themselves in reserve. "No, thanks," said one. The group was of curious formation. Two were prominent local business men; one was the district-attorney; and one was a professional gambler of the kind known as "square." But a scrutiny of the group would not have enabled an observer to pick the gambler from the men of more reputable pursuits. He was, in fact, a man so delicate in manner, when among people of fair class, and so judicious in his choice of victims, that in the strictly masculine part of the town's life he had come to be explicitly trusted and admired. People called him a thoroughbred. The fear and contempt with which his craft was regarded was undoubtedly the reason that his quiet dignity shone conspicuous above the quiet dignity of men who might be merely hatters, billiard-markers or grocery clerks. Beyond an occasional unwary traveler, who came by rail, this gambler was supposed to prey solely upon reckless and senile farmers, who, when flush with good crops, drove into town in all the pride and confidence of an absolutely invulnerable stupidity. Hearing at times in circuitous fashion of the despoilment of such a farmer, the important men of Romper invariably laughed in contempt of the victim, and if they thought of the wolf at all, it was with a kind of pride at the knowledge that he would never dare think of attacking their wisdom and courage. Besides, it was popular that this gambler had a real wife and two real children in a neat cottage in a suburb, where he led an exemplary home life, and when any one even suggested a discrepancy in his character, the crowd immediately vociferated descriptions of this virtuous family circle. Then men who led exemplary home lives, and men who did not lead exemplary home lives, all subsided in a bunch, remarking that there was nothing more to be said.

However, when a restriction was placed upon him—as, for instance, when a strong clique of members of the new Pollywog Club refused to permit him, even as a spectator, to appear in the rooms of the organization—the candor and gentleness with which he accepted the judgment disarmed many of his foes and made his friends more desperately partisan. He invariably distinguished between himself and a respectable Romper man so quickly and frankly that his manner actually appeared to be a continual broadcast compliment.

And one must not forget to declare the fundamental fact of his entire position in Romper. It is irrefutable that in all affairs outside of his business, in all matters that occur eternally and commonly between man and man, this thieving card-player was so generous, so just, so moral, that, in a contest, he could have put to fight the consciences of nine-tenths of the citizens of Romper.

And so it happened that he was seated in this saloon with the two prominent local merchants and the district-attorney.

The Swede continued to drink raw whisky, meanwhile babbling at the barkeeper and trying to induce him to indulge in potations. "Come on. Have a drink. Come on. What—no? Well, have a little one then. By gawd. I've whipped a man to-night, and I want to celebrate. I whipped him good, too. Gentlemen," the Swede cried to the men at the table, "have a drink?"

"Ssh!" said the barkeeper.

The group at the table, although furtively attentive, had been pretending to be deep in talk, but now a man lifted his eyes toward the Swede and said shortly: "Thanks. We don't want any more."

At this reply the Swede ruffled out his chest like a rooster. "Well," he exploded, "it seems I can't get anybody to drink with me in this town. Seems so, don't it? Well!"

"Ssh!" said the barkeeper.

"Say," snarled the Swede, "don't you try to shut me up. I won't have it. I'm a gentleman, and I want people to drink with me. And I want 'em to drink with me now. *Now*—do you understand?" He rapped the bar with his knuckles.

Years of experience had calloused the bartender. He merely grew sulky. "I hear you," he answered.

"Well," cried the Swede, "listen hard then. See those men over there? Well, they're going to drink with me, and don't you forget it. Now you watch."

"Hi!" yelled the barkeeper, "this won't do!"

"Why won't it?" demanded the Swede. He stalked over to the table, and by chance laid his hand upon the shoulder of the gambler. "How about this?" he asked, wrathfully. "I asked you to drink with me."

The gambler simply twisted his head and spoke over his shoulder. "My friend, I don't know you."

"Oh, hell!" answered the Swede, "come and have a drink."

"Now, my boy," advised the gambler kindly, "take your hand off my shoulder and go 'way and mind your own business." He was a little slim man, and it seemed strange to hear him use this tone of heroic patronage to the burly Swede. The other men at the table said nothing.

"What? You won't drink with me, you little dude! I'll make you then! I'll make you!" The Swede had grasped the gambler frenziedly at the throat, and was dragging him from his chair. The other men sprang up. The barkeeper dashed around the corner of his bar. There was a great tumult, and then was seen a long blade in the hand of the gambler. It shot forward, and a human body, this citadel of virtue, wisdom, power, was pierced as easily as if it had been a melon. The Swede fell with a cry of supreme astonishment.

The prominent merchants and the district-attorney must have at once tumbled out of the place backward. The bartender found himself hanging limply to the arm of a chair and gazing into the eyes of a murderer.

"Henry," said the latter, as he wiped his knife on one of the towels that hung beneath the bar-rail, "you tell 'em where to find me. I'll be home, waiting for 'em." Then he vanished. A moment afterward the barkeeper was in the street dinning through the storm for help, and, moreover, companionship.

The corpse of the Swede, alone in the saloon, had its eyes fixed upon a dreadful legend that dwelt a-top of the cash-machine. "This registers the amount of your purchase."

IX

Months later, the cowboy was frying pork over the stove of a little ranch near the Dakota line, when there was a quick thud of hoofs outside, and, presently, the Easterner entered with the letters and the papers.

"Well," said the Easterner at once, "the chap that killed the Swede has got three years. Wasn't much, was it?"

"He has? Three years?" The cowboy poised his pan of pork, while he ruminated upon the news. "Three years. That ain't much."

"No. It was a light sentence," replied the Easterner as he unbuckled his spurs. "Seems there was a good deal of sympathy for him in Romper."

"If the bartender had been any good," observed the cowboy thoughtfully, "he would have gone in and cracked that there Dutchman on the head with a bottle in the beginnin' of it and stopped all this here murderin'."

"Yes, a thousand things might have happened," said the Easterner tartly.

The cowboy returned his pan of pork to the fire, but his philosophy continued. "It's funny, ain't it? If he hadn't said Johnnie was cheatin' he'd be alive this minute. He was an awful fool. Game played for fun, too. Not for money. I believe he was crazy."

"I feel sorry for that gambler," said the Easterner.

"Oh, so do I," said the cowboy. "He don't deserve none of it for killin' who he did."

"The Swede might not have been killed if everything had been square."

"Might not have been killed?" exclaimed the cowboy. "Everythin' square? Why, when he said that Johnnie was cheatin' and acted like such a jackass? And then in the saloon he fairly walked up to git hurt?" With these arguments the cowboy browbeat the Easterner and reduced him to rage.

"You're a fool!" cried the Easterner viciously. "You're a bigger jackass than the Swede by a million majority. Now let me tell you one thing. Let me tell you something. Listen! Johnnie was cheating!"

" 'Johnnie,' " said the cowboy blankly. There was a minute of silence, and then he said robustly: "Why, no. The game was only for fun."

"Fun or not," said the Easterner, "Johnnie was cheating. I saw him. I know it. I saw him. And I refused to stand up and be a man. I let the Swede fight it out alone. And you—you were simply puffing around the place and wanting to fight. And then old Scully himself! We are all in it! This poor gambler isn't even a noun. He is kind of an adverb. Every sin is the result of a collaboration. We, five of us, have collaborated in the murder of this Swede. Usually there are from a dozen to forty women really involved in every murder, but in this case it seems to be only five men—you, I, Johnnie, old Scully, and that fool of an unfortunate gambler came merely as a culmination, the apex of a human movement, and gets all the punishment."

The cowboy, injured and rebellious, cried out blindly into this fog of mysterious theory. "Well, I didn't do anythin', did I?"

Twelve O'Clock

"Where were you at twelve o'clock, noon, on the 9th of June, 1875?"—*Question on intelligent cross-examination.*

I

"Excuse *me*," said Ben Roddle with graphic gestures to a group of citizens in Nantucket's store. "Excuse *me*. When them fellers in leather pants an' six-shooters ride in, I go home an' set in th' cellar. That's what I do. When you see me pirooting through the streets at th' same time an' occasion as them punchers, you kin put me down fer bein' crazy. Excuse *me*."

"Why, Ben," drawled old Nantucket, "you ain't never really seen 'em turned loose. Why, I kin remember—in th' old days—when——"

"Oh, damn yer old days!" retorted Roddle. Fixing Nantucket with the eye of scorn and contempt, he said: "I suppose you'll be sayin' in a minute that in th' old days you used to kill Injuns, won't you?"

There was some laughter, and Roddle was left free to expand his ideas on the periodic visits of cowboys to the town. "Mason Rickets, he had ten big punkins a-sittin' in front of his store, an' them fellers from the Upside-down-F ranch shot 'em up—shot 'em all up—an' Rickets lyin' on his belly in th' store a-callin' fer 'em to quit it. An' what did they do! Why, they *laughed* at 'im!—just *laughed* at 'im! That don't do a town no good. Now, how would an eastern capiterlist"—(it was the town's humor to be always gassing of phantom investors who were likely to come any moment and pay a thousand prices for everything)—"how would an eastern capiterlist like that? Why, you couldn't see 'im fer th' dust on his trail. Then he'd tell all his friends that their town may be all right, but ther's too much loose-handed shootin' fer my money.' An' he'd be right, too. Them rich fellers, they don't make no bad breaks with their money. They watch it all th' time b'cause they know blame well there ain't hardly room fer their feet fer th' pikers an' tin-horns an' thimble-riggers what are layin' fer 'em. I tell you, one puncher racin' his cow-pony hell-bent-fer-election down Main Street an' yellin' an' shootin' an' nothin' at all done about it, would scare away a whole herd of capiterlists. An' it ain't right. It oughter be stopped."

A pessimistic voice asked: "How you goin' to stop it, Ben?"

"Organize," replied Roddle pompously. "Organize: that's the only way to make these fellers lay down. I——"

From the street sounded a quick scudding of pony hoofs, and a party of cowboys swept past the door. One man, however, was seen to draw rein and dismount. He came clanking into the store. "Mornin', gentlemen," he said, civilly.

"Mornin'," they answered in subdued voices.

He stepped to the counter and said, "Give me a paper of fine cut, please." The group of citizens contemplated him in silence. He certainly did not look threatening. He appeared to be a young man of twenty-five years, with a tan from wind and sun, with a remarkably clear eye from perhaps a period of enforced temperance, a quiet young man who wanted to buy some tobacco. A six-shooter swung low on his hip, but at the moment it looked more decorative than warlike; it seemed merely a part of his odd gala dress—his sombrero with its band of rattlesnake skin, his great flaming neckerchief, his belt of embroidered Mexican leather, his high-heeled boots, his huge spurs. And, above all, his hair had been watered and brushed until it lay as close to his head as the fur lays to a wet cat. Paying for his tobacco, he withdrew.

Ben Roddle resumed his harangue. "Well, there you are! Looks like a calm man now, but in less'n half an hour he'll be as drunk as three bucks an' a squaw, an' then . . . . excuse *me!*"

II

On this day the men of two outfits had come into town, but Ben Roddle's ominous words were not justified at once. The punchers spent most of the morning in an attack on whiskey which was too earnest to be noisy.

At five minutes of eleven, a tall, lank, brick-colored cowboy strode over to Placer's Hotel. Placer's Hotel was a notable place. It was the best hotel within two hundred miles. Its office was filled with arm-chairs and brown papier-maché receptacles. At one end of the room was a wooden counter painted a bright pink, and on this morning a man was behind the counter writing in a ledger. He was the proprietor of the hotel, but his customary humor was so sullen that all strangers immediately wondered why in life he had chosen to play the part of mine host. Near his left hand, double doors opened into the dining-room, which in warm weather was always kept darkened in order to discourage the flies, which was not compassed at all.

Placer, writing in his ledger, did not look up when the tall cowboy entered.

"Mornin', mister," said the latter. "I've come to see if you kin grub-stake th' hull crowd of us fer dinner t'day."

Placer did not then raise his eyes, but with a certain churlishness, as if it annoyed him that his hotel was patronized, he asked: "How many?"

"Oh, about thirty," replied the cowboy. "An' we want th' best dinner you kin raise an' scrape. Everything th' best. We don't care what it costs s'long as we git a good square meal. We'll pay a dollar a head: by God, we will! We won't kick on nothin' in the bill if you do it up fine. If you ain't got it in th' house, russle th' hull town fer it. That's our gait. So you just tear loose, an' we'll——"

At this moment the machinery of a cuckoo-clock on the wall began to whirr, little doors flew open, and a wooden bird appeared and cried, "Cuckoo!" And this was repeated until eleven o'clock had been announced, while the cowboy, stupefied, glassy-eyed, stood with his red throat gulping. At the end he wheeled upon Placer and demanded: *"What in hell is that?"*

Placer revealed by his manner that he had been asked this question too many times. "It's a clock," he answered shortly.

"I know it's a clock," gasped the cowboy: "but what *kind* of a clock?"

"A cuckoo-clock. Can't you see?"

The cowboy, recovering his self-possession by a violent effort, suddenly went shouting into the street. "Boys! Say, boys! Com' 'ere a minute!"

His comrades, comfortably inhabiting a near-by saloon,

heard his stentorian calls, but they merely said to one another: "What's th' matter with Jake?—he's off his nut again."

But Jake burst in upon them with violence. "Boys," he
yelled, "come over to th' hotel! They got a clock with a bird
inside it, an' when it's eleven o'clock or anything like that, th'
bird comes out an' says, '*toot*-toot, *toot*-toot!' that way, as
many times as whatever time of day it is. It's immense! Come
on over!"

The roars of laughter which greeted his proclamation were
of two qualities; some men laughing because they knew all
about cuckoo-clocks, and other men laughing because they
had concluded that the eccentric Jake had been victimized by
some wise child of civilization.

Old Man Crumford, a venerable ruffian who probably had
been born in a corral, was particularly offensive with his
loud guffaws of contempt. "Bird a-comin' out of a clock an'
a-tellin' ye th' time! Haw-haw-haw!" He swallowed his
whiskey. "A bird! a-tellin' ye th' time! Haw-haw! Jake, you
ben up agin some new drink. You ben drinkin' lonely an' got
up agin some snake-medicine licker. A bird a-tellin' ye th'
time! Haw-haw!"

The shrill voice of one of the younger cowboys piped from
the background. "Brace up, Jake. Don't let 'em laugh at ye.
Bring 'em that salt cod-fish of yourn what kin pick out th'
ace."

"Oh, he's only kiddin' us. Don't pay no 'tention to 'im. He
thinks he's smart."

A cowboy whose mother had a cuckoo-clock in her house
in Philadelphia spoke with solemnity. "Jake's a liar. There's
no such clock in the world. What? a bird inside a clock to tell
the time? Change your drink, Jake."

Jake was furious, but his fury took a very icy form. He
bent a withering glance upon the last speaker. "I don't mean
a *live* bird," he said, with terrible dignity. "It's a wooden bird,
an'——"

"A wooden bird!" shouted Old Man Crumford. "Wooden
bird a-tellin' ye th' time! Haw-haw!"

But Jake still paid his frigid attention to the Philadelphian.
"An' if yer sober enough to walk, it ain't such a blame long
ways from here to th' hotel, an' I'll bet my pile agin yours if
you only got two bits."

"I don't want your money, Jake," said the Philadelphian.
"Somebody's been stringin' you—that's all. I wouldn't take

your money." He cleverly appeared to pity the other's inno-
cence.

"You couldn't *git* my money," cried Jake, in sudden hot
anger. "You couldn't git it. Now—since yer so fresh—let's
see how much you got." He clattered some large gold pieces
noisily upon the bar.

The Philadelphian shrugged his shoulders and walked
away. Jake was triumphant. "Any more bluffers 'round
here?" he demanded. "Any more? Any more bluffers?
Where's all these here hot sports? Let 'em step up. Here's my
money—come an' git it."

But they had ended by being afraid. To some of them his
tale was absurd, but still one must be circumspect when a
man throws forty-five dollars in gold upon the bar and bids
the world come and win it. The general feeling was expressed
by Old Man Crumford, when with deference he asked:
"Well, this here bird, Jake—what kinder lookin' bird is it?"

"It's a little brown thing," said Jake briefly. Apparently he
almost disdained to answer.

"Well—how does it work?" asked the old man meekly.

"Why in blazes don't you go an' look at it?" yelled Jake.
"Want me to paint it in iles fer you? Go an' look!"

III

Placer was writing in his ledger. He heard a great trample
of feet and clink of spurs on the porch, and there entered
quietly the band of cowboys, some of them swaying a trifle,
and these last being the most painfully decorous of all. Jake
was in advance. He waved his hand toward the clock. "There
she is," he said laconically. The cowboys drew up and stared.
There was some giggling, but a serious voice said half-au-
dibly, "I don't see no bird."

Jake politely addressed the landlord. "Mister, I've fetched
these here friends of mine in here to see yer clock—"

Placer looked up suddenly. "Well, they can see it, can't
they?" he asked in sarcasm. Jake, abashed, retreated to his
fellows.

There was a period of silence. From time to time the men
shifted their feet. Finally, Old Man Crumford leaned toward
Jake, and in a penetrating whisper demanded, "Where's th'
bird?" Some frolicsome spirits on the outskirts began to call
"Bird! Bird!" as men at a political meeting call for a particular speaker.

Jake removed his big hat and nervously mopped his brow.

The young cowboy with the shrill voice again spoke from the skirts of the crowd. "Jake, is ther' sure-'nough a bird in that thing?"

"Yes. Didn't I tell you once?"

"Then," said the shrill-voiced man, in a tone of conviction, "it ain't a clock at all. It's a bird-cage."

"I tell you it's a clock," cried the maddened Jake, but his retort could hardly be heard above the howls of glee and derision which greeted the words of him of the shrill voice.

Old Man Crumford was again rampant. "Wooden bird a-tellin' ye th' time! Haw-haw!"

Amid the confusion Jake went again to Placer. He spoke almost in supplication. "Say, mister, what time does this here thing go off agin?"

Placer lifted his head, looked at the clock, and said: "Noon."

There was a stir near the door, and Big Watson of the Square-X outfit, and at this time very drunk indeed, came shouldering his way through the crowd and cursing everybody. The men gave him much room, for he was notorious as a quarrelsome person when drunk. He paused in front of Jake, and spoke as through a wet blanket. "What's all this— monkeyin' about?"

Jake was already wild at being made a butt for everybody, and he did not give backward. "None a' your damn business, Watson."

"Huh?" growled Watson, with the surprise of a challenged bull.

"I said," repeated Jake distinctly, "it's none a' your damn business."

Watson whipped his revolver half out of its holster. "I'll make it m' business, then, you——"

But Jake had backed a step away, and was holding his left-hand palm outward toward Watson, while in his right he held his six-shooter, its muzzle pointing at the floor. He was shouting in a frenzy,—"No—don't you try it, Watson! Don't you dare try it, or, by Gawd, I'll kill you, sure—*sure!*"

He was aware of a torment of cries about him from fearful men; from men who protested, from men who cried out because they cried out. But he kept his eyes on Watson, and those two glared murder at each other, neither seeming to breathe, fixed like statues.

A loud new voice suddenly rang out: "Hol' on a minute!"

All spectators who had not stampeded turned quickly, and saw Placer standing behind his bright pink counter, with an aimed revolver in each hand.

"Cheese it!" he said. "I won't have no fightin' here. If you want to fight, git out in the street."

Big Watson laughed, and, speeding up his six-shooter like a flash of blue light, he shot Placer through the throat—shot the man as he stood behind his absurd pink counter with his two aimed revolvers in his incompetent hands. With a yell of rage and despair, Jake smote Watson on the pate with his heavy weapon, and knocked him sprawling and bloody. Somewhere a woman shrieked like windy, midnight death. Placer fell behind the counter, and down upon him came his ledger and his inkstand, so that one could not have told blood from ink.

The cowboys did not seem to hear, see, or feel, until they saw numbers of citizens with Winchesters running wildly upon them. Old Man Crumford threw high a passionate hand. "Don't shoot! We'll not fight ye fer 'im."

Nevertheless two or three shots rang, and a cowboy who had been about to gallop off suddenly slumped over on his pony's neck, where he held for a moment like an old sack, and then slid to the ground, while his pony, with flapping rein, fled to the prairie.

"In God's name, don't shoot!" trumpeted Old Man Crumford. "We'll not fight ye fer 'im!"

"It's murder," bawled Ben Roddle.

In the chaotic street it seemed for a moment as if everybody would kill everybody. "Where's the man what done it?" These hot cries seemed to declare a war which would result in an absolute annihilation of one side. But the cowboys were singing out against it. They would fight for nothing—yes— they often fought for nothing—but they would not fight for this dark something.

At last, when a flimsy truce had been made between the inflamed men, all parties went to the hotel. Placer, in some dying whim, had made his way out from behind the pink counter, and, leaving a horrible trail, had travelled to the centre of the room, where he had pitched headlong over the body of Big Watson.

The men lifted the corpse and laid it at the side.

"Who done it?" asked a white, stern man.

A cowboy pointed at Big Watson. "That's him," he said huskily.

There was a curious grim silence, and then suddenly, in the death-chamber, there sounded the loud whirring of the clock's works, little doors flew open, a tiny wooden bird appeared and cried "Cuckoo"—twelve times.

Moonlight on the Snow

I

The town of War Post had an evil name for three hundred miles in every direction. It radiated like the shine from some stupendous light. The citizens of the place had been for years grotesquely proud of their fame as a collection of hard-shooting gentlemen who invariably "got" the men who came up against them. When a citizen went abroad in the land he said, "I'm f'm War Post." And it was as if he had said, "I am the devil himself."

But ultimately it became known to War Post that the serene-browed angel of peace was in the vicinity. The angel was full of projects for taking comparatively useless bits of prairie and sawing them up into town lots, and making chaste and beautiful maps of his handiwork which shook the souls of people who had never been in the West. He commonly traveled here and there in a light wagon, from the tail-board of which he made orations which soared into the empryean regions of true hydrogen gas. Towns far and near listened to his voice and followed him singing, until in all that territory you couldn't throw a stone at a jack-rabbit without hitting the site of a projected mammoth hotel; estimated cost, fifteen thousand dollars. The stern and lonely buttes were given titles like grim veterans awarded tawdry patents of nobility—Cedar Mountain, Red Cliffs, Lookout Peak. And from the East came both the sane and the insane with hope, with courage, with hoarded savings, with cold decks, with Bibles, with knives in boots, with humility and fear, with bland impudence. Most came with their own money; some came with money gained during a moment of inattention on the part of somebody in the East. And high in the air was the serene-browed angel of peace, with his endless gabble and his pretty maps. It was curious to walk out of an evening to the edge of

132

a vast silent sea of prairie, and to reflect that the angel had parceled this infinity into building lots.

But no change had come to War Post. War Post sat with her reputation for bloodshed pressed proudly to her bosom and saw her mean neighbors leap into being as cities. She saw drunken old reprobates selling acres of red-hot dust and becoming wealthy men of affairs, who congratulated themselves on their shrewdness in holding land which, before the boom, they would have sold for enough to buy a treat all 'round in the Straight Flush Saloon—only nobody would have given it.

War Post saw dollars rolling into the coffers of a lot of contemptible men who couldn't shoot straight. She was amazed and indignant. She saw her standard of excellence, her creed, her reason for being great, all tumbling about her ears, and after the preliminary gasps she sat down to think it out.

The first man to voice a conclusion was Bob Hether, the popular barkeeper in Stevenson's Crystal Palace. "It's this here gun-fighter business," he said, leaning on his bar, and, with the gentle, serious eyes of a child, surveying a group of prominent citizens who had come in to drink at the expense of Tom Larpent, a gambler. They solemnly nodded assent. They stood in silence, holding their glasses and thinking.

Larpent was a chief factor in the life of the town. His gambling-house was the biggest institution in War Post. Moreover, he had been educated somewhere, and his slow speech had a certain mordant quality which was apt to puzzle War Post, and men heeded him for the reason that they were not always certain as to what he was saying. "Yes, Bob," he drawled, "I think you are right. The value of human life has to be established before there can be theatres, water-works, street cars, women and babies."

The other men were rather aghast at this cryptic speech, but somebody managed to snigger appreciatively and the tension was eased.

Smith Hanham, who whirled roulette for Larpent, then gave his opinion.

"Well, when all this here coin is floatin' 'round, it 'pears to me we orter git our hooks on some of it. Them little tin-horns over at Crowdger's Corners are up to their necks in it, an' we ain't yit seen a centavo. Not a centavetto. That ain't right. It's all well enough to sit 'round takin' money away from innercent cow-punchers s'long's ther's nothin' better; but when these here speculators come 'long flashin' rolls as big as water-buckets, it's up to us to whirl in an' git some of it."

This became the view of the town, and, since the main stipulation was virtue, War Post resolved to be virtuous. A great meeting was held, at which it was decreed that no man should kill another man under penalty of being at once hanged by the populace. All the influential citizens were present, and asserted their determination to deal out a swift punishment which would take no note of an acquaintance or friendship with the guilty man. Bob Hether made a loud, long speech, in which he declared that he for one would help hang his "own brother" if his "own brother" transgressed this law which now, for the good of the community, must be forever held sacred. Everybody was enthusiastic save a few Mexicans, who did not quite understand; but as they were more than likely to be the victims of any affray in which they were engaged, their silence was not considered ominous.

At half-past ten on the next morning Larpent shot and killed a man who had accused him of cheating at a game. Larpent had then taken a chair by the window.

II

Larpent grew tired of sitting in the chair by the window. He went to his bedroom, which opened off the gambling hall. On the table was a bottle of rye whiskey, of a brand which he specially and secretly imported from the East. He took a long drink; he changed his coat after laving his hands and brushing his hair. He sat down to read, his hand falling familiarly upon an old copy of Scott's "Fair Maid of Perth."

In time he heard the slow trample of many men coming up the stairs. The sound certainly did not indicate haste; in fact, it declared all kinds of hesitation. The crowd poured into the gambling hall; there was low talk; a silence; more low talk. Ultimately somebody rapped diffidently on the door of the bedroom. "Come in," said Larpent. The door swung back and disclosed War Post with a delegation of its best men in the front, and at the rear men who stood on their toes and craned their necks. There was no noise. Larpent looked up casually into the eyes of Bob Hether. "So you've come up to the scratch all right, eh, Bobbie?" he asked kindly. "I was wondering if you would weaken on the blood-curdling speech you made yesterday."

Hether first turned deadly pale and then flushed beet red.

His six-shooter was in his hand, and it appeared for a moment as if his weak fingers would drop it to the floor. "Oh, never mind," said Larpent in the same tone of kindly patronage. "The community must and shall hold this law forever sacred; and your own brother lives in Connecticut, doesn't he?" He laid down his book and arose. He unbuckled his revolver belt and tossed it on the bed. A look of impatience had come suddenly upon his face. "Well, you don't want me to be master of ceremonies at my own hanging, do you? Why don't somebody say something or do something? You stand around like a lot of bottles. Where's your tree, for instance? You know there isn't a tree between here and the river. Damned little jack-rabbit town hasn't even got a tree for its hanging. Hello, Coats, you live in Crowdger's Corners, don't you? Well, you keep out of this thing, then. The Corners has had its boom, and this is a speculation in real estate which is the business solely of the citizens of War Post."

The behavior of the crowd became extraordinary. Men began to back away; eye did not meet eye; they were victims of an inexplicable influence; it was as if they had heard sinister laughter from a gloom. "I know," said Larpent considerately, "that this isn't as if you were going to hang a comparative stranger. In a sense, this is an intimate affair. I know full well you could go out and jerk a comparative stranger into kingdom come and make a sort of festal occasion of it. But when it comes to performing the same office for an old friend, even the ferocious Bobbie Hether stands around on one leg like a damned white-livered coward. In short, my milk-fed patriots: you seem fat-headed enough to believe that I am going to hang myself if you wait long enough; but unfortunately I am going to allow you to conduct your own real-estate speculations. It seems to me there should be enough men here who understand the value of corner lots in a safe and godly town, and hence should be anxious to hurry this business."

The icy tones had ceased, and the crowd breathed a great sigh, as if it had been freed of a physical pain. But still no one seemed to know where to reach for the scruff of this weird situation. Finally there was some jostling on the outskirts of the crowd, and some men were seen to be pushing old Billie Simpson forward amid some protests. Simpson was, on occasion, the voice of the town. Somewhere in his past he had been a Baptist preacher. He had fallen far, very far, and the only remnant of his former dignity was a fatal facility of speech when half drunk. War Post used him on those state occasions when it became bitten with a desire to "do the thing up in style." So the citizens pushed the blear-eyed old ruffian forward until he stood hemming and hawing in front of Larpent. It was evident at once that he was brutally sober, and hence wholly unfitted for whatever task had been planned for him. A dozen times he croaked like a frog, meanwhile wiping the back of his hand rapidly across his mouth. At last he managed to stammer, "Mister Larpent——"

In some indescribable manner Larpent made his attitude of respectful attention to be grossly contemptuous and insulting. "Yes, Mister Simpson?"

"Er—now—Mister Larpent," began the old man hoarsely, "we wanted to know——" Then obviously feeling that there was a detail which he had forgotten, he turned to the crowd and whispered, "Where is it?" Many men precipitately cleared themselves out of the way, and down this lane Larpent had an unobstructed view of the body of the man he had slain. Old Simpson again began to croak like a frog, "Mister Larpent."

"Yes, Mister Simpson."

"Do you—er—do you—admit——"

"Oh, certainly," said the gambler good-humoredly. "There can be no doubt of it, Mister Simpson, although, with your well-known ability to fog things, you may later possibly prove that you did it yourself. I shot him because he was too officious. Not quite enough men are shot on that account, Mister Simpson. As one fitted in every way by nature to be consummately officious, I hope you will agree with me, Mister Simpson."

Men were plucking old Simpson by the sleeve and giving him directions. One could hear him say, "What?" "Yes." "All right." "What?" "All right." In the end he turned hurriedly upon Larpent and blurted out, "Well, I guess we're goin' to hang you."

Larpent bowed. "I had a suspicion that you would," he said in a pleasant voice. "There has been an air of determination about the entire proceeding, Mister Simpson."

There was an awkward moment. "Well—well—well, come ahead——"

Larpent courteously relieved a general embarrassment. "Why, of course. We must be moving. Clergy first, Mister Simpson. I'll take my old friend, Bobbie Hether, on my right hand, and we'll march soberly to the business, thus lending a certain dignity to this outing of real-estate speculators."

"Tom," quavered Bob Hether, "for Gawd's sake, keep your mout' shut."

"He invokes the deity," remarked Larpent placidly. "But, no; my last few minutes I am resolved to devote to inquiries as to the welfare of my friends. Now, you, for instance, my dear Bobbie, present to-day the lamentable appearance of a rattlesnake that has been four times killed and then left in the sun to rot. It is the effect of friendship upon a highly delicate system. You suffer? It is cruel. Never mind; you will feel better presently."

III

War Post had always risen superior to her lack of a tree by making use of a fixed wooden crane which appeared over a second-story window on the front of Pigrim's general store. This crane had a long tackle always ready for hoisting merchandise to the store's loft. Larpent, coming in the midst of a slow-moving throng, cocked a bright bird-like eye at this crane.

"Mm—yes," he said.

Men began to work frantically. They called each to each in voices strenuous but low. They were in a panic to have the thing finished. Larpent's cold ironical survey drove them mad, and it entered the minds of some that it would be felicitous to hang him before he could talk more. But he occupied the time in pleasant discourse. "I see that Smith Hanham is not here. Perhaps some undue tenderness of sentiment keeps him away. Such feeling are entirely unnecessary. Don't you think so, Bobbie? Note the feverish industry with which the renegade parson works at the rope. You will never be hung, Simpson. You will be shot for fooling too near a petticoat which doesn't belong to you—the same old habit which got you flung out of the Church, you red-eyed old satyr. Ah, the Cross Trail stage coach approaches. What a situation!" The crowd turned uneasily to follow his glance, and saw, truly enough, the dusty rickety old vehicle coming at the gallop of four lean horses. Ike Boston was driving the coach, and far away he had seen and defined the throng in front of Pigrim's store. First calling out excited information to his passengers, who were all inside, he began to lash his horses and yell. As a result he rattled wildly up to the scene just as they were arranging the rope around Larpent's neck.

"Whoa!" said he to his horses.

The inhabitants of War Post peered at the windows of the coach and saw therein six pale, horror-stricken faces. The men at the rope stood hesitating. Larpent smiled blandly. There was a silence. At last a broken voice cried from the coach: "Driver! Driver! What is it? What is it?"

Ike Boston spat between the wheel horses and mumbled that he s'posed anybody could see, less'n they were blind. The door of the coach opened and out stepped a beautiful young lady. She was followed by two little girls hand clasped in hand, and a white-haired old gentleman with a venerable and peaceful face. And the rough West stood in naked immorality before the eyes of the gentle East. The leather-faced men of War Post had never imagined such perfection of feminine charm, such radiance; and as the illumined eyes of the girl wandered doubtfully, fearfully, toward the man with the rope around his neck, a certain majority of the practiced ruffians tried to look as if they were having nothing to do with the proceedings.

"Oh," she said, in a low voice, "what are you going to do?"

At first none made reply; but ultimately a hero managed to break the harrowing stillness by stammering out, "Nothin'!" And then, as if aghast at his own prominence, he shied behind the shoulders of a big neighbor.

"Oh, I know," she said, "but it's wicked. Don't you see how wicked it is? Papa, do say something to them."

The clear, deliberate tones of Tom Larpent suddenly made every one stiffen. During the early part of the interruption he had seated himself upon the steps of Pilgrim's store, in which position he had maintained a slightly bored air. He now was standing with the rope around his neck and bowing. He looked handsome and distinguished and—a devil. A devil as cold as moonlight upon the ice. "You are quite right, miss. They are going to hang me, but I can give you my word that the affair is perfectly regular. I killed a man this morning, and you see these people here who look like a fine collection of premier scoundrels are really engaged in forcing a real-estate boom. In short, they are speculators, land barons, and not the children of infamy which you no doubt took them for at first."

"O—oh!" she said, and shuddered.

Her father now spoke haughtily. "What has this man done? Why do you hang him without a trial, even if you have fair proofs?"

The crowd had been afraid to speak to the young lady, but

a dozen voices answered her father. "Why, he admits it."
"Didn't ye hear?" "There ain't no doubt about it." "No!" "He
sez he did."

The old man looked at the smiling gambler. "Do you admit that you committed murder?"

Larpent answered slowly. "For the first question in a temporary acquaintance that is a fairly strong beginning. Do you
wish me to speak as man to man, or to one who has some
kind of official authority to meddle in a thing that is none of
his affair?"

"I—ah—I," stuttered the other. "Ah—man to man."

"Then," said Larpent, "I have to inform you that this
morning, at about 10:30, a man was shot and killed in my
gambling house. He was engaged in the exciting business of
trying to grab some money out of which he claimed I had
swindled him. The details are not interesting."

The old gentleman waved his arm in a gesture of terror
and despair and tottered toward the coach; the young lady
fainted; the two little girls wailed. Larpent sat on the steps
with the rope around his neck.

IV

The chief function of War Post was to prey upon the
bands of cowboys who, when they had been paid, rode gayly
into town to look for sin. To this end there were in War Post
many thugs and thieves. There was treachery and obscenity
and merciless greed in every direction. Even Mexico was
levied upon to furnish a kind of ruffian which appears infrequently in the northern races. War Post was not good; it was
not tender; it was not chivalrous; but——

But——

There was a quality to the situation in front of Pigrim's
store which made War Post wish to stampede. There were
the two children, their angelic faces turned toward the sky,
weeping in the last anguish of fear; there was the beautiful
form of the young lady prostrate in the dust of the road, with
her trembling father bending over her; on the steps sat Larpent, waiting, with a derisive smile, while from time to time
he turned his head in the rope to make a forked-tongued remark as to the character and bearing of some acquaintance.
All the simplicity of a mere lynching was gone from this
thing. Through some bewildering inner power of its own it
had carried out of the hands of its inaugurators and was

marching along like a great drama and they were only spectators. To them it was ungovernable; they could do no more than stand on one foot and wonder.

Some were heartily sick of everything and wished to run away. Some were so interested in the new aspect that they had forgotten why they had originally come to the front of Pigrim's store. There were the poets. A large practical class wished to establish at once the identity of the new comers. Who were they? Where did they come from? Where were they going to? It was truthfully argued that they were the parson for the new church at Crowdger's Corners, with his family.

And a fourth class—a dark-browed, muttering class—wished to go at once to the root of all disturbance by killing Ike Boston for trundling up his old omnibus and dumping out upon their ordinary lynching party such a load of tears and inexperience and sentimental argument. In low tones they addressed vitriolic reproaches.

"But how'd I know?" he protested, almost with tears. "How'd I know ther'd be all this here kick up?"

But Larpent suddenly created a great stir. He stood up, and his face was inspired with a new, strong resolution. "Look here, boys," he said decisively, "you hang me to-morrow. Or, anyhow, later on to-day. We can't keep frightening the young lady and those two poor babies out of their wits. Ease off on the rope, Simpson, you blackguard! Frightening women and children is your game, but I'm not going to stand it. Ike Boston, take your passengers on to Crowdger's Corners, and tell the young lady that, owing to her influence, the boys changed their minds about making me swing. Somebody lift the rope where it's caught under my ear, will you? Boys, when you want me you'll find me in the Crystal Palace."

His tone was so authoritative that some obeyed him at once involuntarily; but, as a matter of fact, his plan met with general approval. War Post heaved a great sigh of relief. Why had nobody thought earlier of so easy a way out of all these here tears?

V

Larpent went to the Crystal Palace, where he took his comfort like a gentleman, conversing with his friends and drinking. At nightfall two men rode into town, flung their bridles over a convenient post and clanked into the Crystal

Palace. War Post knew them in a glance. Talk ceased and there was a watchful squaring back.

The foremost was Jack Potter, a famous town marshal of Yellow Sky, but now sheriff of the county; the other was Scratchy Wilson, once a no less famous desperado. They were both two-handed men of terrific prowess and courage, but War Post could hardly believe her eyes at view of this daring invasion. It was unprecedented.

Potter went straight to the bar, behind which frowned Bobbie Hether.

"You know a man by the name of Larpent?"

"Supposin' I do?" said Bobbie sourly.

"Well, I want him. Is he in the saloon?"

"Maybe he is an' maybe he isn't," said Bobbie.

Potter went back among the glinting eyes of the citizens. "Gentlemen, I want a man named Larpent. Is he here?"

War Post was sullen, but Larpent answered lazily for himself. "Why, you must mean me. My name is Larpent. What do you want?"

"I've got a warrant for your arrest."

There was a movement all over the room as if a puff of wind had come. The swing of a hand would have brought on a murderous mêlée. But after an instant the rigidity was broken by Larpent's laughter.

"Why, you're sold, sheriff!" he cried. "I've got a previous engagement. The boys are going to hang me to-night."

If Potter was surprised he betrayed nothing.

"The boys won't hang you to-night, Larpent," he said calmly, "because I'm goin' to take you in to Yellow Sky."

Larpent was looking at the warrant. "Only grand larceny," he observed. "But still, you know, I've promised these people to appear at their performance."

"You're goin' in with me," said the impassive sheriff.

"You bet he is, sheriff!" cried an enthusiastic voice, and it belonged to Bobbie Hether. The barkeeper moved down inside his rail, and, inspired like a prophet, he began a harangue to the citizens of War Post. "Now, look here, boys, that's jest what we want, ain't it? Here we were goin' to hang Tom Larpent jest for the reputation of the town, like. 'Long comes Sheriff Potter, the reg-u-lerly cons-ti-tuted officer of the law, an' he says, 'No; the man's mine.' Now, we want to make the reputation of the town as a law-abidin' place, so what do we say to Sheriff Potter? We says, 'A-a-ll right, sheriff; you're reg'lar; we ain't; he's your man.' But supposin' we go to fightin' over it? Then what becomes of the reputation of the town which we was goin' to swing Tom Larpent for?"

The immediate opposition to these views came from a source which a stranger might have difficulty in imagining. Men's foreheads grew thick with lines of obstinacy and disapproval. They were perfectly willing to hang Larpent yesterday, to-day, or tomorrow as a detail in a set of circumstances at War Post; but when some outsider from the alien town of Yellow Sky came into the sacred precincts of War Post and proclaimed the intention of extracting a citizen for cause, any citizen for any cause, the stomach of War Post was fed with a clan's blood, and her children gathered under one invisible banner, prepared to fight as few people in few ages were enabled to fight for their—points of view. There was a guttural murmuring.

"No; hold on!" screamed Bobbie, flinging up his hands. "He'll come clear all right. Tom," he appealed wildly to Larpent, "you never committed no—— ——low-down grand larceny?"

"No," said Larpent coldly.

"But how was it? Can't you tell us how it was?"

Larpent answered with plain reluctance. He waved his hand to indicate that it was all of little consequence. "Well, he was a tenderfoot, and he played poker with me, and he couldn't play quite good enough. But he thought he could; he could play extremely well, he thought. So he lost his money. I thought he'd squeal."

"Boys," begged Bobbie, "let the sheriff take him."

Some answered at once, "Yes!" Others continued to mutter. The sheriff had held his hand because, like all quiet and honest men, he did not wish to perturb any progress toward a peaceful solution; but now he decided to take the scene by the nose and make it obey him.

"Gentlemen," he said formally, "this man is comin' with me. Larpent, get up and come along."

This might have been the beginning, but it was practically the end. The two opinions in the minds of War Post fought in the air and, like a snow-squall, discouraged all action. Amid general confusion Jack Potter and Scratchy Wilson moved to the door with their prisoner. The last thing seen by the men in the Crystal Palace was the bronze countenance of Jack Potter as he backed from the place.

A man filled with belated thought suddenly cried out, "Well, they'll hang him fer this here shootin' game, anyhow."

Bobbie Hether looked disdain upon the speaker.

"Will they! An' where'll they get their witnesses? From here, do y' think? No; not a single one. All he's up against is a case of grand larceny; and——even supposin' he done it—— what in hell does grand larceny amount to?"

SKETCHES
AND EARLY STORIES

The Last of the Mohicans

Few of the old, gnarled and weather-beaten inhabitants of the pines and boulders of Sullivan County are great readers of books or students of literature. On the contrary, the man who subscribes for the county's weekly newspaper is the man who has attained sufficient position to enable him to leave his farm labors for literary pursuits. The historical traditions of the region have been handed down from generation to generation, at the firesides in the old homesteads. The aged grandsire recites legends to his grandson; and when the grandson's head is silvered he takes his corn-cob pipe from his mouth and transfixes his children and his children's children with stirring tales of hunter's exploit and Indian battle. Historians are wary of this form of procedure. Insignificant facts, told from mouth to mouth down the years, have been known to become of positively appalling importance by the time they have passed from behind the last corn-cob in the last chimney corner. Nevertheless, most of these fireside stories are verified by books written by learned men, who have dived into piles of mouldy documents and dusty chronicles to establish their facts.

This gives the great Sullivan County thunderbolt immense weight. And they hurl it at no less a head than that which once evolved from its inner recesses the famous Leatherstocking Tales. The old story-tellers of this district are continually shaking metaphorical fists at *The Last of the Mohicans* of J. Fenimore Cooper. Tell them that they are aiming their shafts at one of the standard novels of American literature and they scornfully sneer; endeavor to oppose them with the intricacies of Indian history and they shriek defiance. No consideration for the author, the literature or the readers can stay their hands, and they claim without reservation that the last of the Mohicans, the real and only authentic last of the Mohicans, was a demoralized, dilapidated inhabitant of Sullivan County.

The work in question is of course a visionary tale and the historical value of the plot is not a question of importance. But when the two heroes of Sullivan County and J. Fenimore Cooper, respectively, are compared, the pathos lies in the contrast, and the lover of the noble and fictional Uncas is overcome with great sadness. Even as Cooper claims that his Uncas was the last of the children of the Turtle, so do the sages of Sullivan County roar from out their rockbound fastnesses that their nondescript Indian was the last of the children of the Turtle. The pathos lies in the contrast between the noble savage of fiction and the sworn-to-claimant of Sullivan County.

All know well the character of Cooper's hero, Uncas, that bronze god in a North American wilderness, that warrior with the eye of the eagle, the ear of the fox, the tread of the catlike panther, and the tongue of the wise serpent of fable. Over his dead body a warrior cries:

"Why has thou left us, pride of the Wapanachki? Thy time has been like that of the sun when in the trees; thy glory brighter than his light at noonday. Thou art gone, youthful warrior, but a hundred Wyandots are clearing the briers from thy path to the world of spirits. Who that saw thee in battle would believe that thou couldst die? Who before thee has ever shown Uttawa the way into the fight? Thy feet were like the wings of eagles; thine arm heavier than falling branches from the pine; and thy voice like the Manitto when he speaks in the clouds. The tongue of Uttawa is weak and his heart exceedingly heavy. Pride of the Wapanachki, why hast thou left us?"

The last of the Mohicans supported by Sullivan County is a totally different character. They have forgotten his name. From their description of him he was no warrior who yearned after the blood of his enemies as the hart panteth for the water-brooks; on the contrary he developed a craving for the rum of the white men which rose superior to all other anxieties. He had the emblematic Turtle tattooed somewhere under his shirtfront. Arrayed in tattered, torn and ragged garments which some white man had thrown off, he wandered listlessly from village to village and from house to house, his only ambition being to beg, borrow or steal a drink. The settlers helped him because they knew his story. They knew of the long line of mighty sachems sleeping under the pines of the mountains. He was a veritable "poor Indian." He dragged through his wretched life in helpless misery. No one could be more alone in the world than he and when he died there was no one to call him pride of anything nor to inquire why he had left them.

Not Much of a Hero

It is supposed to be a poor tombstone that cannot sing praises. In a thousand graveyards the prevailing sentiment is: "Here lies a good man." Some years ago the people of this place erected a monument which they inscribed to "Tom Quick, the Indian Slayer, or the Avenger of the Delaware." After considerable speechmaking and celebrating, they unveiled the stone upon which was inscribed the following touching tribute to the life and character of the great Delaware Valley pioneer: "Tom Quick was the first white child born within the present borough of Milford."

As he has long been known in history as a righteous avenger inflamed with just wrath against his enemies, the silence of the marble upon those virtues which nearly all dead men are said to have possessed is astonishing. Why the worthy gentlemen who had the matter in hand failed to mention any of those qualities or deeds by which "Tom" Quick made fame, but simply mentioned a fact for which he apparently was quite irresponsible, is, possibly, an unintentional rebuke to those who have delighted to honor those qualities of pitiless cruelty which rendered him famous. His exemplary character has made his memory popular in many parts of the valley. A local writer in Port Jervis some years ago was asked to dramatize a life of "Tom" Quick. He agreed and began a course of reading on his subject. But after much study he was compelled to acknowledge that he could not make Quick's popular qualities run in a noble and virtuous groove. He gave up the idea of making Quick the hero and introduced him as a secondary character, as a monomaniac upon the subject of Indians. The little boys living about Milford must be much agitated over the coldness of the monument's inscription, for Quick was a boys' hero. He has been a subject for the graphic and brilliant pens of the talented novelists of the dime and five-cent school. Youths going westward to massacre the devoted red man with a fell purpose and a small-calibre revolver always carry a cheap edition of Tom Quick's alleged biography, which is, when they are at a loss how to proceed, a valuable book of reference. In these volumes all the known ways to kill Indians are practically demonstrated. The hero is pictured as a gory-handed avenger of an advanced type who goes about seeking how many Indians he can devour within a given time. He is a paragon of virtue and slaughters savages in a very high and exalted manner. He also says "b'ar" and "thar" and speaks about getting his "har riz." He is a "dead shot" and perforates Indians with great rapidity and regularity, while they, it seems, persist in offering themselves as targets with much abandon and shoot at him with desperate wildness, never coming within several yards of their aim.

Historians are, as a rule, unsentimental. The aesthetic people, the lovers of the beautiful, the poetic dreamers, have always claimed that Quick during his lifetime killed one hundred Indians. The local historians stoutly assert that he only killed fifteen at the most. But certainly there must be some glory in fifteen Indians and when the manner in which the historians say Quick killed his Indians is taken into consideration it is not surprising that Quick occupies a unique place in history. He was born in Milford as above-mentioned, where his parents had settled in 1733. His father built mills and owned other valuable real-estate in the town, but "Tom" loved the woods and the mountains and chose rather to spend his time wandering with red companions than staying in or near the settlements. He became a veritable Indian in his habits. Until the French and Indian War he lived in perfect amity with the savages, sharing their amusements and pursuits. During this war, however, some savages shot "Tom's" father from ambush. His friendship turned immediately to the deadliest hatred and he swore that he would kill every redskin that crossed his path; he would hunt them as long as one of them remained east of the Alleghanies. The first Indian to be killed by Quick was named Muskwink. After the French and Indian War this Indian returned to the Valley of the Neversink. One day Quick went to a tavern near the junction of the Neversink and Delaware rivers. There he met Muskwink, who was, as usual, intoxicated. The Indian approached "Tom" and told him with great glee that he was of the party that killed Quick's father. He said he had scalped the old man with his own hand. He described laughingly the dying agonies of Quick's father, and mimicked his cries and groans. "Tom" was immediately worked up to the convulsive fury of an enraged panther. He snatched an old musket from the wall and pointing it at Muskwink's breast, drove him out of the house in advance of himself. After proceeding with his prisoner about a mile from the tavern, he shot him in the back, dragged the body into the bushes and left it.

At another time "Tom" and two other white men went into ambush in a thicket which overlooked some rocks where Indians often fished. Three Indians came to the rocks and were attacked by the white men. One was killed by a blow on the head with a club. Another was shot through the head and through the hand, while the third jumped into the river to save his life.

On one occasion Quick and a number of other white hunters sought shelter for the night in the log cabin of a man named Showers. An Indian arrived later and asked permission to stay all night. Showers agreed and the Indian, rolling himself in his blanket, lay down among the white hunters. In the middle of the night there was an explosion. When the hunters hastily struck a light they discovered Quick with a smoking rifle in his hand standing over the body of the Indian, who had been shot dead in his sleep.

Some time after the killing of Muskwink, an Indian with his squaw and three children was paddling down the Delaware River in a canoe. When the family was passing through Butler's Rift "Tom" Quick rose from where he lay concealed in the tall reed-grass on the shore and aiming his rifle at them commanded them to come ashore. When they had come near he shot the man, tomahawked the woman and the two eldest children and knocked the babe's brains out against a tree.

Quick made a statement to his nephew that he had killed an indefinite number of Indians. He said he would lie in the woods and wait until he heard a rifle go off. Then he would creep stealthily in the direction of the sound and would often find an Indian skinning a deer or a bear. He said that it was an easy matter then to put a ball through the red man's head or heart.

Another tale told of him smacks somewhat of the impossible and yet should be recognized as a unique method of fighting Indians. It seems that the tribes used to send small parties of their young warriors to kill this implacable hater of their race. A party of these Indians once met Quick in the woods. He was splitting a long log. They announced to him their intention of killing him. He parleyed with them for some time. Finally he seemed to agree to their plan, but requested that he be allowed, as his last act on earth, to split that log. They agreed for certain reasons only known to themselves. He drove a wedge in the end and then he begged as another favor that they assist him in splitting the log. Again they innocently and guilelessly agreed. Arranging themselves in a long line down the side of the log, the imbecile redskins placed their fingers in the crack held open by the wedge and began to heave. "Tom" then calmly knocked out the wedge, the log closed up and their fingers were all caught tight and fast. They, of course, danced about like so many kittens whose claws were caught in balls of yarn. "Tom" enjoyed their peculiar gyrations and listened to their passionate comments for a while and then proceeded to cut them up in small pieces with his axe. It is a notable fact that no one in the history of the country has ever discovered that kind of an Indian except "Tom" Quick in this alleged adventure. Quick finally died from old age in his bed quietly.

Apparently, if these adventures of his can be taken as examples, "Tom" Quick was not an "Indian fighter." He was merely an Indian killer. There are three views to be taken of "Tom" Quick. The deeds which are accredited to him may be fiction ones and he may have been one of those sturdy and bronzed woodsmen who cleared the path of civilization. Or the accounts may be true and he a monomaniac upon the subject of Indians as suggested by the dramatist. Or the accounts may be true and he a man whose hands were stained with unoffending blood, purely and simply a murderer.

Billie Atkins Went to Omaha

Billie Atkins is a traveler. He has seen the cold blue gleam of the Northern lakes, the tangled green thickets of Florida and the white peaks of the Rockies. All this has he seen and much more, for he has been a tramp for sixteen years.

One winter evening when the "sitting room" of a lodging house just off the Bowery was thronged with loungers Billie came in, mellow with drink and in the eloquent stage. He chose to charm them with a description of a journey from Denver to Omaha. They all listened with appreciation, for when Billie is quite drunk he tells a tale with indescribable gestures and humorous emotions that makes one feel that, after all, the buffets of fate are rather more comic than otherwise.

It seems that when Billie was in Denver last winter it suddenly occurred to him that he wished to be in Omaha. He did not deem it necessary to explain this fancy: he merely announced that he happened to be in Denver last winter and that then it occurred to him that he wished to be in Omaha. Apparently these ideas come to his class like bolts of compelling lightning. After that swift thought, it was impossible for Denver to contain him; he must away to Omaha. When the night express on the Union Pacific pulled out Billie "made a great sneak" behind some freight cars and climbed onto the "blind" end of the baggage car.

It was a very dark night and Billie congratulated himself that he had not been discovered. He huddled to a little heap on the car platform and thought, with a woman's longing, of Omaha.

However, it was not long before an icy stream of water struck Billie a startling blow in the face, and as he raised his eyes he saw in the red glare from the engine a very jocular fireman crouching on the coal and holding the nozzle of a small hose in his hand. And at frequent intervals during the night this jocular fireman would climb up on the coal and play the hose on Billie. The drenched tramp changed his position and curled himself up into a little ball and swore graphically, all to no purpose. The fireman persisted with his hose and when he thought that Billie was getting too comfortable he came back to the rear of the tender and doused him with a pailful of very cold water.

But Billie stuck to his position. For one reason, the express went too fast for him to get safely off, and for another reason he wished to go to Omaha.

The train rushed into the cold gray of dawn on the prairies. The biting chill of the morning made Billie shake in his wet clothes. He adjusted himself on the edge of the rocking car platform where he could catch the first rays of the sun. And it was this change of position that got him into certain difficulties. At about eight o'clock the express went roaring through a little village. Billie, sunning himself on the edge of the steps, espied three old farmers seated on the porch of the village store. They grinned at him and waved their arms.

"I taut they was jest givin' me er jolly," said Billie, "so I waved me hand at 'em an' gives 'em er laugh, an' th' train went on. But it turned out they wasn't motionin' t' me at all, but was all th' while givin' er tip t' th' brakey that I was on th' blind. An' 'fore I knew it th' brakey came over th' top, or aroun' th' side, or somehow, an' I was a-gittin' kicked in th' neck.

" 'Gitoffahere! gitoffahere!'

"I was dead escared b'cause th' train was goin' hell bentin'.

" 'Gitoffahere! gitoffahere!'

" 'Oh, please, mister,' I sez, 'I can't git off—th' train's goin' too fast.'

"But he kept on kickin' me fer a while til finally he got tired an' stopped th' train b'cause I could a-never got off th' way she was runnin'. By this time th' passengers in all th' cars got onto it that they was puttin' er bum off th' blind, an' when I got down off th' step, I see every winder in th' train was fuller heads, an' they gimme er great laugh until I had t' turn me back an' walk off."

As it happened, the nearest station to where Billie then found himself was eighteen miles distant. He dried his clothes as best he could and then swore along the tracks for a mile or two. But it was weary business—tramping along in the vast vacancy of the plains. Billie got tired and lay down to wait for a freight train. After a time one came and as the long string of boxcars thundered past him, he made another "great sneak" and a carefully calculated run and grab. He got safely on the little step and then he began to do what he called "ridin' th' ladder." That is to say, he clung to the little iron ladder that is fastened to the end of each car. He remained hanging there while the long train crept slowly over the plains.

He did not dare to show himself above the top of the car for fear of the brakeman. He considered himself safe down between the ends of the jolting cars, but once, as he chanced to look toward the sky, he saw a burly brakeman leaning on the brakewheel and regarding him.

"Come up here," said the brakeman.

Billie climbed painfully to the top of the car.

"Got any money?" said the brakeman.

"No," replied Billie.

"Well, then, gitoffahere," said the brakeman, and Billie received another installment of kicks. He went down the ladder and puckered his mouth and drew in his breath, preparatory to getting off the car, but the train had arrived at a small grade and Billie became frightened. The little wheels were all a-humming and the cars lurched like boats on the sea.

"Oh, please, mister," said Billie, "I can't git off. It's a-goin' too fast."

The brakeman swore and began the interesting operation of treading, with his brass toed boots, on Billie's fingers. Billie hung hard. He cast glances of despair at the rapid fleeting ground and shifted his grip often. But presently the brakeman's heels came down with extraordinary force and Billie involuntarily released his hold.

He fell in a heap and rolled over and over. His face and body were scratched and bruised, and on the top of his head there was a contusion that fitted like a new derby. His clothes had been rags, but they were now exaggerated out of all semblance of clothes. He sat up and looked at the departing train. "Gawd-dernit," he said, "I'll never git t' Omaha at this rate."

Presently Billie developed a most superhuman hunger. He saw the houses of a village some distance away, and he made for them, resolved to have something to eat if it cost a life. But still he knew he would be arrested if he appeared on the streets of any well organized, respectable town in the trousers he was then obliged to wear. He was in a quandry until by good fortune he perceived a pair of brown overalls hanging on a line in the rear of an isolated house.

He "made a great sneak on 'em." This sort of thing requires patience, but not more than an hour later, he bore off a large square of cloth which he had torn from one leg of the overalls. At another house he knocked at the door and when a woman came he stood very carefully facing her and requested a needle and thread. She gave them to him, and he waited until she had shut the door before he turned and went away.

He retired then into a thick growing patch of sunflowers on the outskirts of the town and started in to sew the piece of overall to his trousers. He had not been engaged long at his task before "two hundred kids" accumulated in front of the sunflower patch and began to throw stones at him. For some time the sky was darkened by a shower of missiles of all sizes. Occasionally Billie, without his trousers, would make little forays, yelling savage threats. These would compel the boys to retire some distance, but they always returned again with renewed ardor. Billie thought he would never get his trousers mended.

But this adventure was the cause of his again meeting Black John Randolph, who Billie said was "th' whitest pardner" he ever had. While he was engaged in conflict with the horde of boys a negro came running down the road and began to belabor them with a boot blacking kit. The boys ran off, and Billie saw with delight that his rescuer was Black John Randolph, whom he had known in Memphis.

Billie, unmolested, sewed his trousers. Then he told Black John that he was hungry, and the two swooped down on the town. Black John shined shoes until dark. He shined for all the available citizens of the place. Billie stood around and watched. The earnings were sixty cents. They spent it all for gingerbread, for it seems that Billie had developed a sudden marvelous longing for gingerbread.

Having feasted, Billie decided to make another attempt for Omaha. He and Black John went to the railroad yard and there they discovered an east-bound freight car that was empty save for one tramp and seven cans of peaches. They parleyed with the tramp and induced him to give up his claim to two-thirds of the car. They settled very comfortably, and that night Billie was again on his way to Omaha. The three of them lived for twenty-four hours on canned peaches, and would have been happy ever after no doubt if it had not happened that their freight car was presently switched off to a side line, and sent careering off in the wrong direction.

When Billie discovered this he gave a whoop and fell out of the car, for he was very particular about walking, and he did not wish to be dragged far from the main line. He trudged back to it, and there discovered a lumber car that contained about forty tramps.

This force managed to overawe the trainmen for a time and compel a free ride for a few miles, but presently the engine was stopped, and the trainmen formed in war array and advanced with clubs.

Billie had had experience in such matters. He "made a sneak." He repaired to a coal car and cuddled among the coal. He buried his body completely, and of his head only his nose and his eyes could have been seen.

The trainmen spread the tramps out over the prairie in a wide fleeing circle, as when a stone is hurled into a placid creek. They remained cursing in their beards, and the train went on.

Billie, snug in his bed, smiled without disarranging the coal that covered his mouth, and thought of Omaha.

But in an hour or two he got impatient, and upreared his head to look at the scenery. An eagle eyed brakeman espied him.

"Got any money?"

"No."

"Well, then, gitoffahere."

Billie got off. The brakeman continued to throw coal at him until the train had hauled him beyond range.

"Hully mack'rel," said Billy, "I'll never git t' Omaha."

He was quite discouraged. He lay down on a bank beside the track to think, and while there he went to sleep. When he awoke a freight train was thundering past him. Still half asleep, he made a dash and a grab. He was up the ladder and on top of the car before he had recovered all of his faculties. A brakeman charged on him.

"Got any money?"

"No, but, please, mister, won't yeh please let me stay on yer train fer a little ways? I'm awful tired, an' I wanta git t' Omaha."

The brakeman reflected. Then he searched Billie's pockets, and finding half a plug of tobacco, took possession of it. He decided to let Billie ride for a time.

Billie perched on top of the car and admired the changing

scenery while the train went twenty miles. Then the brakeman induced him to get off, considering no doubt that a
twenty mile ride was sufficient in exchange for a half plug of
tobacco.

The rest of the trip is incoherent, like the detailed accounts
of great battles. Billie boarded trains and got thrown off on
his head, on his left shoulder, on his right shoulder, on his
hands and knees. He struck the ground slanting, straight from
above and full sideways. His clothes were shredded and torn
like the sails of a gale blown brig. His skin was tattooed with
bloody lines, crosses, triangles, and all the devices known to
geometry. But he wouldn't walk, and he was bound to reach
Omaha. So he let the trainmen use him as a projectile with
which to bombard the picturesque Western landscape.

And eventually he reached Omaha. One night, when it was
snowing and cold winds whistled among the city's chimneys,
he arrived in a coal car. He was filled with glee that he had
reached the place of his endeavor. He could not repress his
pride when he thought of the conquered miles. He went forth
from the coal car with a blithe step.

The police would not let him stand on a corner nor sit
down anywhere. They drove him about for two or three
hours, until he happened to think of the railroad station. He
went there, and was just getting into a nice doze by the warm
red stove in the waiting room, when an official of some kind
took him by the collar, and leading him calmly to the door,
kicked him out into the snow. After that he was ejected from
four saloons in rapid succession.

"Hully mack'rel!" he said, as he stood in the snow and
quavered and trembled.

Until three o'clock in the morning various industrious policemen kept him moving from place to place as if he were
pawn in a game of chess, until finally Billie became desperate
and approached an officer in this fashion:

"Say, mister, won't yeh please arrest me? I wanta go t' jail
so's I kin sleep."

"What?"

"I say, won't yer please arrest me? I wanta go to t' jail so's
I kin sleep."

The policeman studied Billie for a moment. Then he made
an impatient gesture.

"Oh, can't yeh arrest yerself? The jail's a long ways from
here, an' I don't wanta take yeh way up there."

"Sure—I kin," said Billie. "Where is it?"

The policeman gave him directions, and Billie started for the jail.

He had considerable difficulty in finding it. He was often obliged to accost people in the street.

"Please, mister, can yeh tell me where the jail is?"

At last he found it, and after a short parley, they admitted him. They gave him permission to sleep on a sort of an iron slab swung by four chains from the ceiling. Billie sank down upon this couch and arrayed his meager rags about his form. Before he was completely in the arms of the slumber god, however, he made a remark expressive of a new desire, a sudden born longing. "Hully mack'rel. I mus' start back fer Denver in th' mornin'."

In a Park Row Restaurant

"Whenever I come into a place of this sort I am reminded of the Battle of Gettysburg," remarked the stranger. To make me hear him he had to raise his voice considerably, for we were seated in one of the Park Row restaurants during the noon-hour rush. "I think that if a squadron of Napoleon's dragoons charged into this place they would be trampled under foot before they could get a biscuit. They were great soldiers, no doubt, but they would at once perceive that there were many things about sweep and dash and fire of war of which they were totally ignorant.

"I come in here for the excitement. You know, when I was Sheriff, long ago, of one of the gayest counties of Nevada, I lived a life that was full of thrills, for the citizens could not quite comprehend the uses of a sheriff, and did not like to see him busy himself in other people's affairs continually. One man originated a popular philosophy, in which he asserted that if a man required pastime, it was really better to shoot the sheriff than any other person, for then it would be quite impossible for the sheriff to organize a posse and pursue the assassin. The period which followed the promulgation of this theory gave me habits which I fear I can never outwear. I require fever and exhilaration in life, and when I come in here it carries me back to the old days."

I was obliged to put my head far forward, or I could never have heard the stranger's remarks. Crowds of men were swarming in from streets and invading the comfort of seated men in order that they might hang their hats and overcoats upon the long rows of hooks that lined the sides of the room. The finding of vacant chairs became a serious business. Men dashed to and fro in swift searches. Some of those already seated were eating with terrible speed or else casting impatient or tempestuous glances at the waiters.

Meanwhile the waiters dashed about the room as if a monster pursued them and they sought escape wildly through the walls. It was like the scattering and scampering of a lot of water bugs, when one splashes the surface of the brook with a pebble. Withal, they carried incredible masses of dishes and threaded their swift ways with rare skill. Perspiration stood upon their foreheads, and their breaths came strainedly. They served customers with such speed and violence that it often resembled a personal assault. The crumbs from the previous diner were swept off with one fierce motion of a napkin. A waiter struck two blows at the table and left there a knife and a fork. And then came the viands in a volley, thumped down in haste, causing men to look sharp to see if their trousers were safe.

There was in the air an endless clatter of dishes, loud and bewilderingly rapid, like the gallop of a thousand horses. From afar back, at the places of communication to the kitchen, there came the sound of a continual roaring altercation, hoarse and vehement, like the cries of the officers of a regiment under attack. A mist of steam fluttered where the waiters crowded and jostled about the huge copper coffee urns. Over in one corner a man who toiled there like a foundryman was continually assailed by sharp cries. "Brown th' wheat!" An endless string of men were already filing past the cashier, and, even in these moments, this latter was a marvel of self possession and deftness. As the spring doors clashed to and fro, one heard the interminable thunder of the street, and through the window, partially obscured by displayed vegetables and roasts and pies, could be seen the great avenue, a picture in gray tones, save where a bit of green park gleamed, the foreground occupied by this great typical turmoil of car and cab, truck and mail van, wedging their way through an opposing army of the same kind and surrounded on all sides by the mobs of hurrying people.

"A man might come in here with a very creditable stomach and lose his head and get indigestion," resumed the stranger, thoughtfully. "It is astonishing how fast a man can eat when he tries. This air is surcharged with appetites. I have seen very orderly, slow moving men become possessed with the spirit of this rush, lose control of themselves and all at once begin to dine like madmen. It is impossible not to feel the effect of this impetuous atmosphere.

"When consommé grows popular in these places all breweries will have to begin turning out soups. I am reminded of the introduction of canned soup into my town in the West. When the boys found that they could not get full on it they wanted to lynch the proprietor of the supply store for selling an inferior article, but a drummer who happened to be in town explained to them that it was a temperance drink.

"It is plain that if the waiters here could only be put upon a raised platform and provided with repeating rifles that would shoot corn-muffins, butter cakes, Irish stews or any delicacy of the season, the strain of this strife would be greatly lessened. As long as the waiters were competent marksmen, the meals here would be conducted with great expedition. The only difficulty would be when for instance a waiter made an error and gave an Irish stew to the wrong man. The latter would have considerable difficulty in passing it along to the right one. Of course the system would cause awkward blunders for a time. You can imagine an important gentleman in a white waist-coat getting up to procure the bill-of-fare from an adjacent table and by chance intercepting a hamburger-steak bound for a man down by the door. The man down by the door would refuse to pay for a steak that had never come into his possession.

"In some such manner thousands of people could be accommodated in restaurants that at present during the noon hour can feed only a few hundred. Of course eloquent pickets would have to be stationed in the distance to intercept any unsuspecting gentleman from the West who might consider the gunnery of the waiters in a personal way and resent what would look to them like an assault. I remember that my old friend Jim Wilkinson, the ex-sheriff of Tin Can, Nevada, got very drunk one night and wandered into the business end of the bowling alley there. Of course he thought that they were shooting at him and in reply he killed three of the best bowlers in Tin Can."

A Christmas Dinner Won in Battle

Tom had set up a plumbing shop in the prairie town of Levelville as soon as the people learned to care more about sanitary conditions than they did about the brand of tobacco smoked by the inhabitants of Mars. Nevertheless he was a wise young man for he was only one week ahead of the surveyors. A railroad, like a magic wand, was going to touch Levelville and change it to a great city. In an incredibly short time, the town had a hotel, a mayor, a board of aldermen and more than a hundred real estate agents, besides a blue print of the plans for a street railway three miles long. When the cow boys rode in with their customary noise to celebrate the fact that they had been paid, their efforts were discouraged by new policemen in uniform. Levelville had become a dignified city.

As the town expanded in marvelous circles out over the prairies, Tom bestrode the froth of the wave of progress. He was soon one of the first citizens. These waves carry men to fortune with sudden sweeping movements, and Tom had the courage, the temerity and the assurance to hold his seat like a knight errant.

In the democratic and genial atmosphere of this primary boom, he became an intimate acquaintance of Colonel Fortman, the president of the railroad, and with more courage, temerity and assurance, had already fallen violently in love with his daughter, the incomparable Mildred. He carried his intimacy with the colonel so far as to once save his life from the flying might of the 5.30 express. It seems that the colonel had ordered the engineer of the 5.30 to make his time under all circumstances; to make his time if he had to run through fire, blood and earthquake. The engineer decided that the usual rule relating to the speed of trains when passing through freight yards could not concern an express that was ordered to slow down for nothing but the wrath of heaven and in consequence, at the time of this incident, the 5.30 was shrieking through the Levelville freight yard at fifty miles an hour, roaring over the switches and screaming along the lines of box cars. The colonel and Tom were coming from the shops. They had just rounded the corner of a car and stepped out upon the main track when this whirring, boiling, howling demon of an express came down upon them. Tom had an instant in which to drag his companion off the rails; the train whistled past them like an enormous projectile. "Damn that fellow—he's making his time," panted the old colonel gazing after the long speeding shadow with its two green lights. Later he said very soberly: "I'm much obliged to you for that Tom, old boy."

When Tom went to him a year later, however, to ask for the hand of Mildred, the colonel replied: "My dear man, I think you are insane. Mildred will have over a million dollars at my death, and while I don't mean to push the money part of it too far forward, yet Mildred with her beauty, her family name and her wealth, can marry the finest in the land. There isn't anyone too great for her. So you see, my dear man, it is impossible that she could consider you for a moment."

Whereupon Tom lost his temper. He had the indignation of a good, sound-minded, fearless-eyed young fellow who is assured of his love and assured almost of the love of the girl. Moreover, it filled him with unspeakable rage to be called "My dear man."

They then accused each other of motives of which neither were guilty, and Tom went away. It was a serious quarrel. The colonel told Tom never to dare to cross his threshold. They passed each other on the street without a wink of an eye to disclose the fact that one knew that the other existed. As time went on the colonel became more massively aristocratic and more impenetrably stern. Levelville had developed about five grades of society, and the Fortmans mingled warily with the dozen families that formed the highest and iciest grades. Once when the colonel and Mildred were driving through town, the girl bowed to a young man who passed them.

"Who the deuce was that?" said the colonel airily. "Seems to me I ought to know that fellow."

"That's the man that saved your life from the 5.30," replied Mildred.

"See here, young lady," cried the colonel angrily, "don't you take his part against me."

About a year later came the great railway strike. The papers of the city foreshadowed it vaguely from time to time, but no one apparently took the matter in a serious way. There had been threats and rumors of threats but the general public had seemed to view them as idle bombast. At last, however, the true situation displayed itself suddenly and vividly. Almost the entire force of the great P. C. C. and W. U. system went on strike. The people of the city awoke one morning to find the grey sky of dawn splashed with a bright crimson color. The strikers had set ablaze one of the company's shops in the suburbs and the light from it flashed out a red ominous signal of warning foretelling the woe and despair of the struggle that was to ensue. Rumors came that the men usually so sober, industrious and imperturbable were running in a wild mob, raving and destroying. Whereupon, the people who had laughed to scorn any idea of being prepared for this upheaval began to assiduously abuse the authorities for not being ready to meet it.

That morning Tom, in his shirt sleeves, went into the back part of his shop to direct some of his workmen about a certain job, and when he came out he was well covered by as honest a coating of grime and soot as was ever worn by journeyman. He went to the sink to dispose of this adornment and while there he heard his men talking of the strike. One was saying: "Yes, sir; sure as th' dickens! They say they're goin' t' burn th' president's house an' everybody in it." Tom's body stiffened at these words. He felt himself turn cold. A moment later he left the shop forgetting his coat, forgetting his covering of soot and grime.

In the main streets of the city there was no evident change. The horses of the jangling street cars still slipped and strained in the deep mud into which the snow had been churned. The store windows were gay with the color of Christmas. Innumerable turkeys hung before each butcher's shop. Upon the walks the business men had formed into little eager groups discussing the domestic calamity. Against the leaden-hued sky, over the tops of the buildings, arose a great leaning pillar of smoke marking the spot upon which stood the burning shop.

Tom hurried on through that part of town which was composed of little narrow streets with tiny grey houses on either side. There he saw a concourse of Slavs, Polacs, Italians and Hungarians, laborers of the company, floundering about in the mud and raving, conducting a riot in their own inimitable way. They seemed as blood-thirsty, pitiless, mad, as starved wolves. And Tom presented a figure no less grim as he ran through the crowd, coatless and now indeed hatless, with pale skin showing through the grime. He went until he came to a stretch of commons across which he could see the Fortman's house standing serenely with no evidences of riot about it. He moderated his pace then.

When he had gone about half way across this little snow-covered common, he looked back, for he heard cries. Across the white fields, winding along the muddy road, there came a strange procession. It resembled a parade of Parisians at the time of the first revolution. Fists were wildly waving and at times hoarse voices rang out. It was as if this crowd was delirious from drink. As it came nearer Tom could see women—gaunt and ragged creatures with inflamed visages and rolling eyes. There were men with dark sinister faces whom Tom had never before seen. They had emergd from the earth, so to speak, to engage in this carousal of violence. And from this procession there came continual threatening ejaculations, shrill cries for revenge, and querulous voices of hate, that made a sort of barbaric hymn, a pagan chant of savage battle and death.

Tom waited for them. Those in the lead evidently considered him to be one of their number since his face was grimed and his garments dishevelled. One gigantic man with bare and brawny arms and throat, gave him invitation with a fierce smile. "Come ahn, Swipsey, while we go roast 'em."

A raving grey-haired woman, struggling in the mud, sang a song which consisted of one endless line:

"We'll burn th' foxes out,
We'll burn th' foxes out,
We'll burn th' foxes out."

As for the others, they babbled and screamed in a vast variety of foreign tongues. Tom walked along with them listening to the cries that came from the terrible little army, marching with clenched fists and with gleaming eyes fastened upon the mansion that upreared so calmly before them.

When they arrived, they hesitated a moment, as if awed by the impassive silence of the structure with closed shutters and barred doors, which stolidly and indifferently confronted them.

Then from the centre of the crowd came the voice of the grey-headed old woman: "Break in th' door! Break in th' door!" And then it was that Tom displayed the desperation born of his devotion to the girl within the house. Although he was perhaps braver than most men, he had none of that magnificent fortitude, that gorgeous tranquility amid upheavals and perils which is the attribute of people in plays; but he stepped up on the porch and faced the throng. His face was wondrously pallid and his hands trembled but he said: "You fellows can't come in here."

There came a great sarcastic howl from the crowd. "Can't we?" They broke into laughter at this wildly ridiculous thing. The brawny, bare-armed giant seized Tom by the arm. "Get outa th' way, you yap," he said between his teeth. In an instant Tom was punched and pulled and knocked this way and that way, and amid the pain of these moments he was conscious that members of the mob were delivering thunderous blows upon the huge doors. Directly indeed they crashed down and he felt the crowd sweep past him and into the house. He clung to a railing; he had no more sense of balance than a feather. A blow in the head had made him feel that the ground swirled and heaved around him. He had no further interest in rioting, and such scenes of excitement. Gazing out over the common he saw two patrol wagons, loaded with policemen, and the lashed horses galloping in the mud. He wondered dimly why they were in such a hurry.

But at that moment a scream rang from the house out through the open doors. He knew the voice and, like an electric shock it aroused him from his semi-stupor. Once more alive, he turned and charged into the house as valiant and as full of rage as a Roman. Pandemonium reigned within. There came yells and roars, splinterings, cracklings, crashes. The scream of Mildred again rang out; this time he knew it came from the dining-room before whose closed door, four men were as busy as miners with improvised pick and drill.

Tom grasped a heavy oaken chair that stood ornamentally in the hall and, elevating it above his head, ran madly at the four men. When he was almost upon them, he let the chair fly. It seemed to strike all of them. A heavy oak chair of the old English type is one of the most destructive of weapons. Still, there seemed to be enough of the men left for they flew at him from all sides like dragons. In the dark of the hallway, Tom put down his head and half-closed his eyes and plied his fists. He knew he had but a moment in which to stand up, but there was a sort of grim joy in knowing that the most terrific din of this affray was going straight through the dining-room door, and into the heart of Mildred and when she knew that her deliverer was—— He saw a stretch of blood-red sky flame under his lids and then sank to the floor, blind, deaf, and nerveless.

When the old colonel arrived in one of the patrol wagons, he did not wait to see the police attack in front but ran around to the rear. As he passed the dining-room windows he saw his wife's face. He shouted, and when they opened a window he clambered with great agility into the room. For a minute they deluged each other with shouts of joy and tears. Then finally the old colonel said: "But they did not get in here. How was that?"

"Oh, papa," said Mildred, "they were trying to break in when somebody came and fought dreadfully with them and made them stop."

"Heavens, who could it have been?" said the colonel. He went to the door and opened it. A group of police became visible hurrying about the wide hall but near the colonel's feet lay a body with a white still face.

"Why, it's—it's——" ejaculated the colonel in great agitation.

"It's Tom," cried Mildred.

When Tom came to his senses he found that his fingers were clasped tightly by a soft white hand which by some occult power of lovers knew at once.

"Tom," said Mildred.

And the old colonel from further away said: "Tom, my boy!"

But Tom was something of an obstinate young man. So as soon as he felt himself recovered sufficiently, he arose and went unsteadily toward the door.

"Tom, where are you going?" cried Mildred.

"Where are you going, Tom?" called the colonel.

"I'm going home," said Tom doggedly. "I didn't intend to cross this threshold—I——" He swayed unsteadily and seemed about to fall. Mildred screamed and ran toward him. She made a prisoner of him. "You shall not go home," she told him.

"Well," began Tom weakly yet persistently, "I——"

"No, no, Tom," said the colonel, "you are to eat a Christmas dinner with us to-morrow and then I wish to talk with you about—about——"

"About what?" said Tom.

"About—about—damnitall, about marrying my daughter," cried the colonel.

From London Impressions

There was to be noticed in this band of rescuers a young man in evening clothes and a top-hat . . . Now in America a young man in evening clothes and a top-hat may be a terrible object. He is not likely to do violence, but he is likely to do impassivity and indifference to the point where they become worse than violence. There are certain of the more idle phases of civilization to which America has not yet awakened—and it is a matter of no moment if she remains unaware. This matter of hats is one of them. I recall a legend recited to me by an esteemed friend, ex-Sheriff of Tin Can, Nevada. Jim Cortright, one of the best gun-fighters in town, went on a journey to Chicago and while there he procured a top-hat. He was quite sure how Tin Can would accept this innovation, but he relied on the celerity with which he could get a six-shooter into action. One Sunday Jim examined his guns with his usual care, placed the top-hat on the back of his head, and sauntered coolly out into the streets of Tin Can.

Now, while Jim was in Chicago, some progressive citizens had decided that Tin Can needed a bowling alley. The carpenters went to work the next morning and an order for the balls and pins was telegraphed to Denver. In three days the whole population was concentrated at the new alley betting their outfits and their lives.

It has since been accounted very unfortunate that Jim Cortright had not learned of bowling alleys at his mother's knee nor even later in the mines. This portion of his mind was singularly belated. He might have been an Apache for all he knew of bowling alleys.

In his careless stroll through the town, his hands not far from his belt and his eyes going sideways in order to see who would shoot first at the hat, he came upon this long low shanty where Tin Can was betting itself hoarse over a game between a team from the ranks of Excelsior Hose Company

No. I and a team composed from the habitués of the "Red Light" saloon.

Jim, in blank ignorance of bowling phenomena, wandered casually through a little door into what must always be termed the wrong end of a bowling-alley. Of course he saw that the supreme moment had come. They were not only shooting at the hat and at him, but the low-down cusses were using the most extraordinary and hellish ammunition. Still perfectly undaunted, however, Jim retorted with his two Colts and killed three of the best bowlers in Tin Can.

The ex-Sheriff vouched for this story. He himself had gone headlong through the door at the firing of the first shot with that simple courtesy which leads Western men to donate the fighters plenty of room. He said that afterward the hat was the cause of a number of other fights, and that finally a delegation of prominent citizens were obliged to wait upon Cortright and ask him if he wouldn't take that thing away somewheres and bury it. Jim pointed out to them that it was his hat and that he would regard it as a cowardly concession if he submitted to their dictation in the matter of his headgear. He added that he purposed to continue to wear his top-hat on every occasion when he happened to feel that the wearing of a top-hat was a joy and a solace to him.

The delegation sadly retired and announced to the town that Jim Cortright had openly defied them and had declared his purpose of forcing his top-hat on the pained attention of Tin Can whenever he chose. Jim Cortright's Plug Hat became a phrase with considerable meaning to it.

However, the whole affair ended in a great passionate outburst of popular revolution. Spike Foster was a friend of Cortright, and one day when the latter was indisposed Spike came to him and borrowed the hat. He had been drinking heavily at the "Red Light," and was in a supremely reckless mood. With the terrible gear hanging jauntily over his eye and his two guns drawn, he walked straight out into the middle of the square in front of the Palace Hotel, and drew the attention of all Tin Can by a blood-curdling imitation of the yowl of a mountain lion.

This was when the long-suffering populace arose as one man. The top-hat had been flaunted once too often. When Spike Foster's friends came to carry him away they found nearly a hundred and fifty men shooting busily at a mark, and the mark was the hat. My informant told me that he believed he owed his popularity in Tin Can, and subsequently his election to the distinguished office of Sheriff, to the active and prominent part he had taken in the proceedings.

The enmity to the top-hat expressed by this convincing anecdote exists in the American West at present, I think, in the perfection of its strength; but disapproval is not now displayed by volleys from the citizens, save in the most aggravating cases. It is at present usually a matter of mere jibe and general contempt. The East, however, despite a great deal of kicking and gouging, is having the top-hat stuffed slowly and carefully down its throat, and there now exist many young men who consider that they could not successfully conduct their lives without this furniture.

REPORTS
AND LETTERS

Nebraska's Bitter Fight for Life

The vast prairies in this section of Nebraska contain a people who are engaged in a bitter and deadly fight for existence. Some of the reports telegraphed to the East have made it appear that the entire State of Nebraska is a desert. In reality the situation is serious, but it does not include the whole State. However, people feel that thirty counties in pain and destitution is sufficient.

The blot that is laid upon the map of the State begins in the north beyond Custer county. It is there about fifty miles wide. It slowly widens then in a southward direction until when it crosses the Platte River it is over a hundred miles wide. The country to the north and to the west of this blot is one of the finest grazing grounds in the world and the cattlemen there are not suffering. Valentine is in this portion which is exempt. To the eastward, the blot shades off until one finds moderate crops.

In June, 1894, the bounteous prolific prairies of this portion of Nebraska were a-shine with the young and tender green of growing corn. Round and fat cattle filled the barnyards of the farmers. The trees that were congregated about the little homesteads were of the vivid and brave hue of healthy and vigorous vegetation. The towns were alive with the commerce of an industrious and hopeful community. These mighty brown fields stretching for miles under the imperial blue sky of Nebraska had made a promise to the farmer. It was to compensate him for his great labor, his patience, his sacrifices. Under the cool, blue dome the winds gently rustled the arrays of waist-high stalks.

Then, on one day about the first of July there came a menace from the southward. The sun had been growing prophetically more fierce day by day, and in July there began these winds from the south, mild at first and subtle like the breaths of the panting countries of the tropics. The corn in the fields underwent a preliminary quiver from this breeze burdened with an omen of death. In the following days it became stronger, more threatening. The farmers turned anxious eyes toward their fields where the corn was beginning to rustle with a dry and crackling sound which went up from the prairie like cries.

Then from the southern horizon came the scream of a wind hot as an oven's fury. Its valor was great in the presence of the sun. It came when the burning disc appeared in the east and it weakened when the blood-red, molten mass vanished in the west. From day to day, it raged like a pestilence. The leaves of the corn and of the trees turned yellow and sapless like leather. For a time they stood the blasts in the agony of a futile resistance. The farmers helpless, with no weapon against this terrible and inscrutable wrath of nature, were spectators at the strangling of their hopes, their ambitions, all that they could look to from their labor. It was as if upon the massive altar of the earth, their homes and their families were being offered in sacrifice to the wrath of some blind and pitiless deity.

The country died. In the rage of the wind, the trees struggled, gasped through each curled and scorched leaf, then, at last, ceased to exist, and there remained only the bowed and bare skeletons of trees. The corn shivering as from fever, bent and swayed abjectly for a time, then one by one the yellow and tinder-like stalks, twisted and pulled by the rage of the hot breath, died in the fields and the vast and sometimes beautiful prairies were brown and naked.

In a few weeks this prosperous and garden-like country was brought to a condition of despair, but still this furnace-wind swept along the dead land, whirling great clouds of dust, straws, blades of grass. A farmer, gazing from a window, was confronted by a swirling tempest of dust that intervened between his vision and his scorched fields. The soil of the roads turned to powder in this tempest, and men traveling against the winds found all the difficulties of some hideous and unnatural snow storm. At nightfall the winds always vanished and the sky which had glistened like a steel shield became of a soft blue, as the purple shadows of a merciful night advanced from the west.

These farmers now found themselves existing in a virtual desert. The earth from which they had wrested each morsel which they had put into their mouths had now abandoned them. Nature made light of her obligation under the toil of these men. This vast tract was not a fit place for the nomads of Sahara.

And yet, for the most part, there was no wavering, no absence of faith in the ultimate success of the beautiful soil. Some few despaired at once and went to make new homes in the north, in the south, in the east, in the west. But the greater proportion of the people of this stricken district were men who loved their homes, their farms, their neighborhoods, their counties. They had become rooted in this soil, which so seldom failed them in compensation for their untiring and persistent toil. They could not move all the complexities of their social life and their laboring life. The magic of home held them from traveling toward the promise of other lands. And upon these people there came the weight of the strange and unspeakable punishment of nature. They are a fearless folk, completely American. Their absolute types are now sitting about New England dinner tables. They summoned their strength for a long war with cold and hunger. Prosperity was at the distance of a new crop of 1895. It was to be from August to August. Between these months loomed the great white barrier of the winter of 1894–95. It was a supreme battle to which to look forward. It required the profound and dogged courage of the American peoples who have come into the West to carve farms, railroads, towns, cities, in the heart of a world fortified by enormous distances.

The weakest were, of course, the first to cry out at the pain of it. Farmers, morally certain of the success of the crop, had already gone into debt for groceries and supplies. The hot winds left these men without crops and without credit. They were instantly confronted with want. They stood for a time reluctant. Then family by family they drove away to other States where there might be people who would give their great muscular hands opportunity to earn food for their wives and little children.

Then came the struggle of the ones who stood fast. They were soon driven to bay by nature, now the pitiless enemy. They were sturdy and dauntless. When the cry for help came from their lips it was to be the groan from between the clenched teeth. Men began to offer to work at the rate of twenty-five cents a day, but, presently, in the towns no one had work for them, and, after a time, barely anyone had twenty-five cents a day which they dared invest in labor. Life in the little towns halted. The wide roads, which had once been so busy, became the dry veins of the dead land.

Meanwhile, the chill and tempest of the inevitable winter had gathered in the north and swept down upon the devastated country. The prairies turned bleak and desolate.

The wind was a direct counter-part of the summer. It came down like wolves of ice. And then was the time that from this district came that first wail, half impotent rage, half despair. The men went to feed the starving cattle in their tiny allowances in clothes that enabled the wind to turn their bodies red and then blue with cold. The women shivered in the houses where fuel was as scarce as flour, and where flour was sometimes as scarce as diamonds.

The cry for aid was heard everywhere. The people of a dozen States responded in a lavish way and almost at once. A relief commission was appointed by Governor Holcomb at Lincoln to receive the supplies and distribute them to the people in want. The railroad companies granted transportation to the cars that came in loaded with coal and flour from Iowa and Minnesota, fruit from California, groceries and clothing from New York and Ohio, and almost everything possible from Georgia and Louisiana. The relief commission became involved in a mighty tangle. It was obliged to contend with enormous difficulties.

Sometimes a car arrives in Lincoln practically in pawn. It has accumulated the freight charges of perhaps half a dozen railroads. The commission then corresponds and corresponds with railroads to get the charges remitted. It is usually the fault of the people sending the car who can arrange for free and quick transportation by telegraphing the commission in Lincoln a list of what their car, or cars, contain. The commission will then arrange all transportation.

A facetious freight agent in the East labelled one carload of food: "Outfit for emigrants." This car reached the people who needed it only after the most extraordinary delays and after many mistakes and explanations and re-explanations. Meanwhile, a certain minority began to make war upon the commission at the expense of the honest and needy majority. Men resorted to all manner of tricks in order to seduce the commission into giving them supplies which they did not need. Also various unscrupulous persons received donations of provisions from the East and then sold them to the people at a very low rate it is true, but certainly at the most obvious of profits. The commission detected one man selling a donated carload of coal at the price of forty cents per ton. They discovered another man who had collected some two thousand dollars from charitable folk in other States, and of this sum he really gave to the people about eight hundred dollars. The commission was obliged to make long wars upon all these men who wished to practice upon the misery of the farmers.

As is mentioned above, this stricken district does not include in any manner the entire State of Nebraska, but, nevertheless, certain counties that are not in the drought portion had no apparent hesitation about vociferously shouting for relief. When the State Legislature appropriated one hundred and fifty thousand dollars to help the starving districts, one or two counties in the east at once sent delegations to the capital to apply for a part of it. They said, ingenuously, that it was the State's money and they wanted their share of it.

To one town in the northern part of the State there was sent from the East a carload of coal. The citizens simply apportioned it on the basis of so much per capita. They appointed a committee to transport the coal from the car to each man's residence. It was the fortune of this committee finally to get into the office of a citizen who was fairly prosperous.

"Where do yeh want yer coal put?" they said, with a clever and sly wink.

"What coal?"

"Why, our coal! Your coal! The coal what was sent here."

"Git out 'a here! If you put any coal in my cellar I'll kill some of yeh."

They argued for a long time. They did not dare to leave anyone out of the conspiracy. He could then tell of it. Having failed with him, they went to his wife and tried to get her to allow them to put the coal in the cellar. In this also they were not successful.

These are a part of the difficulties with which the commission fights. Its obligation is to direct all supplies from the generous and pitying inhabitants of other States into the correct paths to reach the suffering. To do this over a territory covering many hundreds of square miles, and which is but meagrely connected by railroads, is not an easy task.

L. P. Ludden, the secretary and general manager of the commission, works early and late and always. In his office at Lincoln he can be seen at any time when people are usually awake working over the correspondence of the bureau. He is confronted each mail by a heap of letters that is as high as a warehouse. He told the writer of this article that he had not seen his children for three weeks, save when they were asleep. He always looked into their room when he arrived home late at night and always before he left early in the morning.

But he is the most unpopular man in the State of Nebraska. He is honest, conscientious and loyal; he is hardworking and has great executive ability. He struggles heroically with the thugs who wish to filch supplies, and with the virtuous but misguided philanthropists who write to learn of the folks that received their fifty cents and who expect a full record of this event.

From a hundred towns whose citizens are in despair for their families, arises a cry against Ludden. From a hundred towns whose citizens do not need relief and in consequence do not get it, there arises a cry against Ludden. The little newspapers print the uncompromising sentence: "Ludden must go!" Delegations call upon the governor and tell him that the situation would be mitigated if they could only have relief from Ludden. Members of the legislature prodded by their rural constituents, arise and demand an explanation of the presence in office of Ludden. And yet this man with the square jaw and the straight set lips hangs on in the indomitable manner of a man of the soil. He remains in front of the tales concerning him; merely turns them into his bureau and an explanation comes out by the regular machinery of his system, to which he has imparted his personal quality of inevitableness. Once, grown tired of the abuse, he asked of the governor leave to resign, but the governor said that it would be impossible now to appoint a new man without some great and disastrous halt of the machinery. Ludden returned to his post and to the abuse.

But in this vast area of desolated land there has been no benefit derived from the intrigues and scufflings at Lincoln which is two hundred miles away from the scene of the suffering. This town of Eddyville is in the heart of the stricken territory. The thermometer at this time registers eighteen degrees below zero. The temperature of the room which is the writer's bedchamber is precisely one and a half degrees below zero. Over the wide white expanses of prairie, the icy winds from the north shriek, whirling high sheets of snow and enveloping the house in white clouds of it. The tempest forces fine stinging flakes between the rattling sashes of the window that fronts the storm. The air has remained gloomy the entire day. From other windows can be seen the snowflakes fleeing into the south, traversing as level a line as bullets, speeding like the wind. The people in the sod houses are much more comfortable than those who live in frame dwellings. Many of these latter are high upon ridges of the prairie and the fingers of the storm clutch madly at them. The sod houses huddle close to the ground and their thick walls restrain the heat of the scant wood-fire from escaping.

Eddyville is a typical town of the drought district. Approaching it over the prairie, one sees a row of little houses, blocked upon the sky. Most of them are one storied. Some of the stores have little square false-fronts. The buildings straggle at irregular intervals along the street and a little board sidewalk connects them. On all sides stretches the wind-swept prairie.

This town was once a live little place. From behind the low hillocks, the farmers came jogging behind their sturdy teams. The keepers of the three or four stores did a thriving trade. But at this time the village lies as inanimate as a corpse. In the rears of the stores, a few men perhaps, sit listlessly by the stoves. The people of the farms remain close in-doors during this storm. They have not enough warm clothing to venture into the terrible blasts. One can drive past house after house without seeing signs of life unless it be a weak curl of smoke scudding away from a chimney. Occasionally, too, one finds a deserted homestead, a desolate and unhappy thing upon the desolate and unhappy prairie.

And for miles around this town lie the countless acres of the drought-pestered district.

Some distance from here a man was obliged to leave his wife and baby and go into the eastern part of the State to make a frenzied search for work that might be capable of furnishing them with food. The woman lived alone with her baby until the provisions were gone. She had received a despairing letter from her husband. He was still unable to get work. Everybody was searching for it; none had it to give. Meanwhile he had ventured a prodigious distance from home.

The nearest neighbor was three miles away. She put her baby in its little ramshackle carriage and traveled the three miles. The family there shared with her as long as they could—two or three days. Then she went on to the next house. There, too, with the quality of mercy which comes with incredible suffering, they shared with her. From house to house she went pushing her baby-carriage. She received a meal here, three meals here, a meal and a bed here. The baby was a weak and puny child.

During this swirling storm, the horses huddle abjectly and stolidly in the fields, their backs humped and turned toward the eye of the wind, their heads near the ground, their manes blowing over their eyes. Ice crusts their soft noses. The writer asked a farmer this morning: "How will your horses get through the winter?"

"I don't know," he replied, calmly. "I ain't got nothing to give 'em. I got to turn 'em out and let 'em russle for theirselves. Of course if they get enough to live on, all right, an' if they don't they'll have to starve."

"And suppose there are a few more big storms like this one?"

"Well, I don't suppose there'll be a horse left round here by ploughin' time then. The people ain't got nothin' to feed 'em upon in the spring. A horse'll russle for himself in the snow, an' then when th' spring rains comes, he'll go all to pieces unless he gets good nursin' and feedin'. But we won't have nothin' to give 'em."

Horses are, as a usual thing, cheaper in this country than good saddles, but at this time, there is a fair proportion of men who would willingly give away their favorite horses if they could thus insure the animals warm barns and plenty of feed.

But the people cannot afford to think now of these minor affections of their hearts.

The writer rode forty-five miles through the country, recently. The air turned the driver a dark shade, until he resembled some kind of a purple Indian from Brazil, and the team became completely coated with snow and ice, as if their little brown bodies were in quaint ulsters. They became dull and stupid in the storm. Under the driver's flogging they barely stirred, holding their heads dejectedly, with an expression of unutterable patient weariness. Six men were met upon the road. They strode along silently with patches of ice upon their beards. The fields were for the most part swept bare of snow, and there appeared then the short stumps of the corn, where the hot winds of the summer had gnawed the stalks away.

Yet this is not in any sense a type of a Nebraska storm. It is phenomenal. It is typical only of the misfortunes of this part of the State. It is commensurate with other things, that this tempest should come at precisely the time when it will be remarkable if certain of the people endure it.

Eddyville received a consignment of aid recently. There

were eighty sacks of flour and a dozen boxes of clothing. Four miles about the little village the farmers came with their old wagons and their ill-fed horses. Some of them blushed when they went before the local committee to sign their names and get the charity. They were strong, fine, sturdy men, not bended like the Eastern farmer but erect and agile. Their faces occasionally expressed the subtle inner tragedy which relief of food and clothing at this time can do but little to lighten. The street was again lively, but there was an elemental mournfulness in the little crowd. They spoke of the weather a great deal.

Two days afterward the building where the remainder of the relief stores had been put away, burned to the ground.

A farmer in Lincoln county recently said: "No, I didn't get no aid. I hadter drive twenty-five miles t' git my flour, an' then drive back agin an' I didn't think th' team would stand it, they been poor-fed so long. Besides I'd hadter put up a dollar to keep th' team over night an' I didn't have none. I hain't had no aid!"

"How did you get along?"

"Don't git along, stranger. Who the hell told you I did get along?"

In the meantime, the business men in the eastern part of the State, particularly in the splendid cities of Omaha and Lincoln, are beginning to feel the great depression resulting from extraordinary accounts which have plastered the entire State as a place of woe. Visitors to the country have looked from car-windows to see the famine-stricken bodies of the farmers lying in the fields and have trod lightly in the streets of Omaha to keep from crushing the bodies of babes. But the point should be emphasized that the grievous condition is confined to a comparatively narrow section of the western part of the State.

Governor Holcomb said to the writer: "It is true that there is much misery in the State, but there is not the universal privation which has been declared. Crop failure was unknown until 1890 when the farmers lost much of their labor, but at that time, and in 1893, when a partial loss was experienced, the eastern half of the State was able to take care of the western half where the failure was pronounced.

"This year has been so complete a failure as to reduce many to extreme poverty, but I do not think that there are more than twenty per cent at present in need. Great irrigation enterprises that are now being inaugurated will, no doubt, eliminate the cause of failure in large districts of the western part of the State. The grain that is produced and stock that is raised in this State put it in the front rank of the great agricultural commonwealths. I have no doubt that in a year or two her barns will be overflowing. I see nothing in the present situation nor in the history of the State as I have observed it for sixteen years that ought to discourage those who contemplate coming here to make homes. In the western part of the State, a vast amount of unwise speculation has caused great losses, but that part of the country cannot be excelled for grazing, and irrigation will, no doubt, render it safe and profitable for agriculture. In the greater part of the State, the people are suffering no more than a large percentage of the agricultural districts of other States. It has been brought about as much by the general national depression as by local causes."

It is probable that a few years will see the farms in the great Platte River valley watered by irrigation, but districts that have not an affluence of water will depend upon windmills. The wells in this State never fail during a drought. They furnish an abundance of cool and good water. Some farmers plan to build little storage reservoirs upon the hillocks of the prairie. They are made by simply throwing up banks of earth, and then allowing cattle to trample the interiors until a hard and water-tight bottom is formed. In this manner a farmer will be in a degree independent of the most terrible droughts.

Taking the years in groups of five the rainfall was at its lowest from 1885 to 1890 when the general average was 22.34 inches. The general average for 1891, 1892 and 1893 was 23.85 inches. But 1894 now enters the contest with a record of but 13.10 inches. People are now shouting that Nebraska is to become arid. In past years when rainfalls were enormous they shouted that Nebraska was to become a great pond.

The final quality of these farmers who have remained in this portion of the State is their faith in the ultimate victory of the land and their industry. They have a determination to wait until nature, with her mystic processes, restores to them the prosperity and bounty of former years. "If a man stays right by this country, he'll come out all right in the end."

Almost any man in the district will cease speaking of his woes to recite the beauties of the times when the great rolling prairies are green and golden with the splendor of young corn, the streams are silver in the light of the sun, and when from the wide roads and the little homesteads there arises the soundless essence of a hymn from the happy and prosperous people.

But then there now is looming the eventual catastrophe that would surely depopulate the country. These besieged farmers are battling with their condition with an eye to the rest and success of next August. But if they can procure no money with which to buy seed when spring comes around, the calamity that ensues is an eternal one, as far as they and their farms here are concerned. They have no resort then but to load their families in wagons behind their hungry horses and set out to conquer these great distances, which like walls shut them from the charitable care of other and more fortunate communities.

In the meantime, they depend upon their endurance, their capacity to help each other, and their steadfast and unyielding courage.

Galveston, Texas, in 1895

It is the fortune of travellers to take note of differences and publish them to their friends. It is the differences that are supposed to be valuable. The travellers seek them bravely, and cudgel their wits to find means to unearth them. But in this search they are confronted continually by the resemblances and the intrusion of commonplace and most obvious similarity into a field that is being ploughed in the romantic fashion is what causes an occasional resort to the imagination.

The winter found a cowboy in south-western Nebraska who had just ended a journey from Kansas City, and he swore bitterly as he remembered how little boys in Kansas City followed him about in order to contemplate his wide-brimmed hat. His vivid description of this incident would have been instructive to many Eastern readers. The fact that little boys in Kansas City could be profoundly interested in the sight of a wide-hatted cowboy would amaze a certain proportion of the populace. Where then can one expect cowboys if not in Kansas City? As a matter of truth, however, a steam boiler with four legs and a tail, galloping down the main street of the town, would create no more enthusiasm there than a real cow-puncher. For years the farmers have been driving the cattlemen back, back toward the mountains and into Kansas, and Nebraska has come to an almost universal condition of yellow trolly-cars with clanging gongs and whirring wheels, and conductors who don't give a curse for the public. And travellers tumbling over each other in their haste to trumpet the radical differences between Eastern and Western life have created a generally wrong opinion. No one has yet dared to declare that if a man drew three trays in Syracuse, N.Y., in many a Western city the man would be blessed with a full house. The declaration has no commercial value. There is a distinct fascination in being aware that in some parts of the world there are purple pigs, and children who are born with china mugs dangling where their ears should be. It is this fact which makes men sometimes grab tradition in wonder; color and attach contemporaneous date-lines to it. It is this fact which has kept the sweeping march of the West from being chronicled in any particularly true manner.

In a word, it is the passion for differences which has prevented a general knowledge of the resemblances.

If a man comes to Galveston resolved to discover every curious thing possible, and to display every point where Galveston differed from other parts of the universe, he would have the usual difficulty in shutting his eyes to the similarities. Galveston is often original, full of distinctive characters. But it is not like a town in the moon. There are, of course, a thousand details of street color and life which are thoroughly typical of any American city. The square brick business blocks, the mazes of telegraph wires, the trolly-cars clamoring up and down the streets, the passing crowd, the slight fringe of reflective and reposeful men on the curb, all disappoint the traveller, and he goes out in the sand somewhere and digs in order to learn if all Galveston clams are not schooner-rigged.

Accounts of these variations are quaint and interesting reading, to be sure, but then, after all, there are the great and elemental facts of American life. The cities differ as peas—in complexion, in size, in temperature—but the fundamental part, the composition, remains.

There has been a wide education in distinctions. It might be furtively suggested that the American people did not thoroughly know their mighty kinship, their universal emotions, their identical view-points upon many matters about which little is said. Of course, when the foreign element is injected very strongly, a town becomes strange, unfathomable, wearing a sort of guilty air which puzzles the American eye. There begins then a great diversity, and peas become turnips, and the differences are profound. With them, however, this prelude has nothing to do. It is a mere attempt to impress a reader with the importance of remembering that an illustration of Galveston streets can easily be obtained in Maine. Also, that the Gulf of Mexico could be mistaken for the Atlantic Ocean, and that its name is not printed upon it in tall red letters, notwithstanding the legend which has been supported by the geographies.

There are but three lifts in the buildings of Galveston. This is not because the people are skilled climbers; it is because the buildings are for the most part not high.

A certain Colonel Menard bought this end of the island of Galveston from the Republic of Texas in 1838 for fifty thousand dollars. He had a premonition of the value of wide streets for the city of his dreams, and he established a minimum width of seventy feet. The widest of the avenues is one hundred and fifty feet. The fact that this is not extraordinary for 1898 does not prevent it from being marvellous as municipal forethought in 1838.

In 1874 the United States Government decided to erect stone jetties at the entrance to the harbor of Galveston in order to deepen the water on the outer and inner bars, whose shallowness compelled deep-water ships to remain outside and use lighters to transfer their cargoes to the wharves of the city. Work on the jetties was in progress when I was in Galveston in 1895—in fact, two long, low black fingers of stone stretched into the Gulf. There are men still living who had confidence in the Governmental decision of 1874, and these men now point with pride to the jetties and say that the United States Government is nothing if not inevitable.

The soundings at mean low tide were thirteen feet on the inner bar and about twelve feet on the outer bar. At present there is twenty-three feet of water where once was the inner bar, and as the jetties have crept toward the sea they have achieved eighteen feet of water in the channel of the outer bar at mean low tide. The plan is to gain a depth of thirty feet. The cost is to be about seven million dollars.

Undoubtedly in 1874 the people of Galveston celebrated the decision of the Government with great applause, and prepared to welcome mammoth steamers at the wharves during the next spring. It was in 1889, however, that matters took conclusive form. In 1895 the prayer of Galveston materialised.

In 1889, Iowa, Nebraska, Missouri, Kansas, California, Arkansas, Texas, Wyoming, and New Mexico began a serious pursuit of Congress. Certain products of these States and Territories could not be exported with profit, owing to the high rate for transportation to Eastern ports. They demanded a harbor on the coast of Texas with a depth and area sufficient for great sea-crossing steamers. The board of army engineers which was appointed by Congress decided on Galveston as the point. The plan was to obtain by means of artificial constructions a volume and velocity of tidal flow that would maintain a navigable channel. The jetties are seven thousand feet apart, in order to allow ample room for the escape of the enormous flow of water from the inner bar.

Galveston has always been substantial and undeviating in its amount of business. Soon after the war it attained a commercial solidity, and its progress has been steady but quite slow. The citizens now, however, are lying in wait for a real Western boom. Those products of the West which have been walled in by the railroad transportation rates to Eastern ports are now expected to pass through Galveston. An air of hope pervades the countenance of each business man. The city, however, expected 1,500,000 bales of cotton last season, and the Chamber of Commerce has already celebrated the fact.

A train approaches the Island of Galveston by means of a long steel bridge across a bay, which glitters like burnished metal in the winter-time sunlight. The vast number of white two-storied frame houses in the outskirts remind one of New England, if it were not that the island is level as a floor. Later, in the commercial part of the town, appear the conventional business houses and the trolly-cars. Far up the cross-streets is the faint upheaval of the surf of the breeze-blown Gulf, and in the other direction the cotton steamers are arrayed with a fresco upon their black sides of dusky chuckling stevedores handling the huge bales amid a continual and foreign conversation, in which all the subtle and incomprehensible gossip of their social relations goes from mouth to mouth, the bales leaving little tufts of cotton all over their clothing.

Galveston has a rather extraordinary number of very wealthy people. Along the finely-paved drives their residences can be seen, modern for the most part and poor in architecture. Occasionally, however, one comes upon a typical Southern mansion, its galleries giving it a solemn shade and its whole air one of fine and enduring dignity. The palms standing in the grounds of these houses seem to pause at this time of year, and patiently abide the coming of the hot breath of summer. They still remain of a steadfast green and their color is a wine.

Underfoot the grass is of a yellow hue, here and there patched with a faint impending verdancy. The famous snowstorm here this winter played havoc with the color of the vegetation, and one can now observe the gradual recovery of the trees, the shrubbery, the grass. In this vivid sunlight their vitality becomes enormous.

This storm also had a great effect upon the minds of the citizens. They would not have been more astonished if it had rained suspender buttons. The writer read descriptions of this storm in the newspapers of the date. Since his arrival here he has listened to 574 accounts of it.

Galveston has the aspect of a seaport. New York is not a seaport; a seaport is, however, a certain detail of New York. But in Galveston the docks, the ships, the sailors, are a large element in the life of the town. Also, one can sometimes find here that marvellous type the American sailor. American seamen are not numerous enough to ever depreciate in value. A town that can produce a copy of the American sailor should encase him in bronze and unveil him on the Fourth of July. A veteran of the waves explained to the writer the reason that American youths do not go to sea. He said it was because saddles are too expensive. The writer congratulated the veteran of the waves upon his lucid explanation of this great question.

Galveston has its own summer resorts. In the heat of the season, life becomes sluggish in the streets. Men move about with an extraordinary caution as if they expected to be shot as they approached each corner.

At the beach, however, there is a large hotel which overflows with humanity, and in front is, perhaps, the most comfortable structure in the way of bath-houses known to the race. Many of the rooms are ranged about the foot of a large dome. A gallery connects them, but the principal floor to this structure is the sea itself, to which a flight of steps leads. Galveston's 35,000 people divide among themselves in summer a reliable wind from the Gulf.

There is a distinctly cosmopolitan character to Galveston's people. There are men from everywhere. The city does not represent Texas. It is unmistakably American, but in a general manner. Certain Texas differentiations are not observable in this city.

Withal, the people have the Southern frankness, the honesty which enables them to meet a stranger without deep suspicion, and they are the masters of a hospitality which is instructive to cynics.

Stephen Crane in Texas

"Ah," they said, "you are going to San Anton? I wish I was. There's a town for you."

From all manner of people, business men, consumptive men, curious men and wealthy men, there came an exhibition of a profound affection for San Antonio. It seemed to symbolize for them the poetry of life in Texas.

There is an eloquent description of the city which makes it consist of three old ruins and a row of Mexicans sitting in the sun. The author, of course, visited San Antonio in the year 1101. While this is undoubtedly a masterly literary effect, one can feel glad that after all we don't steer our ships according to these literary effects.

At first the city presents a totally modern aspect to the astonished visitor. The principal streets are lanes between rows of handsome business blocks, and upon them proceeds with important uproar the terrible and almighty trolley car. The prevailing type of citizen is not seated in the sun; on the contrary he is making his way with the speed and intentness of one who competes in a community that is commercially in earnest. And the victorious derby hat of the North spreads its wings in the holy place of legends.

This is the dominant quality. This is the principal color of San Antonio. Later one begins to see that these edifices of stone and brick and iron are reared on ashes, upon the ambitions of a race. It expresses again the victory of the North. The serene Anglo-Saxon erects business blocks upon the dreams of the transient monks; he strings telegraph wires across the face of their sky of hope; and over the energy, the efforts, the accomplishments of these pious fathers of the early church passes the wheel, the hoof, the heel.

Here, and there, however, one finds in the main part of the town, little old buildings, yellow with age, solemn and severe in outline, that have escaped by a miracle or by a historical importance, the whirl of the modern life. In the Mexican quarter there remains, too, much of the old character, but despite the tenderness which San Antonio feels for these monuments, the unprotected mass of them must get trampled into shapeless dust which lies always behind the march of this terrible century. The feet of the years will go through many old roofs.

Trolley cars are merciless animals. They gorge themselves with relics. They make really coherent history look like an omelet. If a trolley car had trolleyed around Jericho, the city would not have fallen; it would have exploded.

Centuries ago the white and gold banner of Spain came up out of the sea and the Indians, mere dots of black on the vast Texan plain, saw a moving glitter of silver warriors on the horizon's edge. There came then the long battle of soldier and priest, side by side, against these stubborn barbaric hordes, who wished to retain both their gods and their lands. Sword and crozier made frenzied circles in the air. The soldiers varied their fights with the Indians by fighting the French, and both the Indians and the French occasionally polished their armor for them with great neatness and skill.

During interval of peace and interval of war, toiled the pious monks, erecting missions, digging ditches, making farms and cudgeling their Indians in and out of the church. Sometimes, when the venerable fathers ran short of Indians to convert, the soldiers went on expeditions and returned dragging in a few score. The settlement prospered. Upon the gently rolling plains, the mission churches with their yellow stone towers outlined upon the sky, called with their bells at evening a multitude of friars and meek Indians and gleaming soldiers to service in the shadows before the flaming candles, the solemn shrine, the slow-pacing, chanting priests. And wicked and hopeless Indians, hearing these bells, scudded off into the blue twilight of the prairie.

The ruins of these missions are now besieged in the valley south of the city by indomitable thickets of mesquite. They rear their battered heads, their soundless towers, over dead forms, the groves of monks; and of the Spanish soldiers not one so much as flourishes a dagger.

Time has torn at these pale yellow structures and overturned walls and towers here and there, defaced this and obliterated that. Relic hunters with their singular rapacity have dragged down little saints from their niches and pulled important stones from arches. They have performed offices of destruction of which the wind and the rain of the innumerable years was not capable. They are part of the general scheme of attack by nature.

The wind blows because it is the wind, the rain beats because it is the rain, the relic hunters hunt because they are relic hunters. Who can fathom the ways of nature? She thrusts her spear in the eye of Tradition and her agents feed on his locks. A little guide-book published here contains one of these "Good friend, forbear——" orations. But still this desperate massacre of the beautiful carvings goes on and it would take the ghosts of the monks with the ghosts of scourges, the phantoms of soldiers with the phantoms of swords, a scowling, spectral party, to stop the destruction. In the meantime, these portentous monuments to the oil, the profound convictions of the fathers, remain stolid and unyielding, with the bravery of stone, until it appears like the last stand of an army. Many years will charge them before the courage will abate which was injected into the mortar by the skillful monks.

It is something of a habit among the newspaper men and others who write here to say: "Well, there's a good market for Alamo stuff, now." Or perhaps they say: "Too bad! Alamo stuff isn't going very strong, now." Literary aspirants of the locality as soon as they finish writing about Her Eyes, begin on the Alamo. Statistics show that 69,710 writers of the state of Texas have begun at the Alamo.

Notwithstanding this fact, the Alamo remains the greatest memorial to courage which civilization has allowed to stand. The quaint and curious little building fronts on one of the most populous plazas of the city and because of Travis, Crockett, Bowie and their comrades, it maintains dignity amid the taller modern structures which front it. It is the tomb of the fiery emotions of Texans who refused to admit that numbers and Mexicans were arguments. Whether the swirl of life, the crowd upon the streets, pauses to look or not, the spirit that lives in this building, its air of contemplative silence, is as eloquent as an old battle flag.

The first Americans to visit San Antonio arrived in irons. This was the year 1800. There were eleven of them. They had fought one hundred and fifty Spanish soldiers on the eastern frontier and, by one of those incomprehensible chances which so often decides the color of battles, they had lost the fight. Afterward, Americans began to filter down through Louisiana until in 1834 there were enough of them to openly disagree with the young federal government in the

City of Mexico, although there was not really any great number of them. Santa Anna didn't give a tin whistle for the people of Texas. He assured himself that he was capable of managing the republic of Mexico, and after coming to this decision he said to himself that that part of it which formed the state of Texas had better remain quiet with the others. In writing of what followed, a Mexican sergeant says: "The Texans fought like devils."

There was a culmination at the old Mission of the Alamo in 1836. This structure then consisted of a rectangular stone parapet 190 feet long and about 120 feet wide, with the existing Church of the Alamo in the southeast corner. Colonel William B. Travis, David Crockett and Colonel Bowie, whose monument is a knife with a peculiar blade, were in this enclosure with a garrison of something like one hundred and fifty men when they heard that Santa Anna was marching against them with an army of 4,000. The Texans shut themselves in the mission, and when Santa Anna demanded their surrender they fired a cannon and inaugurated the most appalling conflict of the continent.

Once Colonel Travis called his men together during a lull of the battle and said to them: "Our fate is sealed. * * * Our friends were evidently not informed of our perilous situation in time to save us. Doubtless they would have been here by this time if they had expected any considerable force of the enemy. * * * Then we must die."

He pointed out to them the three ways of being killed— surrendering to the enemy and being executed, making a rush through the enemy's lines and getting shot before they could inflict much damage, or of staying in the Alamo and holding out to the last, making themselves into a huge and terrible porcupine to be swallowed by the Mexican god of war. All the men save one adopted the last plan with their colonel.

This minority was a man named Rose. "I'm not prepared to die, and shall not do so if I can avoid it." He was some kind of a dogged philosopher. Perhaps he said: "What's the use?" There is a strange inverted courage in the manner in which he faced his companions with this sudden and short refusal in the midst of a general exhibition of supreme bravery. "No," he said. He bade them adieu and climbed the wall. Upon its top he turned to look down at the upturned faces of his silent comrades.

After the battle there were 521 dead Mexicans mingled with the corpses of the Texans.

The Mexicans form a certain large part of the population of San Antonio. Modern inventions have driven them toward the suburbs, but they are still seen upon the main streets in the ratio of one to eight and in their distant quarter of course they swarm. A small percentage have reached positions of business eminence.

The men wear for the most part wide-brimmed hats with peaked crowns, and under these shelters appear their brown faces and the inevitable cigarettes. The remainder of their apparel has become rather Americanized, but the hat of romance is still superior. Many of the young girls are pretty, and all of the old ones are ugly. These latter squat like clay images, and the lines upon their faces and especially about the eyes, make it appear as if they were always staring into the eye of a blinding sun.

Upon one of the plazas, Mexican vendors with open-air stands sell food that tastes exactly like pounded fire-brick from hades—chili con carne, tamales, enchiladas, chili verde, frijoles. In the soft atmosphere of the southern night, the cheap glass bottles upon the stands shine like crystal and the lamps glow with a tender radiance. A hum of conversation ascends from the strolling visitors who are at their social shrine.

The prairie about San Antonio is wrinkled into long low hills, like immense waves, and upon them spreads a wilderness of the persistent mesquite, a bush that grows in defiance of everything. Some forty years ago the mesquite first assailed the prairies about the city, and now from various high points it can be seen to extend to the joining of earth and sky. The individual bushes do not grow close together, and roads and bridle paths cut through the dwarf forest in all directions. A certain class of Mexicans dwell in hovels amid the mesquite.

In the Mexican quarter of the town the gambling houses are crowded nightly, and before the serene dealers lie little stacks of silver dollars. A Mexican may not be able to raise enough money to buy beef tea for his dying grandmother, but he can always stake himself for a game of monte.

Upon a hillock of the prairie in the outskirts of the city is situated the government military post, Fort Sam Houston. There are four beautiful yellow and blue squadrons of cavalry, two beautiful red and blue batteries of light artillery and six beautiful white and blue companies of infantry. Officers' row resembles a collection of Newport cottages. There are magnificent lawns and gardens. The presence of so many officers of the line besides the gorgeous members of the staff of the commanding general, imparts a certain brilliant quality to San Antonio society. The drills upon the wide parade ground make a citizen proud.

'Mid Cactus and Mesquite

The train rolled out of the Americanisms of San Antonio—the coal and lumber yards, the lines of freight cars, the innumerable tracks and black cinder paths—and into the southern expanses of mesquite.

In the smoking compartment, the capitalist from Chicago said to the archaeologist from Boston: "Well, here we go." The archaeologist smiled with placid joy.

The brown wilderness of mesquite drifted steadily and for hours past the car-windows. Occasionally a little ranch appeared half-buried in the bushes.

In the door-yard of one some little calicoed babies were playing and in the door-way itself a woman stood leaning her head against the post of it and regarding the train listlessly. Pale, worn, dejected, in her old and soiled gown, she was of a type to be seen North, East, South, West.

"That'll be one of our best glimpses of American civilization," observed the archaeologist then.

Cactus plants spread their broad pulpy leaves on the soil of reddish brown in the shade of the mesquite bushes. A thin silvery vapor appeared at the horizon.

"Say, I met my first Mexican, day before yesterday," said the capitalist. "Coming over from New Orleans. He was a peach. He could really talk more of the English language than any man I've ever heard. He talked like a mill-wheel. He had the happy social faculty of making everybody intent upon his conversation. You couldn't help it, you know. He put every sentence in the form of a question. 'San Anton' fine town—uh? F-i-n-n-e—uh? Gude beesness there—uh? Yes gude place for beesness—uh?' We all had to keep saying 'yes,' or 'certainly' or 'you bet your life,' at intervals of about three seconds."

"I went to school with some Cubans up North when I was a boy," said the archaeologist, "and they taught me to swear in Spanish. I'm all right in that. I can——"

"Don't you understand the conversational part at all?" demanded the capitalist.

"No," replied the archaeologist.

"Got friends in the City of Mexico?"

"No!"

"Well, by jiminy, you're going to have a daisy time!"

"Why, do you speak the language?"

"No!"

"Got any friends in the city?"

"No."

"Thunder."

These mutual acknowledgements riveted the two men together. In this invasion, in which they were both facing the unknown, an acquaintance was a prize.

As the train went on over the astonishing brown sea of mesquite, there began to appear little prophecies of Mexico. A Mexican woman, perhaps, crouched in the door of a hut, her bare arms folded, her knees almost touching her chin, her head leaned against the door-post. Or perhaps a dusky sheep-herder in peaked sombrero and clothes the color of tan-bark, standing beside the track, his inscrutable visage turned toward the train. A cloud of white dust rising above the dull-colored bushes denoted the position of his flock. Over this lonely wilderness vast silence hung, a speckless sky, ignorant of bird or cloud.

"Look at this," said the capitalist.

"Look at that," said the archaeologist.

These premonitory signs threw them into fever of anticipation. "Say, how much longer before we get to Laredo?" The conductor grinned. He recognized some usual, some typical aspect in this impatience. "Oh, a long time yet."

But then finally when the whole prairie had turned a faint preparatory shadow-blue, some one told them: "See those low hills off yonder? Well, they're beyond the Rio Grande."

"Get out—are they?"

A sheep-herder with his flock raising pale dust-clouds over the lonely mesquite could no longer interest them. Their eyes were fastened on the low hills beyond the Rio Grande.

"There it is! There's the river!"

"Ah, no, it ain't!"

"I say it is."

Ultimately the train manœuvered through some low hills and into sight of low-roofed houses across stretches of sand. Presently it stopped at a long wooden station. A score of Mexican urchins were congregated to see the arrival. Some twenty yards away stood a train composed of an engine, a mail and baggage car, a Pullman and three day coaches marked first, second and third class in Spanish. "There she is, my boy," said the capitalist. "There's the Aztec Limited. There's the train that's going to take us to the land of flowers and visions and all that."

There was a general charge upon the ticket office to get American money changed to Mexican money. It was a beautiful game. Two Mexican dollars were given for every American dollar. The passengers bid good-bye to their portraits of the national bird, with exultant smiles. They examined with interest the new bills which were quite gay with red and purple and green. As for the silver dollar, the face of it intended to represent a cap of liberty with rays of glory shooting from it, but it looked to be on the contrary a picture of an exploding bomb. The capitalist from Chicago jingled his coin with glee. "Doubled my money!"

"All aboard," said the conductor for the last time. Thereafter he said: "Vamanos." The train swung around the curve and toward the river. A soldier in blue fatigue uniform from the adjacent barracks, a portly German regardant at the entrance of his saloon, an elaborate and beautiful Anglo-Saxon oath from the top of a lumber pile, a vision of red and white and blue at the top of a distant staff, and the train was upon the high bridge that connects one nation with another.

Laredo appeared like a city veritably built upon sand. Little plats of vivid green grass appeared incredible upon this apparent waste. They looked like the grass mats of the theatrical stage. An old stone belfry arose above the low roofs. The river, shallow and quite narrow, flowed between wide banks of sand which seemed to express the stream's former records.

In Nuevo Laredo, there was a throng upon the platform— Mexican women, muffled in old shawls, and men, wrapped closely in dark-hued serapes. Over the heads of the men towered the peaked sombreros of fame. It was a preliminary picture painted in dark colors.

There was also a man in tan shoes and trousers of violent English check. When a gentleman of Spanish descent is important, he springs his knee-joint forward to its limit with each step. This gentleman was springing his knee-joints as if they were of no consequence, as if he had a new pair at his service.

"You have only hand baggage," said the conductor. "You won't have to get out."

Presently, the gentleman in tan shoes entered the car, springing his knee-joints frightfully. He caused the porter to let down all the upper berths while he fumbled among the blankets and mattresses. The archaeologist and the capitalist had their valises already open and the gentleman paused in his knee-springing flight and gently peered in them. "All right," he said approvingly and pasted upon each of them a label which bore some formidable Mexican legend. Then he knee-springed himself away.

The train again invaded a wilderness of mesquite. It was amazing. The travellers had somehow expected a radical change the moment they were well across the Rio Grande. On the contrary, southern Texas was being repeated. They leaned close to the pane and stared into the mystic south. In the rear, however, Texas was represented by a long narrow line of blue hills, built up from the plain like a step.

Infrequently horsemen, shepherds, hovels appeared in the mesquite. Once, upon a small hillock a graveyard came into view and over each grave was a black cross. These somber emblems, lined against the pale sky, were given an inexpressibly mournful and fantastic horror from their color, new in this lonely land of brown bushes. The track swung to the westward and extended as straight as a rapier blade toward the rose-colored sky from whence the sun had vanished. The shadows of the mesquite deepened.

Presently the train paused at a village. Enough light remained to bring clearly into view some square yellow huts from whose rectangular doors there poured masses of crimson rays from the household fires. In these shimmering glows, dark and sinister shadows moved. The archaeologist and the capitalists were quite alone at this time in the sleeping-car and there was room for their enthusiasm, their ejaculations. Once they saw a black outline of a man upon one of these red canvasses. His legs were crossed, his arms were folded in his serape, his hat resembled a charlotte russe. He leaned negligently against the door-post. This figure justified to them all their preconceptions. He was more than a painting. He was the proving of certain romances, songs, narratives. He renewed their faith. They scrutinized him until the train moved away.

They wanted mountains. They clamored for mountains. "How soon, conductor, will we see any mountains?" The conductor indicated a long shadow in the pallor of the afterglow. Faint, delicate, it resembled the light rain-clouds of a faraway shower.

The train, rattling rhythmically, continued toward the far horizon. The deep mystery of night upon the mesquite prairie settled upon it like a warning to halt. The windows presented black expanses. At the little stations, calling voices could be heard from the profound gloom. Cloaked figures moved in the glimmer of lanterns.

The two travellers, hungry for color, form, action, strove to penetrate with their glances these black curtains of darkness which intervened between them and the new and strange life. At last, however, the capitalist settled down in the smoking compartment and recounted at length the extraordinary attributes of his children in Chicago.

Before they retired they went out to the platform and gazed into the south where the mountain range, still outlined against the soft sky, had grown portentously large. To those upon the train, the black prairie seemed to heave like a sea and these mountains rose out of it like islands. In the west, a great star shone forth. "It is as large as a cheese," said the capitalist.

The archaeologist asserted the next morning that he had awakened at midnight and contemplated Monterey. It appeared, he said, as a high wall and a distant row of lights. When the capitalist awoke, the train was proceeding through a great wide valley which was radiant in the morning sunshine. Mountain ranges, wrinkled, crumpled, bare of everything save sage-brush, loomed on either side. Their little peaks were yellow in the light and their sides were of the faintest carmine tint, heavily interspersed with shadows. The wide, flat plain itself was grown thickly with sage-brush, but date palms were sufficiently numerous to make it look at times like a bed of some monstrous asparagus.

At every station a gorgeous little crowd had gathered to receive the train. Some were merely curious and others had various designs on the traveller—to beg from him or to sell to him. Indian women walked along the line of cars and held baskets of fruit toward the windows. Their broad, stolid faces were suddenly lit with a new commercial glow at the arrival of this trainful of victims. The men remained motionless and reposeful in their serapes. Back from the stations one could see the groups of white, flat-roofed adobe houses. From where a white road stretched over the desert toward the mountains, there usually arose a high, shining cloud of dust from the hoofs of some caballero's charger.

As this train conquered more and more miles toward its sunny destination, a regular progression in color could be noted. At Nuevo Laredo the prevailing tones in the dress of the people were brown, black and grey. Later an occasional purple or crimson serape was interpolated. And later still, the purple, the crimson and the other vivid hues became the typical colors, and even the trousers of dark cloth were replaced by dusty white cotton ones. A horseman in a red serape and a tall sombrero of maroon or pearl or yellow was vivid as an individual, but a dozen or two of them reposeful in the shade of some desert railway station made a chromatic delirium. In Mexico the atmosphere seldom softens anything. It devotes its energy to making high lights, bringing everything forward, making colors fairly volcanic.

The bare feet of the women pattered to and fro along the row of car windows. Their cajoling voices were always soft and musical. The fierce sun of the desert beat down upon their baskets, wherein the fruit and food was exposed to each feverish ray.

From time to time across this lonely sunbeaten expanse, from which a storm of fine, dry dust ascended upon any provocation at all, the train passed walls made of comparatively small stones which extended for miles over the plain and then ascended the distant mountains in an undeviating line. They exposed the most incredible and apparently stupid labor. To see a stone wall beginning high and wide and extending to the horizon in a thin, monotonous thread, makes one think of the innumerable hands that toiled at the stones to divide one extent of sage-brush from another. Occasionally the low roof of a hacienda could be seen, surrounded by outbuildings and buried in trees. These walls marked the boundary of each hacienda's domain.

"Certain times of year," said the conductor, "there is nothing for the Indian peons to do, and as the rancheros have to feed 'em and keep 'em anyhow, you know, why they set 'em to building these stone walls."

The archaeologist and the capitalist gazed with a new interest at the groups of dusty-footed peons at the little stations. The clusters of adobe huts wherein some of them dwelt resembled the pictures of Palestine tombs. Withal, they smiled amiably, contentedly, their white teeth gleaming.

When the train roared past the stone monument that marked the Tropic of Cancer, the two travellers leaned out dangerously.

"Look at that, would you?"

"Well, I'm hanged!"

They stared at it with awed glances. "Well, well, so that's it, is it?" When the southern face of the monument was presented, they saw the legend, "Zona Torrida."

"Thunder, ain't this great."

Finally, the valley grew narrower. The track wound near the bases of hills. Through occasional passes could be seen other ranges, leaden-hued, in the distance. The sage-brushes became scarce and the cactus began to grow with a greater courage. The young green of other and unknown plants became visible. Greyish dust in swirling masses marked the passage of the train.

At San Luis Potosi, the two travellers disembarked and again assailed one of those American restaurants which are located at convenient points. Roast chicken, tender steaks, chops, eggs, biscuit, pickles, cheese, pie, coffee, and just outside in blaring sunshine there was dust and Mexicans and a heathen chatter—a sort of an atmosphere of chili con carne, tortillas, tamales. The two travellers approached this table with a religious air as if they had encountered a shrine.

All the afternoon the cactus continued to improve in sizes. It now appeared that the natives made a sort of a picket fence of one variety and shade trees from another. The brown faces of Indian women and babes peered from these masses of prickly green.

At Atotonilco, a church with red-tiled towers appeared surrounded by poplar trees that resembled hearse plumes, and in the stream that flowed near there was a multitude of heads with long black hair. A vast variety of feminine garments decorated the bushes that skirted the creek. A baby, brown as a water-jar and of the shape of an alderman, paraded the bank in utter indifference or ignorance or defiance.

At various times old beggars, grey and bent, tottered painfully with outstretched hats begging for centavos in voices that expressed the last degree of chill despair. Their clothing hung in the most supernatural tatters. It seemed miraculous that such fragments could stay upon human bodies. With some unerring inexplainable instinct they steered for the capitalist. He swore and blushed each time. "They take me for an easy thing," he said wrathfully. "No—I won't—get out—go away." The unmolested archaeologist laughed.

The churches north of Monterey had been for the most part small and meek structures surmounted by thin wooden crosses. They were now more impressive, with double towers of stone and in the midst of gardens and dependent buildings. Once the archaeologist espied a grey and solemn ruin of a chapel. The old walls and belfry appeared in the midst of a thicket of regardless cactus. He at once recited to the capitalist the entire history of Cortez and the Aztecs.

At night-fall, the train paused at a station where the entire village had come down to see it and gossip. There appeared to be no great lighting of streets. Two or three little lamps burned at the station and a soldier, or a policeman, carried a lantern which feebly illuminated his club and the bright steel of his revolver. In the profound gloom, the girls walked arm and arm, three or four abreast, and giggled. Bands of hoodlums scouted the darkness. One could hear their shrill catcalls. Some pedlers came with flaring torches and tried to sell things.

In the early morning hours, the two travellers scrambled from their berths to discover that the train was high in air. It had begun its great climb of the mountains. Below and on the left, a vast plain of green and yellow fields was spread out like a checkered cloth. Here and there were tiny white villages, churches, haciendas. And beyond this plain arose the peak of Nevado de Toluca for 15,000 feet. Its eastern face was sun-smitten with gold and its snowy sides were shadowed with rose. The color of gold made it appear that this peak was staring with a high serene eternal glance into the East at the approach of the endless suns. And no one feels like talking in the presence of these mountains that stand like gods on the world, for fear that they might hear. Slowly the train wound around the face of the cliff.

When you come to this country, do not confuse the Mexican cakes with pieces of iron ore. They are not pieces of iron ore. They are cakes.

At a mountain station to which the train had climbed in some wonderful fashion, the travellers breakfasted upon cakes and coffee. The conductor, tall, strong, as clear-headed and as clear-eyed, as thoroughly a type of the American railroad man as if he were in charge of the Pennsylvania Limited, sat at the head of the table and harangued the attendant peon. The capitalist took a bite of cake and said "Gawd!"

This little plateau was covered with yellow grass which extended to the bases of the hills that were on all sides. These hills were grown thickly with pines, fragrant, gently waving in the cool breeze. Upon the station platform a cavalry officer, under a grey sombrero heavily ladened with silver braid, conversed with a swarthy trooper. Over the little plain, a native in a red blanket was driving a number of small donkeys who were each carrying an enormous load of fresh hay.

The conductor again yelled out a password to a Chinese lodge and the train renewed its attack upon these extraordinary ridges which intervened between it and its victory. The passengers prepared themselves. Every car window was hung full of heads that were for the most part surmounted by huge sombreros. A man with such a large roll of matting strapped to his back that he looked like a perambulating sentry-box, leaned upon his staff in the roadway and stared at the two engines. Puffing, panting, heaving, they strained like thoroughbred animals, with every steel muscle of their bodies and slowly the train was hauled up this tilted track.

In and out among the hills it went, higher and higher. Often two steel rails were visible far below on the other side of a ravine. It seemed incredible that ten minutes before, the train had been at that place.

In the depths of the valley, a brook brawled over the rocks. A man in dusty white garments lay asleep in the shade of a pine.

At last the whistle gave a triumphant howl. The summit—10,000 feet above the sea—was reached. A winding slide, a sort of tremendous toboggan affair began. Around and around among the hills glided the train. Little flat white villages displayed themselves in the valleys. The maguey plant, from which the Mexicans make their celebrated tanglefoot, flourished its lance-point leaves in long rows. The hills were checkered to their summits with brown fields. The train swinging steadily down the mountains crossed one stream thirteen times on bridges dizzily high.

Suddenly two white peaks, afar off, raised above the horizon, peering over the ridge. The capitalist nearly fell off the train. Popocatepetl and Ixtaccihuatl, the two giant mountains, clothed in snow that was like wool, were marked upon the sky. A glimpse was had of a vast green plain. In this distance, the castle of Chapultepec resembled a low thunder cloud.

Presently the train was among long white walls, green lawns, high shade trees. The passengers began their preparations for disembarking as the train manœuvered through the switches. At last there came a depot heavily fringed with people, an omnibus, a dozen cabs and a soldier in a uniform that fitted him like a bird cage. White dust arose high toward the blue sky. In some tall grass on the other side of the track, a little cricket suddenly chirped. The two travellers with shining eyes climbed out of the car. "A-a-ah," they said in a prolonged sigh of delight. The city of the Aztecs was in their power.

Stephen Crane in Mexico

City of Mexico, May 18.—Two Americans were standing on a street corner in this city not long ago, gazing thoughtfully at the paintings on the exterior wall of a pulque shop—stout maidens in scant vestments lovingly confronting a brimming glass, kings out of all proportion draining goblets to more stout maidens—the whole a wild mass of red, green, blue, yellow, purple, like a concert hall curtain in a mining town.

Far up the street six men in white cotton shirts and short trousers became visible. They were bent forward and upon their shoulders there was some kind of an enormous black thing. They moved at a shambling trot.

The two Americans lazily wondered about the enormous black thing, but the distance defeated them. The six men, however, were approaching at an unvarying pace, and at last one American was enabled to cry out: "Holy poker, it's a piano!"

There was a shuffling sound of sandals upon the stones. In the vivid yellow sunlight the black surface of the piano glistened. The six brown faces were stolid and unworried beneath it.

They passed. The burden and its carriers grew smaller and smaller. The two Americans went out to the curb and remained intent spectators until the six men and the piano were expressed by a faint blur.

When you first come to Mexico and you see a donkey so loaded that little of him but a furry nose and four short legs appear to the eye, you wonder at it. Later, when you see a haystack approaching with nothing under it but a pair of thin human legs, you begin to understand the local point of view. The Indian probably reasons: "Well, I can carry this load. The burro, then, he should carry many times this much." The burro, born in slavery, dying in slavery, generation upon generation, he with his wobbly legs, sore back, and ridiculous little face, reasons not at all. He carries as much as he can, and when he can carry it no further, he falls down.

The Indians, however, must have credit for considerable ingenuity because of the way they have invented of assisting a fallen donkey to its feet. The Aztecs are known to have had many great mechanical contrivances, and this no doubt is part of their science which has filtered down through the centuries.

When a burdened donkey falls down a half dozen Indians gather around it and brace themselves. Then they take clubs and hammer the everlasting daylights out of the donkey. They also swear in Mexican. Mexican is a very capable language for the purposes of profanity. A good swearer here can bring rain in thirty minutes.

It is a great thing to hear the thump, thump, of the clubs and the howling of the natives, and to see the little legs of the donkey quiver and to see him roll his eyes. Finally, after they have hammered him out as flat as a drum head, it flashes upon them suddenly that the burro cannot get up until they remove his load. Well, then, at last they remove his load and the donkey, not much larger than a kitten at best, and now disheveled, weak and tottering, struggles gratefully to his feet.

But, on the other hand, it is possible to see at times—perhaps in the shade of an old wall where branches hang over and look down—the tender communion of two sympathetic spirits. The man pats affectionately the soft muzzle of the donkey. The donkey—ah, who can describe that air so sage, so profoundly reflective, and yet so kind, so forgiving, so unassuming. The countenance of a donkey expresses all manly virtues even as the sunlight expresses all colors.

Perhaps the master falls asleep, and, in that case, the donkey still stands as immovable, as patient, as the stone dogs that guarded the temple of the sun.

A wonderful proportion of the freight-carrying business of this city is conducted by the Indian porters. The donkeys are the great general freight cars and hay wagons for the rural districts, but they do not appear prominently in the strictly local business of the city. It is a strange fact also that of ten wagons that pass you upon the street nine will be cabs and private carriages. The tenth may be a huge American wagon belonging to one of the express companies. It is only fair to state, however, that the odds are in favor of it being another cab or carriage.

The transportation of the city's goods is then left practically in the hands of the Indian porters. They are to be seen at all times trotting to and fro, laden and free. They have acquited all manner of contrivances for distributing the weight of their burdens. Their favorite plan is to pass a broad band over their foreheads and then leaning forward precariously, they amble along with the most enormous loads.

Sometimes they have a sort of table with two handles on each end. Two men, of course, manage this machine. It is the favorite vehicle for moving furniture.

When a man sits down who has been traversing a long road with a heavy bundle he would find considerable agony in the struggle to get upon his feet again with his freight strapped to his back if it were not for a long staff which he carries. He plants the point of this staff on the ground between his knees, and then climbs up it, so to speak, hand over hand.

They have undoubtedly developed what must be called the carrying instinct. Occasionally you may see a porter, unburdened, walking unsteadily as if his centre of balance had been shuffled around so much that he is doubtful. He resembles then an unballasted ship. Place a trunk upon his back and he is as steady as a church.

If you put in his care a contrivance with fifty wheels he would not trundle it along the ground. This plan would not occur to him. No, he would shoulder it. Most bicycles are light enough in weight, but they are rather unhandy articles to carry for long distances. Yet if you send one by a porter he will most certainly carry it on his shoulder. It would fatigue him to roll it along the road.

But there are other things odd here beside the street porters. Yesterday some thieves stole three iron balconies from off the second-story front of a house in the Calle del Sol. The police did not catch the miscreants. Who, indeed, is instructed in the art of catching thieves who steal iron balconies from the second-story fronts of houses?

The people directly concerned went out in the street and assured themselves that the house remained. Then they were satisfied.

As a matter of truth, the thieves of the city are almost always petty fellows, who go about stealing trifling articles and spend much time and finesse in acquiring things that a dignified American crook wouldn't kick with his foot. In truth, the City of Mexico is really one of the safest cities in the world at any hour of the day or night. However, the small-minded and really harmless class who vend birds, canes, opals, lottery tickets, paper flowers and general merchandise upon the streets are able and industrious enough in the art of piracy to satisfy the ordinary intellect.

Those profound minds who make the guide books have warned the traveler very lucidly. After exhaustive thought, the writer has been able to deduct the following elementary rules from what they have to say upon the matter:

I. Do not buy anything at all from street venders.

II. When buying from street venders give the exact sum charged. Do not delude yourself with the idea of getting any change back.

III. When buying from street venders divide by ten the price demanded for any article, and offer it.

IV. Do not buy anything at all from street venders.

It is not easy to go wrong when you have one of these protective volumes within reach, but then the guide book has long been subject to popular ridicule and there is not the universal devotion to its pages which it clearly deserves. Strangers upon entering Mexico should at once acquire a guide book, and then if they fail to gain the deepest knowledge of the country and its inhabitants, they may lay it to their own inability to understand the English language in its purest form. There are tourists now in this hotel who have only been in the city two days, but who, in this time, have devoted themselves so earnestly to their guide books that they are able to draw maps of how Mexico looked before the flood.

It is never just to condemn a class and, in returning to the street venders, it is but fair to record an extraordinary instance of the gentleness, humanity and fine capability of pity in one of their number. An American lady was strolling in a public park one afternoon when she observed a vender with four little plum-colored birds seated quietly and peacefully upon his brown hand.

"Oh look at those dear little birds," she cried to her escort. "How tame they are!"

Her escort, too, was struck with admiration and astonishment and they went close to the little birds. They saw their happy, restful countenances and with what wealth of love they looked up into the face of their owner.

The lady bought two of these birds, although she hated to wound their little hearts by tearing them away from their master.

When she got to her room she closed the door and the windows, and then reached into the wicker cage and brought out one of the pets, for she wished to gain their affection, too, and teach them to sit upon her finger.

The little bird which she brought out made a desperate attempt to perch upon her finger, but suddenly toppled off and fell to the floor with a sound like that made by a water-soaked bean bag.

The loving vender had filled his birds full of shot. This accounted for their happy, restful countenances and their very apparent resolution never to desert the adored finger of their master.

In an hour both the little birds died. You would die too if your stomach was full of shot.

The men who sell opals are particularly seductive. They polish their wares and boil them in oil and do everything to give them a false quality. When they come around in the evening and unfold a square of black paper, revealing a little group of stones that gleam with green and red fires, it is very dispiriting to know that if one bought one would be cheated.

The other day a vender upholding a scarfpin of marvelous brilliancy approached a tourist.

"How much?" demanded the latter.

"Twelve dollars," replied the vender. "Cheap! Very cheap! Only $12."

The tourist looked at the stone and said: "Twelve dollars! No! One dollar."

"Yes, yes," cried the vender eagerly. "One dollar! Yes, yes; you can have it for $1! Take it!"

But the tourist laughed and passed on.

The fact remains, however, that the hotels, the restaurants and the cabs are absolutely cheap and almost always fair. If a man consults reputable shopkeepers when he wishes to buy Mexican goods, and gives a proper number of hours each day to the study of guide books, the City of Mexico is a place of joy. The climate is seldom hot and seldom cold. And to those gentlemen from the States whose minds have a sort of liquid quality, it is necessary merely to say that if you go out into the street and yell: "Gimme a Manhattan!" about forty American bartenders will appear of a sudden and say: "Yes, sir."

From The City of Mexico

. . . The stranger to the city is at once interested in the architecture of the buildings. They are not ruins but they have somehow the dignity of ruins. There is probably no structure in the city of the character that a man of the North would erect. Viewing them as a mass, they are two-storied and plain with heavily barred windows from which the senoritas can gaze down at the street. In the principal part of the town, however, there are innumerable fine old houses with large shaded courts and simple stern decorations that must be echoes of the talent of the Aztecs. There is nothing of the modern in them. They are never incoherent, never over-done. The ornamentation is always a part of the structure. It grows there. It has not been plastered on from a distance. Galleries wind about the sides of the silent and shadowed patios.

Commerce has however waged a long war upon these structures and a vast number of them have succumbed. Signs are plastered on their exteriors and the old courts are given over to the gentle hum of Mexican business. It is not unusual for the offices of a commission merchant or of a dealer of any kind to be located in a building that was once the palace of some Mexican notable and the massive doors, the broad stair-way, the wide galleries, have become in this strange evolution as familiar to messenger boys and porters as they were once perhaps to generals and statesmen. The old palace of the Emperor Iturbide is now a hotel over-run with American tourists. The Mexican National Railroad has its general offices in a building that was the palace of a bygone governor of the city and the American Club has the finest of club-houses because it gained control of a handsome old palace.

There is a certain American aspect to the main business part of the town. Men with undeniable New England faces confront one constantly. The business signs are often American and there is a little group of cafes where everything from the aprons of the waiters to the liquids dispensed are American. One hears in this neighborhood more English than Spanish. Even the native business purpose changes under this influence and they bid for the American coin. "American Barber-shop," "The American Tailor," "American Restaurant" are signs which flatter the tourist's eye. There is nothing so universal as the reputation of Americans for ability to spend money. There can be no doubt that the Zulus upon the approach of an American citizen begin to lay all manner of traps.

Nevertheless there is a sort of a final adjustment. There is an American who runs a merry-go-round in one of the parks here. It is the usual device with a catarrhal orchestrion and a whirl of wooden goats, and ponies and giraffes. But his machine is surrounded at all times by fascinated natives and he makes money by the basketful. The circus too which is really a more creditable organization than any we see in the States, is crowded nightly. It is a small circus. It does not attempt to have simultaneous performances in fifty-nine rings but everything is first-class and the American circus people attain reputations among the populace second only to the most adored of the bull-fighters.

The bull-fighters, by the way, are a most impressive type to be seen upon the streets. There is a certain uniformity about their apparel. They wear flat-topped glazed hats like the seamen of years ago and little short jackets. They are always clean-shaven and the set of the lips wherein lies the revelation of character, can easily be studied. They move confidently, proudly, with a magnificent self-possession. People turn to stare after them. There is in their faces something cold, sinister, merciless. There is history there too, a history of fiery action, of peril, of escape. Yet you would know, you would know without being told that you are gazing at an executioner, a kind of moral assassin.

The faces of the priests are perhaps still more portentous, for the countenances of the bull-fighters are obvious but those of the priests are inscrutable.

The Viga Canal

The Viga Canal leads out to the floating gardens. The canal is really a canal but the floating gardens are not floating gardens at all. We took a cab and rattled our bones loose over the stones of streets where innumerble natives in serape and sombrero thronged about pulque shops that were also innumerable. Brown porters in cotton shirts and trousers trotted out of the way of the cab, moving huge burdens with rare ease. The women seated upon the curb with their babes, glanced up at the rumble of wheels. There were dashes of red and purple from the clothes of the people against the white and yellow background of the low adobe buildings. Into the clear cool afternoon air arose the squawling cries of the vendors of melons, saints, flowers.

At the canal, there was a sudden fierce assault of boatmen that was like a charge of desperate infantry. Behind them, their boats crowded each other at the wharf and the canal lay placid to where upon the further shore, long lazy blades of grass bended to the water like swooning things. At the pulque shop, the cabman paused for a drink before his return drive.

The boatmen beseeched, prayed, appealed. There could have been no more clamor around the feet of the ancient brown gods of Mexico. They almost shed tears; they wriggled in an ecstasy of commercial expectation. They smote their bare breasts and each swore himself to be the incomparable boatman of the Viga. Above their howls arose the tinkle of a street-car as the driver lashed his mules toward the city.

The fortunate boatman fairly trembled in his anxiety to get his craft out into the canal before his freight could change their minds. He pushed frantically with his pole and the boat, built precisely like what we call a scow, moved slowly away.

Great trees lined the shore. The little soiled street-cars passed and passed. Far along the shimmering waters, on which details of the foliage were traced, could be seen countless boatmen, erect in the sterns of their crafts, bending and swaying rhythmically, prodding the bottom with long poles. Out from behind the corner of a garden-wall suddenly appeared Popocatepetl, towering toward the sky, a great cone of creamy hue in the glamor of the sunshine. Then later came Iztaccihuatl, the white woman, of curious shape more camel than woman, its peak confused with clouds. A plain of fervent green stretched toward them. On the other side of the canal, in the shade of a great tree, a mounted gendarme sat immovable and contemplative.

A little canoe made from the trunk of a single tree and narrower than a coffin, approached and the Indian girl in the bow advocated the purchase of tamales while in the stern a tall youth in scant clothing poled away keeping pace with the larger craft.

Frequently there were races. Reposing under the wooden canopies of the boats, people cried to their boatmen. "Hurry up! If you beat that boat ahead, I will give you another real." The laconic Spanish sentences, fortified usually with swift gestures, could always be heard. And under the impetus of these offers, the boatmen struggled hardily, their sandaled feet pattering as they ran along the sides of the boats.

There were often harmless collisions. These boatmen, apprently made blind by the prospective increase in reward, poled sometimes like mad and crashed into boats ahead. Then arose the fervor of Mexican oaths.

Withal, however, they were very skilful, managing their old wooden boxes better than anybody could ever expect of them. And indeed some of them were clever enough to affect the most heroic exertions and gain more pay when in reality they were not injuring their health at all.

At the little village of Santa Anita, everybody disembarked. There was a great babbling crowd in front of the pulque shops. Vivid serapes lighted the effect made by the modest and very economical cotton clothes of the most of the people. In the midst of this uproar, three more mounted gendarmes sat silently, their sabres dangling in their scabbards, their horses poising their ears intently at the throng.

Indian girls with bare brown arms held up flowers for sale, flowers of flaming colors made into wreaths and bouquets. Caballeros, out for a celebration, a carouse, strutted along with these passionate burning flowers of the southland serving as bands to their sombreros. Under the thatched roofs of the pulque shops, more Indian girls served customers with the peculiar beverage and stood by and bantered with them in the universal style. In the narrow street leading away from the canal, the crowd moved hilariously while crouched at the sides of it, a multitude of beggars, decrepit vendors of all kinds, raised unheeded cries. In the midst of the swarming pulque shops, resorts, and gardens, stood a little white church, stern, unapproving, representing the other fundamental aspiration of humanity, a reproach and a warning. The frightened laughter of a girl in a swing could be heard as her lover swung her high, so that she appeared for a moment in her fluttering blue gown and tossing locks, over a fence of tall cactus plants.

A policeman remonstrated with a tottering caballero who wished to kiss a waitress in a pulque shop. A boatman, wailing bitterly, shambled after some riotous youths who had forgotten to pay him. Four men seated around a table were roaring with laughter at the tale of a fifth man. Three old Indian women with bare shoulders and wondrously wrinkled faces squatted on the earthen floor of a saloon and watched the crowd. Little beggars beseeched everybody. "Niña! Niña! Deme un centavo!"

Above the dark formidable hills of the west there was a long flare of crimson, purple, orange, tremendous colors that, in the changes of the sunset, manoeuvred in the sky like armies. Suddenly the little church aroused and its bell clanged persistently, harshly and with an incredible rapidity. People were beginning to saunter back toward the canal.

We procured two native musicians, a violinist and a guitarist and took them with us in our boat. The shadows of the trees in the water grew more portentous. Far to the southeast the two peaks were faint ghostly figures in the heavens. They resembled forms of silver mist in the deep blue of that sky. The boatman lit the candle of a little square lantern and set it in the bottom of the boat. The musicians made some preliminary chords and conversed about being in tune.

Tall trees of some popular variety that always resemble hearse plumes dotted the plain to the westward and as the uproar of colors there faded to a subtle rose, their black solemn outlines intervened like bars across this pink and pallor. A wind, cool and fragrant, reminiscent of flowers and grass and lakes came from those mystic shadows—places whence the two silver peaks had vanished. The boatman held his pole under his arm while he swiftly composed a cigarette.

The musicians played slumberously. We did not wish to hear any too well. It was better to lie and watch the large stars come out and let the music be merely a tale of the past, a recital from the possessions of one's memory, an looking of other songs, other nights. For, after all, the important part of these dreamful times to the wanderer is that they to him with emotional and tender voices of his past. The y low glitter of the lantern at the boatman's feet made h shadow to be a black awful thing that hung angrily over us. There was a sudden shrill yell from the darkness. There had almost been a collision. In the blue velvet of the sky, the stars had gathered in thousands.

Above All Things

Above all things, the stranger finds the occupations of foreign peoples to be trivial and inconsequent. The average mind utterly fails to comprehend the new point of view and that such and such a man should be satisfied to carry bundles or mayhap sit and ponder in the sun all his life in this faraway country seems an abnormally stupid thing. The visitor feels scorn. He swells with a knowledge of his geographical experience. "How futile are the lives of these people," he remarks, "and what incredible ignorance that they should not be aware of their futility." This is the arrogance of the man who has not yet solved himself and discovered his own actual futility.

Yet, indeed, it requires wisdom to see a brown woman in one garment crouched listlessly in the door of a low adobe hut while a naked brown baby sprawls on his stomach in the dust of the roadway—it requires wisdom to see this thing and to see it a million times and yet to say: "Yes, this is important to the scheme of nature. This is part of her economy. It would not be well if it had never been."

It perhaps might be said—if any one dared—that the most worthless literature of the world has been that which has been written by the men of one nation concerning the men of another.

It seems that a man must not devote himself for a time to attempts at psychological perception. He can be sure of two things, form and color. Let him then see all he can but let him not sit in literary judgment on this or that manner of the people. Instinctively he will feel that there are similarities but he will encounter many little gestures, tones, tranquilities, rages, for which his blood, adjusted to another temperature, can possess no interpreting power. The strangers will be indifferent where he expected passion; they will be passionate where he expected calm. These subtle variations will fill him with contempt.

At first it seemed to me the most extraordinary thing that

the lower classes of Indians in this country should insist upon existence at all. Their squalor, their ignorance seemed so absolute that death—no matter what it has in store—would appear as freedom, joy.

The people of the slums of our own cities fill a man with awe. That vast army with its countless faces immovably cynical, that vast army that silently confronts eternal defeat, it makes one afraid. One listens for the first thunder of the rebellion, the moment when this silence shall be broken by a roar of war. Meanwhile one fears this class, their numbers, their wickedness, their might—even their laughter. There is a vast national respect for them. They have it in their power to become terrible. And their silence suggests everything.

They are becoming more and more capable of defining their condition and this increase of knowledge evinces itself in the deepening of those savage and scornful lines which extend from near the nostrils to the corners of the mouth. It is very distressing to observe this growing appreciation of the situation.

I am not venturing to say that this appreciation does not exist in the lower classes of Mexico. No, I am merely going to say that I cannot perceive any evidence of it. I take this last position in order to preserve certain handsome theories which I advanced in the fore part of the article.

It is so human to be envious that of course even these Indians have envied everything from the stars of the sky to the birds, but you cannot ascertain that they feel at all the modern desperate rage at the accident of birth. Of course the Indian can imagine himself a king but he does not apparently feel that there is an injustice in the fact that he was not born a king any more than there is in his not being born a giraffe.

As far as I can perceive him, he is singularly meek and submissive. He has not enough information to be unhappy over his state. Nobody seeks to provide him with it. He is born, he works, he worships, he dies, all on less money than would buy a thoroughbred Newfoundland dog and who dares to enlighten him? Who dares cry out to him that there are plums, plums, plums in the world which belong to him? For my part, I think the apostle would take a formidable responsibility. I would remember that there really was no comfort in the plums after all as far as I had seen them and I would esteem no orations concerning the glitter of plums.

A man is at liberty to be virtuous in almost any position of life. The virtue of the rich is not so superior to the virtue of the poor that we can say that the rich have a great advantage. These Indians are by far the most poverty-stricken class with which I have met but they are not morally the lowest by any means. Indeed, as far as the mere form of religion goes, they are one of the highest. They are exceedingly devout, worshipping with a blind faith that counts a great deal among the theorists.

But according to my view this is not the measure of them. I measure their morality by what evidences of peace and contentment I can detect in the average countenance.

If a man is not given a fair opportunity to be virtuous, if his environment chokes his moral aspirations, I say that he has got the one important cause of complaint and rebellion against society. Of course it is always possible to be a martyr but then we do not wish to be martyrs. Martyrdom offers no inducements to the average mind. We prefer to be treated with justice and then martyrdom is not required. I never could appreciate those grey old gentlemen of history. Why did not they run? I would have run like mad and still respected myself and my religion.

I have said then that a man has the right to rebel if he is not given a fair opportunity to be virtuous. Inversely then, if he possesses this fair opportunity, he cannot rebel, he has no complaint. I am of the opinion that poverty of itself is no cause. It is something above and beyond. For example, there is Collis P. Huntington and William D. Rockefeller—as virtuous as these gentlemen are, I would not say that their virtue is any ways superior to mine for instance. Their opportunities are no greater. They can give more, deny themselves more in quantity but not relatively. We can each give all that we possess and there I am at once their equal.

I do not think however that they would be capable of sacrifices that would be possible to me. So then I envy them nothing. Far from having a grievance against them, I feel that they will confront an ultimate crisis that I, through my opportunities, may altogether avoid. There is in fact no advantage of importance which I can perceive them possessing over me.

It is for these reasons that I refuse to commit judgment upon these lower classes of Mexico. I even refuse to pity them. It is true that at night many of them sleep in heaps in doorways, and spend their days squatting upon the pavements. It is true that their clothing is scant and thin. All manner of things of this kind is true but yet their faces have almost always a certain smoothness, a certain lack of pain, a serene faith. I can feel the superiority of their contentment.

A Letter from Stephen Crane to Willis Brooks Hawkins

[Hartwood, N. Y., about November 5, 1895]

My dear Willis: I always considered [Eugene] Field to be a fine simple spirit and I am glad his death makes you so sad.

I never thought him a western barbarian. I have always believed the western people to be much truer than the eastern people. We in the east are overcome a good deal by a detestable superficial culture which I think is the real barbarism. Culture in it's true sense, I take it, is a comprehension of the man at one's shoulder. It has nothing to do with an adoration for effete jugs and old kettles. This latter is merely an amusement and we live for amusement in the east. Damn the east! I fell in love with the straight out-and-out, sometimes-hideous, often-braggart westerners because I thought them to be the truer men and, by the living piper, we will see in the next fifty years what the west will do. They are serious, those fellows. When they are born they take one big gulp of wind and then they live.

Of course, the east thinks them ridiculous. When they come to congress they display a child-like honesty which makes the old east laugh. And yet—

Garland will wring every westerner by the hand and hail him as a frank honest man. I wont. No, sir. But what I contend for is the atmosphere of the west which really is frank and honest and is bound to make eleven honest men for one pessimistic thief. More glory be with them.

Two Letters from Stephen Crane to Nellie Crouse

I do not suppose you will be overwhelmed with distinction when I tell you that your name is surrounded with much sentiment for me. I was in southern Mexico last winter for a sufficient time to have my face turn the color of a brick side-walk. There was nothing American about me save a large Smith and Wesson revolver and I saw only Indians whom I suspected of loading their tomales [*sic*] with dog. In this state of mind and this physical condition, I arrived one day in the city of Puebla and there I saw an American girl. There was a party of tourists in town and she was of their contingent. I only saw her four times—one in the hotel corridor and three in the street. I had been so long in the mountains and was such an outcast, that the sight of this American girl in a new spring gown nearly caused me to drop dead. She of course never looked in my direction. I never met her. Nevertheless I gained one of those peculiar thrills which a man only acknowledges upon occasion. I ran to the railroad office. I cried: "What is the shortest route to New York." I left Mexico.

I suppose you fail to see how this concerns you in anyway! And no wonder! But this girl who startled me out of my mountaineer senses, resembled you. I have never achieved the enjoyment of seeing you in a new spring gown but this girl became to me not an individual but a sort of a symbol and I have always thought of you with gratitude for the peculiar thrill you gave me in the town of Puebla, Mexico.

Your recent confession that in your heart you like the man of fashion more than you do some other kinds of men came nearer to my own view than perhaps you expected. I have indeed a considerable liking for the man of fashion if he does it well. The trouble to my own mind lies in the fact that the heavy social life demands one's entire devotion. Time after time, I have seen the social lion turn to a lamb and fail—fail at precisely the moment when men should not fail. The world sees this also and it has come to pass that the fashionable man is considerably jeered at. Men who are forever sitting with immovable legs on account of a tea-cup are popularly supposed to be worth little besides. This is true in the main but it is not without brave exceptions, thank heaven. For my part, I like the man who dresses correctly and does the right thing invariably but, oh, he must be more than that, a great deal more. But so seldom is he anymore than correctly-dressed and correctly-speeched, that when I see a man of that kind I usually put him down as a kind of an idiot. Still, as I have said, there are exceptions. There are men of very social habits who nevertheless know how to stand steady when they see cocked revolvers and death comes down and sits on the back of a chair and waits. There are men of very social habits who know good music from bad, good poetry from bad—(a few of 'em)—good drama from bad—(a very few of 'em)—good painting from bad. There are very many of them who know good claret and good poker-playing. There are a few who can treat a woman tenderly not only when they feel amiable but when she most needs tender-treatment. There [are] many who can ride, swim, shoot and sail a boat, a great many. There are an infinitismal [*sic*] number who can keep from yapping in a personal way about women. There are a large number who refuse to haggle over a question of money. There are one or two who invariably mind their own business. There are some who know how to be frank without butchering the feelings of their friends. There is an enormous majority who, upon being insured of safety from detection—become at once the most unconventional of peoples.

In short they are precisely like the remainder of the race, only they devote their minds to riding smoothly. A slight jolt gives them the impression that a mountain has fallen upon them.

I swear by the real aristocrat. The man whose forefathers were men of courage, sympathy and wisdom, is usually one who will stand the strain whatever it may be. He is like a thorough-bred horse. His nerves may be high and he will do a lot of jumping often but in the crises he settles down and becomes the most reliable and enduring of created things.

For the hordes who hang upon the out-skirts of good society and chant 143 masses per day to the social gods and think because they have money they are well-bred—for such people I have a scorn which is very deep and very intense. These people think that polite life is something which is to be studied, a very peculiar science of which knowledge is only gained by long practice whereas what is called "form" is merely a collection of the most rational and just of laws which any properly-born person understands from his cradle. In Hartwood I have a great chance to study the new-rich. The Hartwood Clubhouse is only three miles away and there are some of the new rich in it. May the Lord deliver me from having social aspirations.

I can stand the society man, if he don't interfere with me; I always think the society girl charming but the type that I cant endure is the society matron. Of course there are many exceptions but some I have seen struck me afar off with the peculiar iron-like quality of their thick-headedness and the wild exuberance of their vanity.

On two or three occasions I had some things read at Sherry's and later by chance met people who had been there. I distinctly remember some compliments paid me very graciously and confidently by a woman. Nothing so completely and serenely stupid have I ever witnessed. And the absolutely false tongue of her prattled away for ten minutes in more lies than are usually heard at one time. Of course it was nothing to me if she liked my stuff and it was nothing to her. She was merely being [*sic*] because she indifferently thought it to be correct at that moment, but how those old cats can stand up and lie until there is no breath left in them. Now, they think that is form, mind you, but, good heavens, it isn't. They think that a mere show of complacent idiocy is all that is necessary to a queen of society. Form really is truth, simplicity; when people surround it with falsity, interpret it as meaning: "lies," they become not society leaders but barbarians, savages, beating little silly tom-toms and flourishing little carved wooden goblins. They really defy every creed of this social god, the very diety [*sic*] which they worship.

I am rather apprehensive. I detest dogma and it strikes me that I have expressed too many opinions in this letter. When I express an opinion in writing I am in the habit of considering a long time and then formulating it with a great deal of care. This letter however has been so hasty that I have not always said precisely what I intended to say. But at any rate I hope it will be plain that I strongly admire the social God even if I do despise many of his worshippers.

As for the man with the high aims and things—which you say you like in your soul—but not in your heart—I dont know that he is to my mind any particular improvement on the society man. I shouldn't care to live in the same house with him if he was at all in the habit of talking about them. I get about two letters a day from people who have high literary aims and everywhere I go I seem to meet five or six. They strike me as about the worst and most penetrating kind of bore I know. Of course I, with my meagre successes, would feel like an awful duffer if I was anything but very, very considerate of them but it is getting to be a task. Of course that is not the kind you meant. Still they are certainly people of high aims and there is a ridiculous quality to me in all high ambitions, of men who mean to try to make themselves great because they think it would [be] so nice to be great, to be admired, to be stared at by the mob. "Well," you say, "I didnt mean that kind of high aim either." Tolstoy's aim is, I suppose—I believe—to make himself good. It is an incomparably quixotic task for any man to undertake. He will not succeed; but he will even succeed more than he can ever himself know, and so at his nearest point to success he will be proportionally blind. This is the pay of this kind of greatness.

This letter is certainly not a conscience-smiter but I hope you will reply to it at the same length that you claim for the lost letter.

A Letter from Theodore Roosevelt to Stephen Crane

New York, Aug. 18, 1896

My dear Mr. Crane:—I am much obliged to you for "George's Mother" with your own autograph in the front. I shall keep it with your other books. Some day I shall get you to write your autograph in my "Red Badge of Courage," for much though I like your other books, I think I like that book the best. Some day I want you to write another story of the frontiersman and the Mexican Greaser in which the frontiersman shall come out on top; it is more normal that way! I wish I could have seen Hamlin Garland, but I am leaving in a few days for a three weeks trip in the West.

An Inscription from Stephen Crane to Hamlin Garland

New York City/ July, 1896

[Inscribed in a copy of *George's Mother*]

To Hamlin Garland of the great honest West, from Stephen Crane of the false East

SELECTED BIBLIOGRAPHY

Works by Stephen Crane

Maggie: A Girl of the Streets, 1893   Novel
The Black Riders and Other Lines, 1895   Poems
The Red Badge of Courage: An Episode of the American Civil War, 1895   Novel
George's Mother, 1896   Novel
The Little Regiment and Other Episodes of the American Civil War, 1896   Stories
The Third Violet, 1897   Novel
The Open Boat and Other Tales of Adventure, 1898   Stories
War Is Kind, 1899   Poems
Active Service, 1899   Novel
The Monster and Other Stories, 1899   Stories
Whilomville Stories, 1899   Stories
Wounds in the Rain: War Stories, 1900   Stories
Great Battles of the World, 1901   History
Last Words, 1902   Stories and Travel Reports
The O'Ruddy: A Romance (completed by Robert Barr), 1903   Novel

Biography and Criticism

Beer, Thomas. *Stephen Crane: A Study in American Letters.* New York: Alfred A. Knopf, 1923.
Bergon, Frank. *Stephen Crane's Artistry.* New York: Columbia University Press, 1975, pp. 101-131.
Bernard, Kenneth. " 'The Bride Comes to Yellow Sky': History as Elegy." *The English Record,* 17 (April 1967), 17-20.
Berryman, John. *Stephen Crane.* New York: William Sloane, 1950.
Ferguson, S.C. "Crane's 'The Bride Comes to Yellow Sky.' " *The Explicator,* 21 (March 1963), item 59.
Holton, Milne. *Cylinder of Vision: The Fiction and Journalistic Writing of Stephen Crane.* Baton Rouge: Louisiana State University Press, 1972, pp. 119-146, 225-243.

Katz, Joseph, ed. and introd. *Stephen Crane in the West and Mexico*. Kent, Ohio: The Kent State University Press, 1970, pp. ix-xxv.

Levenson, J.C. "Introduction." In *The Works of Stephen Crane*, V, ed. Fredson Bowers. Charlottesville: The University Press of Virginia, 1970, pp. xv-cxxxii.

Narveson, Robert. " 'Conceit' in 'The Blue Hotel.' " *Prairie Schooner*, 43 (Summer 1969), 187-191.

Pizer, Donald. "Stephen Crane." In *Fifteen American Authors before 1900: Bibliographic Essays on Research and Criticism*, ed. Robert A. Rees and Earl N. Harbert. Madison: University of Wisconsin Press, 1971, pp. 97-138.

Satterwhite, Joseph N. "Stephen Crane's 'The Blue Hotel': The Failure of Understanding." *Modern Fiction Studies*, 2 (Winter 1956-57), 238-241.

Sloate, Bernice. "Stephen Crane in Nebraska." *Prairie Schooner*, 43 (Summer 1969), 192-199.

Solomon, Eric. *Stephen Crane: From Parody to Realism*. Cambridge: Harvard University Press, 1966, pp. 229-282.

Stallman, R.W. *Stephen Crane: A Biography*. New York: George Braziller, 1968.

MENTOR Books of Special Interest

☐ **LOOKING FAR WEST: The Search for the American West in History, Myth, and Literature edited by Frank Bergon and Zeese Papanikolas.** Here in song and story, myth and firsthand report, analysis and eulogy, is an anthology that gives full expression to the West in all its complex meanings. With 16 pages of photographs.
(#ME1645—$2.50)

☐ **ONCE IN THE SADDLE: The Cowboy's Frontier 1866-1896 by Laurence Ivan Seidman.** The legendary wild West—as it really was ... "A superb book!"—The New York Times. Illustrated with photos and drawings of the period.
(#ME1581—$1.75)

☐ **STORIES OF THE AMERICAN EXPERIENCE edited by Leonard Kriegel and Abraham H. Lass.** These stories, by some of the greatest writers America has produced, give vivid insight into both our complex national character and our rich literary heritage. Authors included range from such nineteenth-century masters as Nathaniel Hawthorne and Herman Melville to such moderns as Richard Wright and Nelson Algren. (#ME1605—$2.25)

☐ **THE EXPERIENCE OF THE AMERICAN WOMAN: 30 Stories edited and with an Introduction by Barbara H. Solomon.** A century of great fiction about the place and role of women in America. (#ME1646—$2.50)

☐ **THE MENTOR BOOK OF MAJOR AMERICAN POETS edited by Oscar Williams and Edwin Honig.** From Edward Taylor and Walt Whitman to Hart Crane and W. H. Auden—a compact anthology of three centuries of poetry by 20 great American poets. (#MJ1381—$1.95)

☐ **COLONIAL AMERICAN LITERATURE: From Wilderness to Independence selected and edited, with an Introduction, commentary, and notes by Robert Douglas Mead.** From Indian myths to the Declaration of Independence, this brilliant anthology of pioneer writings describes the creation of our nation. (#MJ1463—$1.95)

SIGNET CLASSICS by American Authors

ℂ

Other SIGNET CLASSICS by American Authors

☐ **THE HOUSE OF THE SEVEN GABLES by Nathaniel Hawthorne.** Afterword by Edward C. Sampson.
(#CY1043—$1.25)

☐ **THE MARBLE FAUN by Nathaniel Hawthorne.** Afterword by Murray Kreiger. (#CW1084—$1.50)

☐ **THE INNOCENTS ABROAD by Mark Twain.** Afterword by Leslie Fiedler. (#CJ1142—$1.95)

☐ **LIFE ON THE MISSISSIPPI by Mark Twain.** Afterword by Leonard Kriegel. (#CQ936—95¢)

☐ **THE JUNGLE by Upton Sinclair.** Foreword by Robert B. Downs. (#CW1102—$1.50)

☐ **LEAVES OF GRASS by Walt Whitman.** Introduction by Gay Wilson Allen. (#CW1042—$1.50)

☐ **LOOKING BACKWARD by Edward Bellamy.** Foreword by Erich Fromm. (#CW870—$1.50)

☐ **MAIN STREET by Sinclair Lewis.** Afterword by Mark Schorer. (#CE1140—$2.25)

☐ **MOBY DICK by Herman Melville.** Afterword by Denham Sutcliffe. (#CE1118—$1.75)

☐ **THE OREGON TRAIL by Francis Parkman.** Foreword by A. B. Guthrie, Jr. (#CW1065—$1.50)

☐ **THE OUTCASTS OF POKER FLAT and Other Tales by Bret Harte.** Introduction by Wallace Stegner. (#CE1161—$1.75)

☐ **THE OX-BOW INCIDENT by Walter Van Tilburg Clark.** Afterword by Walter Prescott Webb. (#CW1007—$1.50)

☐ **THE SCARLET LETTER by Nathaniel Hawthorne.** Foreword by Leo Marx. (#CW1188—$1.50)

☐ **THE TITAN by Theodore Dreiser.** Afterword by John Berryman. (#CJ1060—$1.95)

Ↄ

SIGNET CLASSICS by British Authors

- [ ] **ALICE'S ADVENTURES IN WONDERLAND and THROUGH THE LOOKING GLASS by Lewis Carroll.** Foreword by Horace Gregory. (#CY912—$1.25)

- [ ] **ANIMAL FARM by George Orwell.** Introduction by C. M. Woodhouse. (#CW1028—$1.50)

- [ ] **FAR FROM THE MADDING CROWD by Thomas Hardy.** Aterword by James Wright. Wessex edition.
  (#CY997—$1.25)

- [ ] **GULLIVER'S TRAVELS by Jonathan Swift.** Foreword by Marcus Cunliffe. Illustrated. (#CW1169—$1.50)

- [ ] **HARD TIMES by Charles Dickens.** Afterword by Charles Shapiro. (#CE1152—$1.75)

- [ ] **HEART OF DARKNESS and THE SECRET SHARER by Joseph Conrad.** Introduction by Albert J. Guerard.
  (#CQ1004—95¢)

- [ ] **HUMPHREY CLINKER by Tobias Smollett.** Foreword by Monroe Engel. (#CJ1103—$1.95)

- [ ] **IDYLLS OF THE KING and A Selection of Poems by Alfred Lord Tennyson.** Foreword by George Barker.
  (#CE1181—$1.75)

- [ ] **JANE EYRE by Charlotte Brontë.** Afterword by Arthur Zeiger. (#CW1117—$1.50)

- [ ] **A JOURNAL OF THE PLAGUE YEAR by Daniel Defoe.** Foreword by J. H. Plumb. (#CY927—$1.25)